西厢记

汉英对照

〔元〕王实甫 著
冯萍 译

The Love Notes of the Western Chamber

中国出版集团
中译出版社

图书在版编目（CIP）数据

西厢记：汉英对照/(元)王实甫著；冯萍译．--
北京：中译出版社，2024.3
　ISBN 978-7-5001-7667-1

　Ⅰ.①西… Ⅱ.①王…②冯… Ⅲ.①《西厢记》—
汉、英 Ⅳ.①I237.1

中国国家版本馆CIP数据核字（2023）第257592号

西厢记：汉英对照
XIXIANGJI：HANYING DUIZHAO

出版发行：	中译出版社
地　　址：	北京市西城区新街口外大街28号普天德胜大厦主楼4层
电　　话：	（010）68002876
邮　　编：	100088
责任编辑：	张　旭
特约编辑：	刘育红　王君瑶
封面设计：	黄　浩
排　　版：	聚贤阁
印　　刷：	中煤（北京）印务有限公司
规　　格：	840 mm × 1092 mm　1/32
印　　张：	12
字　　数：	200千字
版　　次：	2024年3月第1版
印　　次：	2024年3月第1次

ISBN 978-7-5001-7667-1
定价：69.00元

版权所有　侵权必究
中　译　出　版　社

译序

《西厢记》是元代王实甫创作的一部杂剧，和西方戏剧一样，分为叙事部分和戏文部分，共有五个场景和二十幕，主要讲述了张生和崔莺莺冲破各种封建礼教的束缚和现实生活的困难险阻，有情人终成眷属的故事。

崔莺莺是前相国之女，但她父亲早逝，留下了母亲、弟弟（父母的养子欢儿）和自己。崔莺莺和母亲本打算把她父亲葬在家乡，但由于路途漫遥，就在普救寺停了下来。这时，书生张生正巧瞥了崔莺莺一眼，便不顾一切地爱上了她。叛军孙飞虎觊觎崔莺莺的美色，把普救寺围了起来，张生向好友白马将军求助，解救了崔莺莺。崔莺莺的母亲在危难之中答应了张生和崔莺莺的婚事，但危机解除之后立马改变了主意。在红娘的帮助下，张生终于和崔莺莺幽会成亲。崔莺莺的母亲知道后，只能决定让张生金榜题名后才能娶她的女儿。张生科举考试一举夺魁，准备迎娶崔莺莺。与此同时，老太太的侄子郑恒诬告张生已经在京另娶。后张生赶到，在红娘和白马将军的帮助下，与崔莺莺有情人终成眷属。

第一次读《西厢记》，就被《西厢记》里华美的辞藻和曲折的故事情节深深吸引。《西厢记》对中国后世文学创作产生了深远的影响。无论是清代曹雪芹的《红楼梦》还是明代笑笑生的《金瓶梅》都引用了《西厢记》中的情节或台词。《西厢记》可以被称为中国古代的第一部罗曼史。

之前读过许渊冲先生翻译的《西厢记》，在感叹之余，也着手自己翻译了一版，尽量保持了作者王实甫的原意，期待可以更好地向西方读者介绍中国文化。在翻译的过程中，我对文中出现的中医名词、古代乐器、古诗词、成语、谚语等进行了细致的推敲，努力在内容和形式上更尊重西方读者阅读戏剧的习惯，同时力求兼顾"信达雅"的原则，希望本书能够帮助英文母语的读者更好地了解中国古代悠扬磅礴的文化。

在中国古代文学史上，那些跨越阶级的爱情故事，诸如小姐与书生、仙女与凡人，大多以悲剧收尾。而《西厢记》却不同，这出戏有一个欢快的结局，昭示着爱情的胜利，表达了人们朴素的愿望，那就是有情人可以终成眷属。

五剧第一本

张君瑞闹道场杂剧

Act One

楔　子

（外扮老夫人上开）老身姓郑，夫主姓崔，官拜前朝相国，不幸因病告殂。只生得个小姐，小字莺莺，年一十九岁，针黹女工，诗词书算，无不能者。老相公在日，曾许下老身之侄，乃郑尚书之长子郑恒为妻。因俺孩儿父丧未满，未得成合。又有个小妮子，是自幼伏侍孩儿的，唤做红娘。一个小厮儿，唤做欢郎。先夫弃世之后，老身与女孩儿扶柩至博陵安葬，因路途有阻，不能得去。来到河中府，将这灵柩寄在普救寺内。这寺是先夫相国修造的，是则天娘娘香火院，况兼法本长老，又是俺相公剃度的和尚，因此俺就这西厢下一座宅子安下。一壁写书附京师去，唤郑恒来，相扶回博陵去。我想先夫在日，食前方丈，从者数百，今日至亲则这三四口儿，好生伤感人也呵。

Prologue

[An actor disguised as an old woman enters. She speaks] "My family name is Zheng. My husband's family name is Cui, who was the former prime minister of the dynasty, however, he died unfortunately out of illness. We only have one daughter, whose nickname is Ying Ying. This year, she is nineteen years old, good at needlework and capable of composing verses and making calculations. When my husband was alive, we have made an engagement between our daughter and my nephew, son of Minister Zheng, named Zheng Heng. As my husband just died less than three years, according to the custom, my daughter's marriage has been delayed. There is a maid servant for my daughter, whose name is Red Maid. Red Maid has served my daughter since she was in her childhood. They almost grow up together. We have adopted a boy when my husband was alive, called Huan Er. When my husband left the world, my daughter and I took his coffin to Bo Ling, hoping to bury the coffin there. However, because of turbulent journey, we are unable to proceed. So we stopped in the He Zhong Prefecture, leaving the coffin in the Pu Jiu Monastery. The monastery was built by my husband when he was the prime minister, in favor of her majesty Wu Zetian. Moreover, the abbot was tonsured by my husband. So my daughter and I settled down in a dwelling in the West Wings of the monastery. I wrote a letter to Zheng Heng in the capital, calling him to forward the coffin to Bo Ling. After writing the letter, I could not help thinking of the days when my husband was still alive. When we dined, the table was full of tasty food. There

【仙吕】【赏花时】夫主京师禄命终刚,子母孤孀途路穷,因此上旅榇在梵王宫。盼不到博陵旧冢,血泪洒杜鹃红。

今日暮春天气,好生困人。不免唤红娘出来分付他。红娘何在?(旦保扮红见科)(夫人云)你看佛殿上没人烧香呵,和小姐闲散心耍一回去来。(红云)谨依严命。(夫人下)(红云)小姐有请。(正旦扮莺莺上)(红云)夫人著俺和姐姐佛殿上闲耍一回去来。(旦唱)

【幺篇】可正是人值残春蒲郡东,门掩重关萧寺中。花落水流红,闲愁万种,无语怨东风。(并下)

were hundreds of servants serving us. At this moment, there are only three or four close relatives left. How sad it is now!"

[Tune of Song of Enjoying Flowers in Company of Fairies] [The Old Lady is appreciating the beautiful flowers in the spring. She sings] "In my husband's officialdom career, he died out of overwork, leaving a helpless daughter and a widowed wife. Now the coffin stays in the monastery. I will be dying anxiously to wait for my relative to come and my tears are shedding on the azalea flowers redder than blood.

This is a good time at the end of the spring. It makes people so tired and sleepy. I will call Red Maid over, and nag her something. Red Maid, where are you?"

[Red Maid enters, wearing an clever look and meets the Old Lady.]

[The Old Lady says] "If there is no one burning incense in the monastery, you may go outside with your lady and have a little fun."

[The Red Maid says] "Yes, my madam."

[The Old Lady exits. The says] "Sister, let's go out!"

[The female Role who acted as Ying Ying enters.]

[Red Maid says] "The old lady asked me to take sissy out and have a little fun in the monastery."

[Ying Ying sings in the same tune with the Old Lady] [Same Tune] "We happened to stay in the Pu Dong Town at the end of the Spring. The door is heavily shut in this shabby monastery. The following stream is tinted red with falling petals. There are hundreds of sorrows in my mind. But I can not blame the East wind." [Exeunt]

第一折

(正末扮骑马引保人上开)小生姓张名珙,字君瑞,本贯西洛人也。先人拜礼部尚书,不幸五旬之上因病身亡。后一年丧母。小生书剑飘零,功名未遂,游于四方。即今贞元十七年二月上旬,唐德宗即位,欲往上朝取应,路经河中府,过蒲关上,有一人姓杜名确,字君实,与小生同郡同学,当初为八拜之交,后弃文就武,遂得武举状元,官拜征西大元帅,统领十万大军,镇守著蒲关。小生就望哥哥一遭,却往京师求进。暗想小生萤窗雪案,刮垢磨光,学成满腹文章,尚在湖海飘零,何日得遂大志也呵!万金宝剑藏秋水,满马春愁压绣鞍。

Scene One

[The male role acted as Zhang Gong rides the horse, following by the Servant Boy enters]

"My family name is Zhang, given name Gong and nick name Jun Rui. I was born in the West Luo City. My father once held the position as General Secretary of the Department of Rites in the court, however, when he was above fifty years old, he died out of sickness. Unfortunately, the next year after my father died, my mother died too. Unable to obtain official ranks, I am pursuing the fame and wondering out of my hometown here and there. I have not returned home for a long time. This is first half of the 17 th year in Zhen Yuan calender, when Tang Dezong is in resign. I am leaving for the capital to attend the imperial civil examination in the court. On the way, I have passed by He Zhong Prefecture. There was a friend in the town, whose family name is Du, given name is Que, and nick name is Jun Shi. He is my sworn brotherhood, my classmates, as well as my fellow countryman. Later, he abandoned pen for the sword, and won the top prize in the military examinations. He was appointed as West Expedition General, commanding one hundred thousand troops, and guarding the pass of Pu. I intend to visit my sworn brother, and at the same time head towards the capital for fame. In the past, when I was poor, I read books under the light of firefly in the summer and snow in the winter. In order to go depth into the book, I read the classic over and over again. I have learned a lot, good at classics and

【仙吕】【点绛唇】游艺中原,脚根无线,如蓬转。望眼连天,日近长安远。

【混江龙】向诗书经传,蠹鱼似不出费钻研。将棘围守暖,把铁砚磨穿。投至得云路鹏程九万里,先受了雪窗萤火二十年。才高难入俗人机,时乖不遂男儿愿。空雕虫篆刻,缀断简残编。

行路之间,早到蒲津。这黄河有九曲,此正古河内之地,你看好形势也呵!

【油葫芦】九曲风涛何处显,则除是此地偏。这河带齐梁分秦晋隘幽燕。雪浪拍长空,天际秋云卷竹索缆浮桥,水上苍龙偃东西溃九州,南北串百川。归舟紧不紧如何见?却便似弩箭乍离弦。

literature, however, I am still wondering around. When shall I realize my ambition? The sword that weighed thousands of gold is buried under the autumn water. I am riding on the embroidered saddle of the horse, with spring sorrows in my mind."

[Tune of Rouged Lips of Fairy Song] "Roaming around and amusing myself in the Central Plain, I am as rootless as floating thistledown. Looking at the horizon in front, I found the sun is even nearer than Chang An City!"

[Tune of Dragon in Troubled Water Song] "Fully reading the classics and poetry, I have devoted myself into study for many years as if a bookworm thirsting for knowledge in the book. My seat is still warm when I left and my ink tone is worn out by my endless studies. I am longing for success and fame, wishing to fly a thousand miles in the sky as if a roc bird. I have studied hard for nearly twenty years. Though I am well learned, I don't have the luck yet. Being poor, my dream is hard to come true. I wasted my talent in poetry writing, and decorating the fragments of books in order to survive. Walking for a long distance, I have arrived in Pu Dong Town long ago. I saw the Yellow River flowing in a zigzag way. Pu Dong Town is located in the north of Yellow River. How magnificent the Yellow River looks like!"

[Tune of Field Cricket Song] "Why can I see the turbulent waves of the zigzag Yellow River? Am I out of the way? The very Yellow River divides the Qi and Liang dynasty, and marks the territory border between Qing and Jing Kingdoms. It is located in strategic place of Yan Kingdom. The white waves beat the long sky, and the

【天下乐】只疑是银河落九天。渊泉云外悬,入东洋不离此径穿。滋洛阳千种花,润梁园万顷田,也曾泛浮槎到日月边。

　　话说间早到城中。这里一座店儿,琴童,接下马者。店小二哥那里?(小二上云)自家是这状元店里小二哥。官人要下呵,俺这里有干净店房。(末云)头房里下,先撒和那马者。小二哥你来,我问你:这里有甚么闲散心处?名山胜境、福地宝坊皆可。(小二云)俺这里有一座寺,名曰普救寺,是则天皇后香火院,盖造非俗:琉璃殿相近青霄,舍利塔直侵云汉。南来北往,三教九流,过者无不瞻仰,则除那里可以君子游玩。(末云)琴童,料持下晌午饭,那里走一遭,便回来也。(童云)安排下饭,撒和了马,等哥哥回家。(下)(法聪上)小僧法聪,是这普救寺法本长老座下弟子。今日师父赴斋去了,著我在寺中,但有探长老的,便

autumn clouds curl with each other. Bamboo bridge floats on the surface of the river, which looks like a blue dragon. In the east and west, the river floods the divine land; in the south and north, it connects hundreds of stream river. Is it necessary to take the boat to go with the river? I feel myself as an arrow shooting from the bows."

[Tune of all over the World Joys Song] "I wonder whether it is the Milk Way falling down from the sky. The source of the fountain is falling from the clouds, and heading towards the East Sea. In order to go into the East sea, I have to pass through this path. There are a thousand flowers in West Luo City, and a thousand miles of good land. However, I have been wandering everywhere even to the moon and the sun. This morning, I have arrived at the town. There is an inn. My servant boy helps me to get off the horse. Where is the innkeeper?"

[The Innkeeper enters and says] "I am the innkeeper. Sir, will you stay here tonight? We have clean rooms."

[Zhang Gong says] "We will settle down in the first rate house. Servant Boy, please feed the horses. Innkeeper, come here. I have some questions for you. Do you know any places around for sightseeing, such as famous mountains, treasured land, and even good monastery."

[The Innkeeper says] "There is a monastery in this town, called Pu Jiu Monastery. It is a monastery that is built in favor of Wu Zetian

记著,待师父回来报知。山门下立地,看有甚么人来。(末上云)却早来到也。(见聪了,聪问云)客官从何来?(末云)小生西洛至此,闻上刹幽雅清爽,一来瞻仰佛像,二来拜谒长老。敢问长老在么?(聪云)俺师父不在寺中,贫僧弟子法聪的便是。请先生方丈拜茶。(末云)既然长老不在呵,不必吃茶。敢烦和尚相引瞻仰一遭,幸甚。(聪云)小僧取钥匙,开了佛殿、钟楼、塔院、罗汉堂、香积厨,盘桓一会,师父敢待回来。(末云)是盖造得好也呵!

empress. It is well built, a palace of colored gaze, which almost approaches to the sky. The dagoba reaches the clouds. People from all walks of life will all come there and worship the Buddha. You should never be disappointed if you visit there."

[Zhang Gong says] "Please arrange for the meal at noon. I will go to visit the monastery, and come back as soon as possible."

[The Servant Boy says] "I will prepare for the meal, feed the horse, and wait for brother to come back." [Exeunt]

[Monk Fa Cong enters and says] "My name is Fa Cong, a disciple of the abbot Fa Ben in the Buddhist monastery. Today, my master has conducted a religious ceremony, leaving me to stay in the monastery. If someone is coming to visit my master, I will write it down and wait for my master's return. I will walk to the gate of the monastery, to see whether someone is coming."

[Zhang Gong says] "I have arrived early."

[Fa Cong greets Zhang Gong and asks] "Sir, where do you come from?"

[Zhang Gong says] "I come from the West Luo City. I heard your monastery elegant and refreshing. I come to worship Buddha, and at the same time to visit the abbot. Could I ask whether the abbot is available now?"

[Fa Cong says] "My master is out at the moment. I can be your guide. My name is Fa Cong, the disciple of my master. Please come and have a cup of tea."

【村里迓鼓】随喜了上方佛殿,早来到下方僧院。行过厨房近西、法堂北、钟楼前面。游了洞房,登了宝塔,将回廊绕遍。数了罗汉,参了菩萨,拜了圣贤。

(莺莺引红娘捻花枝上云)红娘,俺去佛殿耍去来。(末做见科)呀!

正撞著五百年前风流业冤。

【元和令】颠不刺的见了万千,似这般可喜娘的庞儿罕曾见。则著人眼花缭乱口难言,魂灵儿飞在半天。他那里尽人调戏䰀著香肩,只将花笑捻。

【上马娇】这的是兜率宫,休猜做了离恨天。呀,谁想著寺里遇神仙!我见他宜嗔宜喜春风面,

[Zhang Gong says] "Since the abbot is out, don't bother about the tea. I wonder if you could take the trouble and guide me to have a look at the monastery. It will be my greatest honor."

[Fa Cong says] "I will to take out the key and lead you to visit the hall of the monastery, bell tower and sachet kitchen. It will take for a moment. My master may come back soon."

[Zhang Gong claims] "What a well built monastery it is!"

[Tune of Village Drums Song] "Having visited the Buddha hall in the north, I have arrived at monastery in the south. Passing by the kitchen in the west, I visited Buddhist Dharma Hall, with a towering bell in front. After I visited the chambers in the monastery, I have climbed the pagoda, and walked long the winding corridor again and again. I have worshiped bodhisattva, counted the arhats, and showed my respect to the sages." [Ying Ying enters with Red Maid to pick up flowers in the monastery yard. She says] "Red Maid, I will go to the monastery."

[Zhang Gong encounters Ying Ying and claims] "Ah, I happened to meet the predestined lover five hundred years ago."

[Tune of Song of Peace] "Wondering to and fro, and viewing so many things in my life, I never saw such a lovely girl. It makes me bewildered and enchanted. My soul is out of body already. She is standing there, smiling and holding a flower in her hands."

[Tune of Charming on the Horse Song] "This is a Buddhist monastery, but I guess it will turn out to be a place of sorrows. Ah,

偏、宜贴翠花钿。

【胜葫芦】则见他宫样眉儿新月偃，斜侵入鬓云边。

（旦云）红娘，你觑：寂寂僧房人不到，满阶苔衬落花红。（末云）我死也！

未语人前先腼腆，樱桃红绽，玉粳白露，半晌恰方言。

【幺篇】恰便似呖呖莺声花外啭，行一步可人怜。解舞腰肢娇又软，千般袅娜，万般旖旎，似垂柳晚风前。

（红云）那壁有人，咱家去来。（旦回顾觑末）（末云）和尚，恰怎么观音现来？（聪云）休胡说！这是河中开府崔相国的小姐。（末云）世间有这等女子，岂非天姿国色乎？休说那模样儿，则那一对小脚

who can imagine to meet such a goddess in a monastery! She is so beautiful whenever she is happy or angry, with a face smiling as if blowing of spring wind. On the one side of her hair, there hangs a flower shaped hairpin."

[Tune of Better than Gourd Song] "Look at her crescent moon-like eyebrows, which are so long that stretch forward her forehead. [Ying Ying says] "Red Maid, look here. The monks in the monastery are not here. The scenery is so quiet and lonely, with falling petals covering the stairs."

[Zhang Gong says] "Oh, I will die for her. Before she opens her mouth, she stops to think. Her lips is as red as cherry. Her teeth is as white as white dew. She looks so elegant and refined."

[Same Tune] "Her voice sounds like warbler bird chirping. When she walks, she is so delicate and charming. Her waist is so slim and soft when she is dancing, as if a willow branch flowing in the blowing wind."

[Red Maid says] "There is a man looking here. Let's go back."

[Ying Ying looks back before she leaves.] [Zhang Gong asks]

"Little master, where does this Guan Yin come from?"

[Fa Cong says] "Don't talk nonsense. This is the lady from the former prime minister Cui of He Zhong prefecture."

[Zhang Gong says] "I never expect there is such a girl in this world. Doesn't she process peerless beauty in the dynasty? Not to mention

儿，价值百镒之金。(聪云)偌远地，他在那壁，你在这壁，系著长裙儿，你便怎知他脚儿小?(末云)法聪，来来来，你问我怎便知，你觑：

【后庭花】若不是衬残红芳径软，怎显得步香尘底样儿浅。且休题眼角儿留情处，则这脚踪儿将心事传。慢俄延，投至到栊门儿前面，刚那了一步远。刚刚的打个照面，风魔了张解元。似神仙归洞天，空馀下杨柳烟，只闻得鸟雀喧。

【柳叶儿】呀，门掩著梨花深院，粉墙儿高似青天。恨天、天不与人行方便，好著我难消遣，端的是怎留连。小姐呵，则被你兀的不引了人意马心猿。

（聪云）休惹事，河中开府的小姐去远了也。（末唱）

her look, but just look at her pair of small feet. It is worthy of a thousand golden bar."

[Fa Cong asks] "You are so far from her. She is there, and you are here. Moreover, she is wearing long dress, so how do you know she has a pair of small feet?"

[Zhang Gong says] "Fa Cong, come, come. If you asked me how I know, I would tell you. Look!"

[Tune of Backyard flower Song] "See the traces of falling petals on each road side. They look so soft. The foot prints of hers are so shallow and small. The corner of her eyes looks around charmingly, however, her footprints shows there are worries in her mind. Slowly she walked towards the gate of her chamber, though it is just one step away. Just casting a glimpse of the lady at first sight, I am bewitched. The lady must be a goddess returning to the heaven palace, just leaving the willows and polar trees dancing in the wind and birds chirping in the emptiness."

[Tune of Willow Leaves Song] "Ah, the gate is shut. It prevents me from viewing of pear blossom in the deep courtyard. The pink wall is as high as the heaven sky. I hate the heaven, as it can not do convenience of me. It wastes me and makes me tired. Why am I so reluctant to leave? Young lady, you make my heart perturbed.

[Fa Cong says] "Don't make troubles. The lady in the He Zhong prefecture has gone far away."

【寄生草】兰麝香仍在，佩环声渐远。东风摇曳垂杨线，游丝牵惹桃花片，珠帘掩映芙蓉面。你道是河中开府相公家，我道是南海水月观音现。

"十年不识君王面，恰信婵娟解误人。"小生便不往京师去应举也罢。（觑聪云）敢烦和尚对长老说知，有僧房借半间，早晚温习经史，胜如旅邸内冗杂。房金依例拜纳。小生明日自来也。

【赚煞】饿眼望将穿，馋口涎空咽，空著我透骨髓相思病染，怎当他临去秋波那一转。休道是小生，便是铁石人也意惹情牵。近庭轩，花柳争妍，日午当庭塔影圆。春光在眼前，争奈玉人不见，将一座梵王宫疑是武陵源。（下）

[Tune of Parasitic Grass Song] "The scent of blue musk is still lingering in the air. The tinkling of sound of jewelers is gradually disappearing. The East wind blows the willow and polar tree branches, with the silk branches touching the peach petals. The bead curtains hide lady's lotus flower-like face. You told me she is the lady in the He Zhong prefecture, but I thought her as Guan Yin in the south sea who appears!

I have never saw emperor's face in these ten years, but now I believe the beauty will mislead men. I will not go to the capital for the imperial exam. [Zhang Gong looks around and speaks to Fa Cong secretly] "Could you talk to your master if I could stay in the a half room of the monastery Houses? I will review the classics and poetry from morning to evening, which is better than the noisy inn outside. The rent will be paid regularly. I will come here again tomorrow."

[Tune of Pseudo-Epilogue Song] "I am so eager to encounter with the lady again. It makes me suffer from love sickness. I will never forget her glances when she left. Not to mention me, even a stone-hearted person will be softened and fall in love with her. Close to the small room in the yard, the flowers and willows compete in splendor, the shadow of tower is round in the sunlight. The beautiful spring is front of people's eyes, however, the beloved beauty is not by my side. How could I covert a monastery into a heaven of peace and happiness?" [Exeunt]

第二折

（夫人上白）前日长老将钱去与老相公做好事，不见来回话。道与红娘，传著我的言语，去问长老，几时好与老相公做好事？就著他办下东西的当了，来回我话者。（下）（净扮洁上）老僧法本，在这普救寺内做长老。此寺是则天皇后盖造的，后来崩损，又是崔相国重修的。见今崔老夫人领著家眷，扶柩回博陵，因路阻暂寓本寺西厢之下，待路通回博陵迁葬。老夫人处事温俭，治家有方，是是非非，人莫敢犯。夜来老僧赴斋，不知曾有人来望老僧否？（唤聪问科）（聪云）夜来有一秀才，自西洛而来，特谒我师，不遇而返。（洁云）山门外觑著，若再来时，报我知道。（末上云）昨日见了那小姐，倒有顾盼小生之意。今日去问长老借一间僧房，早晚温习经史，倘遇那小姐出来，必当饱看一会。

Scene Two

[The Old Lady enters] "Several days ago, the abbot took the money to redeem the dead soul for my old husband, but he hasn't told me the date to do the ceremony yet. I will send Red Maid to go to the abbot and ask when it will be convenient for him to conduct the funeral for my late husband? If you are told the time, tell me when you are back."[Exeunt]

[Fa Ben enters] "I am an abbot called Fa Ben, the master of this monastery. This monastery was firstly built in favour of Wu Zetian empress, but later it collapsed. Then it is former Prime Minister Cui who rebuilt the monastery. Now, the old lady took her family to live in the western wings of the monastery and intended to carry the coffin to To Ling town. When the road is clear, they will reach Bo Ling and bury the coffin. The old lady is gentle and frugal, who governs the family well. To her, what is right is right, and what is wrong is wrong. No one dares to offend her. Last night, I went outside to do a religious ceremony in the village. I wonder whether someone has come to call on me?"[The abbot calls Fa Cong to come and asks him.]

[Fa Cong says] "Yesterday, there was a young scholar who comes from West Luo City visiting you. As you are absent, he said he would come back."

【中吕】【粉蝶儿】不做周方,埋怨杀你个法聪和尚。借与我半间儿客舍僧房,与我那可憎才居止处门儿相向。虽不能勾窃玉偷香,且将这盼行云眼睛儿打当。

【醉春风】往常时见傅粉的委实羞,画眉的敢是谎。今日多情人一见了有情娘,著小生心儿里早痒痒。迤逗得肠荒,断送得眼乱,引惹得心忙。

(末见聪科)(聪云)师父正望先生来哩,只此少待,小僧通报去。

(洁出见末科)(末云)是好一个和尚呵!

【迎仙客】我则见他头似雪,鬓如霜,面如童,少年得内养。貌堂堂,声朗朗,头直上只少个圆光,却便似捏塑来的僧伽像。

[Fa Ben says] "Wait at the gate of the monastery. If he comes again, please tell me."

[Zhang Gong says] "Since I met the lady yesterday, her image is curved in my mind. Today, I will ask for a chamber to settle down in the monastery and review the classic at the same time. When the lady come, I may have a glance of her."

[Tune of Pink Butterfly Song] "If you do not provide convenience for me, I will not forgive the Fa Cong abbot for all my life. I plan to rent a half room in the guest house of the monastery, which is just facing the room of the lady. Though I could not spend a good time with her, I am able to peep at her secretly."

[Tune of Indulging in the Spring Wind Song] "Usually when I met the lady with powered face, I always feel flustered. However, today when I met the lovable lady, there stirred in me a tortuous impulse. I lost myself, forgetting to eat food, but burnt with anxiety."

[Zhang Gong meets Fa Cong. Fa Cong says] "Sir, my master has been waiting for you now. I will go to inform him."

[Fa Ben comes and meets Zhang Gong] [Zhang Gong sighs] "What an abbot he is!"

[Tune of Welcoming Immortals Guests Song] "I see his hair as white as snow, and grey at temples, however, he has such a ruddy

（洁云）请先生方丈内相见。夜来老僧不在,有失迎迓。望先生恕罪。（末云）小生久闻老和尚清誉,欲来座下听讲,何期昨日不得相遇。今能一见,是小生三生有幸矣。（洁云）先生世家何郡?敢问上姓大名,因甚至此?（末云）小生姓张名珙,字君瑞。

【石榴花】大师一一问行藏,小生仔细诉衷肠。自来西洛是吾乡,宦游在四方,寄居咸阳。先人拜礼部尚书多名望,五旬上因病身亡。

（洁云）老相公弃世,必有所遗。（末唱）平生正直无偏向,止留下四海一空囊。（洁云）老相公在官时浑俗和光。

complexion. His youth has never left him. He is dignified and impressive. His voice is strong and deep. If he had an aureole above his head, he is the very image of Sangha which is made from mud."

[Fa Ben says] "Sir, please come into the abbot room. Yesterday, I was not in the monastery. Please forgive me."

[Zhang Gong says] "I have long heard of your renowned reputation, so I come to hear your preach purposely. However, yesterday you were absent. Today, I finally get an opportunity to meet you. I feel myself very fortunate."

[Fa Ben asks] "May I ask where do you come from? Which city do you live? What is your name? And why are you here?"

[Zhang Gong says] "My family name is Zhang, given name Gong, and nickname Jun Rui."

[Tune of Pomegranate Flower Song] "The abbot asked me the details of my whereabouts, and I answered him with a respect. The West Luo City is my hometown. I wonder around just to attend imperial examination. I once resided in Xian Yang City. My father held the position of General Secretary of the Department of Rites and worked well for his job. However, he died at the age of fifty, out of illness." [Fa Ben says] "As your father died, he must leave you something." [Zhang Gong says] "Throughout my life, I have no bad habits, however, now after roaming around the world, my purse bag is almost empty."

(末唱)

【斗鹌鹑】俺先人甚的是浑俗和光,旳一味风清月朗。

(洁云)先生此一行,必上朝取应去。

(末唱)小生无意求官,有心待听讲。

小生特谒长老,奈路途奔驰,无以相馈——量著穷秀才人情则是纸半张。又没甚七青八黄,尽著你说短论长,一任待掂斤播两。

径禀:有白银一两,与常住公用,略表寸心,望笑留是幸。(洁云)先生客中,何故如此?(末云)物鲜不足辞,但充讲下一茶耳。

【上小楼】小生特来见访,大师何须谦让。

(洁云)老僧决不敢受。

(末唱)

这钱也难买柴薪,不勾斋粮,且备茶汤。

(觑聪云)这一两银,未为厚礼。

[Tune of Fights of Quails Song] "My father keeps a low profile, but doing things. He is an honest and upright official."

[Fa Ben says] "Sir, you said you were on the way to the capital for the imperial examination."

[Zhang Gong answers] "Yes, I am, though I have no ambition to attend officialdom. I have a heart to hear your preach. I intend to visit you purposely, however, the journey is long, and I have nothing to present you as a gift. Being a poor scholar, my presents are nothing but calligraphy and paintings, these pieces of paper."

[Zhang Gong walks towards Fa Ben and presents him.] "I can only offer your one ounce of silver for my expenses in the monastery. This is the gift for you to show my respect. It will be my fortunate if you accept it." [Fa Ben says] "Sir, you are a guest here. Why bother about this?"

[Zhang Gong says] "The gift is too small to be declined. It is just enough for a cup of tea."

[Tune of Ascending the Attic Song] "I come to pay a visit with respect, and there is no need for modest declination."

[Fa Ben says] "I can not accept it."

[Zhang Gong sings] "These money are not enough to buy fuel-wood, nor buy food, but just enough for a cup of tea."

[Zhang Gong looks at Fa Cong secretly] "One ounce of silver is not rich gift.

你若有主张,对艳妆,将言词说上,我将你众和尚死生难忘。

(洁云)先生必有所请。(末云)小生不揣有恳。因恶旅邸冗杂,早晚难以温习经史,欲假一室,晨昏听讲,房金按月任意多少。(洁云)敝寺颇有数间,任先生拣选。

(末唱)

【幺篇】也不要香积厨,枯木堂。远著南轩,离著东墙,靠著西厢。近主廊,过耳房,都皆停当。

(洁云)便不呵,就与老僧同处何如?(末笑云)要恁怎么?你是必休题著长老方丈。

(红上云)老夫人著俺问长老,几时好与老相公做好事,看得停当回话。须索走一遭去来。(见洁科)长老万福。夫人使侍妾来问,几时好与老相公做好事,著看的停当了回话。(末背云)好个女子也呵!

If you are able to accept it, and speak for my sake to that beautiful lady, I will never forget your monks."

[Fa Ben says] "Sir, you must have had some requests."

[Zhang Gong says] "Because of the long tedious journey, I cannot review the classic and history in the crowded inn. I wish I could borrow one room, and devote into study day and night. I will pay the rent for any amount per month."

[Fa Ben says] "This monastery has several empty rooms. You can select any of them.

[Tune of Petty Song] "I don't want the kitchen in the monastery, nor the meditation room, which is far away from the Eastern wall, but I want a room near the West where the anteroom arrests my eyes."

[Fa Ben asks] "I wonder if it is convenient, would you stay in the same room with me?"

[Zhang Gong laughs] "Thank you, dear abbot, but don't mention it."

[The Red Maid enters and says] "The old lady just sent me to inquire the abbot when he is going to conduct a funereal for my late master. When I am told the time, I will reply to the old lady."

[Red Maid meets Fa Ben and says] "Wish you all happiness, abbot. The old lady send me to ask when it is convenient for you to conduct a funereal for my late master? If time is settled, I will reply to her."

[Zhang Gong says secretly] "How clever she looks!"

【脱布衫】大人家举止端详,全没那半点儿轻狂。大师行深深拜了,启朱唇语言得当。

【小梁州】可喜娘的庞儿浅淡妆,穿一套缟素衣裳。胡伶渌老不寻常,偷睛望,眼挫里抹张郎。

【幺篇】若共他多情的小姐同鸳帐,怎舍得他叠被铺床。我将小姐央,夫人快,他不令许放,我亲自写与从良。

　　(洁云)二月十五日可与老相公做好事。(红云)妾与长老同去佛殿看了,却回夫人话。(洁云)先生请少坐,老僧同小娘子看一遭便来。(末云)何故却小生?便同行一遭,又且何如?(洁云)便同行。

[Tune of Doffing off the Clothes Song] "The girl is natural and at ease in her behavior, without any arrogance in her manner. She bowed to the abbot deeply, and conducted herself properly."

[Tune of Small Liang Zhou Song] "The lovely girl wears a slight makeup on the face and a white mourning dress on the body. She is wearing a mischievous and clever smile, whose eyes peeps at Zhang Gong secretly and measures him up and down. But she doesn't speak to him."

[Tune of Petty Song] "If it is possible to marry that lovely lady whom I met last day, I will not to allow this maid to fold our quilts. I myself will write a guarantee, to set her free."

[Fa Ben says] "On february 25th, I am able to conduct a funeral for your late master."

[Red Maid says] "Abbot, could I reply to my old lady, after I go with you to visit the Buddha hall together? I want to see if everything is arranged."

[Fa Ben says] "Sir, Please have a seat for a while. I will go around with this young maid to the old monastery, and come back as soon as possible."

[Zhang Gong says] "My sister, take your time. I will keep a little distance behind."

[Fa Ben says] "What a well mannered scholar!"

[Zhang Gong asks] "I have something to say. Could I put it frankly?"

（末云）著小娘子先行，俺近后些。（洁云）一个有道理的秀才。（末云）小生有一句话说，敢道么？（洁云）便道不妨。

（末唱）

【快活三】崔家女艳妆，莫不是演撒你个老洁郎？

（洁云）俺出家人那有此事？（末）既不沙，却怎睃趁著你头上放毫光？打扮的特来晃。

（洁云）先生是何言语！早是那小娘子不听得哩，若知呵，是甚意思！（红上佛殿科）

（末唱）

【朝天子】过得主廊，引入洞房，好事从天降。

我与你看著门儿，你进去。（洁怒云）先生，此非先王之法言！岂不得罪于圣人之门乎？老僧偌大年纪，焉肯作此等之态！

（末唱）

好模好样忒莽撞。

没则罗便罢，

烦恼则么耶唐三藏？

me for being suspicious of you. In such a big monastery, why are there no other men? It may leave me the impression that the servant maid is too easy to be tricked."

[Fa Ben says] "The old lady governs the family with a strict rule. There is no male coming in or out of the family."

[Zhang Gong says secretly behind] "The bald ass is talking of shit. Even if you are here, I will do what I like to do. If you are strongly against, I will bite the bullet."

[Fa Ben talked to Red Maid] "The Buddhist feasts and Taoist rites have all been prepared. On 15th, the old lady and the young lady can be allowed to burn incense."

[Zhang Gong asks] "Why?"

[Fa Ben says] "It is the filial feeling of young lady to her late father that prompts her to conduct a religious funeral. She did this to repay the deep affection from her parents. This is also the twenty seventh months after the former prime minister died. After that day, the young lady is able to take off the mourning clothes." [Zhang Gong sheds tears too] "How sad it is to lose parents! They gave birth to us and brought us up. It is impossible to repay their affection and kindness. Even as a woman, the young lady has such a heart to show her gratitude to her father. For me who wonders in the world for a dozens of years, I never burn a paper for my dead parents. I wish abbot may show me mercy. I will prepare five thousand tasel, and may you prepare a meal for my decreased parents too! I think old lady will not object if she knows. I just fulfill my duty as a son."

（洁云）法聪，与这先生带一分者。（末背问聪云）那小姐明日来么？（聪云）他父母的勾当，如何不来？（末背云）这五千钱使得有些下落者！

【四边静】人间天上，看莺莺强如做道场。软玉温香，休道是相亲傍，若能勾汤他一汤，到与人消灾障。

（洁云）都到方丈吃茶。（做到科）（末云）小生更衣咱。（末出科云）那小娘子已定出来也，我则在这里等待问他咱。（红辞洁云）我不吃茶了，恐夫人怪来迟，去回话也。（红出科）（末迎红娘祗揖科）小娘子拜揖。（红云）先生万福。（末云）小娘子莫非莺莺小姐的侍妾么？（红云）我便是。何劳先生动问？（末云）小生姓张，名珙，字君瑞，本贯西洛人也。年方二十三岁，正月十七日子时建生。并不曾娶妻……

[Fa Ben says to Fa Cong] "Please prepare one feast for this gentleman."

[Zhang Gong asks Fa Cong secretly] "Will the young lady come tomorrow?"

[Fa Cong says] "It is about her parents' business. How could she be absent for the service of her father?"

[Zhang Gong whispers to himself] "Then, these five thousand tasel is well paid."

[Tune of Four Side Quietness Song] "In the heaven and on the earth, let's see how Ying Ying is going to ask the monks to perform in the ritual rites. She is as fair as a jade. If not having the chance of marrying her, it will bring me good luck and ward off calamities as long as I am able to drink one cup of soup on the feasts."

[Fa Ben says] "Let's come to abbot's room and have a cup of tea."

[Zhang Gong hurries to put on the clothes] "Please excuse me for a moment and allow me to change my clothes." [Zhang Gone goes out and speaks], "That maid is sure to come outside. I just stay here and wait for her to send my respects."

[Red Maid bids goodbye to Fa Ben and says] "I don't eat tea now, afraid that old lady would ask for me. I will go back and reply to her as soon as possible." [Red Maid decides to go outside][Zhang Gong encounters Red Maid and greets her with his hands folding in front] "Good morning, Fair maid."

[Red Maid says] "Sir, wish you all happiness."

[Zhang Gong asks] "Are you the maid of lady Ying Ying?"

（红云）谁问你来？（末云）敢问小姐常出来么？（红怒云）先生是读书君子，孟子曰："男女授受不亲，礼也。"君知"瓜田不纳履，李下不整冠"。道不得个"非礼勿视，非礼勿听，非礼勿言，非礼勿动。"俺夫人治家严肃，有冰霜之操。内无应门五尺之童，年至十二三者，非呼召，不敢辄入中堂。向日莺莺潜出闺房，夫人窥之，召立莺莺于庭下，责之曰："汝为女子，不告而出闺门，倘遇游客小僧私视，岂不自耻？"莺立谢而言曰："今当改过从新，毋敢再犯。"是他亲女，尚然如此，何况以下侍妾乎！先生习先王之道，尊周公之礼，不干己事，何故用心？早是妾身，可以容恕。若夫人知其事呵，决无干休！今后得问

[Red Maid says] "Yes, I am. Why are you asking?"

[Zhang Gong says] "My family name is Zhang, given name Gong, and nickname Jun Rui. I was born in the West Luo City. This year, I am just twenty three years old. I was born between the period of the day from eleven p. m. to one a. m. on lunar january 17th. I haven't married yet..."

[Red Maid stops him.] "Who asked you?"

[Zhang Gong asks] "May I ask how often does your lady go out?"

[Red Maid gets angry. She says] "Sir, you look like an educated gentleman. Haven't you learned of Mencius teaching 'It is not proper for a man and woman to communicate with each other.' This is courtesy between men and women. Have you read of the poem about the gentleman's behavior written by Cao Shi, which says that when a gentleman passes by a watermelon field, he should not lift his shoes. When he passes by the plum trees, he should not tidy up his hat, in order to avoid unnecessary suspicion. There is another saying 'See no evil, hear no evil, speak no evil, move no evil'. My old lady governs the family strictly, paying a lot of attention to my young lady's reputation. In the lady's room, there is no male servant who is taller than five inches. Those male servants who reach twelve or thirteen years old would not be allowed to appear in middle hall of the main room without being asked for. Several days ago, Ying Ying sneaked out of the room secretly. When the old lady knew it, she scolded Ying Ying seriously, 'You are a lady, but you go out of your room. If you met some men peeping at you secretly, don't you feel shameful for yourself?' Ying

的问,不得问的休胡说!(下)(末云)这相思索是害也。

【哨遍】听说罢心怀悒怏,把一天愁都撮在眉尖上。说"夫人节操凛冰霜,不召呼,谁敢辄入中堂!"自思想,比及你心儿里畏惧老母亲威严,小姐呵,你不合临去也回头儿望。待飐下教人怎飐?赤紧的情沾了肺腑,意惹了肝肠。若今生难得有情人,是前世烧了断头香。我得时节手掌儿里奇擎,心坎儿里温存,眼皮儿上供养。

【耍孩儿】当初那巫山远隔如天样,听说罢又在巫山那厢。业身躯虽是立在回廊,魂灵儿已在他行。本待要安排心事传幽客,我子怕漏泄春光与乃堂。夫人怕女孩儿春心荡,怪黄莺儿作对,怨粉蝶儿成双。

Ying hurried to apologized to her mother and promised, 'Sorry, my mother. I will turn a new leaf and never dare to make the same mistake again.' The old lady treated her own daughter like this, not to mention how strict she was with me? Sir, you have well learned the moral law of previous sages, and obeyed the etiquette of Duke Zhou, so it is not your business to ask about Ying Ying. Why do you have such a talk with me? It is lucky of you to meet me, who can tolerant you, but if my old lady learns about it, she will not easily forgive you. In the future, you can ask what you should ask, and not to ask what you shouldn't." [Exit]

[Zhang Gong sighs] "I am afraid that I will die of this love sickness!"

[Tune of Whistle Aloud Song] "After hearing what Red Maid said, I feel so sad and gloomy. The worries are all shown on my knitted eyebrows. Red Maid just said that the old lady pays much attention to the reputation. If not asked, no one dare to enter the middle hall. I am thinking if my lady will be afraid of her strict mother. If so, why did she turn her eyes on me when she went away? What should I do now? The love towards Ying Ying has already deeply curved into my heart, and I am overwhelmed with grief. If I am not able to marry my beloved one in this life, I must have burnt the broken incense in the pre-existence. Ying Ying, when am I able to hold your hands? I miss you dearly day and night. Your image is always floating in my eyes."

[Tune of Playing with the Children Song] "Before I asked Red

【五煞】小姐年纪小,性气刚。张郎倘得相亲傍,乍相逢厌见何郎粉,看邂逅偷将韩寿香。才到是未得风流况,成就了会温存的娇婿,怕甚么能拘束的亲娘。

【四煞】夫人忒虑过,小生空妄想。

郎才女貌合相仿。休直待眉儿浅淡思张敞,春色飘零忆阮郎。非是咱自夸奖,他有德言工貌,小生有恭俭温良。

【三煞】想著他眉儿浅浅描,脸儿淡淡妆,粉香腻玉搓咽项。翠裙鸳绣金莲小,红袖鸾销玉笋长。不想呵其实强,你撇下半天风韵,我拾得万种思量。

Maid, the distance between me and lady is as far as the Wu Mountain. After hearing what Red Maid said, I find the same distance between me and the lady, though she just stays in the next room. Though I am standing in the corridor, my soul has already followed her. I have intended to tell my love sickness to Red Maid, however, I am afraid that my secret is revealed to the old lady. The old lady fears her daughter feeling the first string of love, blaming the yellow warbler in pairs and butterflies flying together."

[Last Stanza] "Red Maid, you are still too young and spirited. You will not listen to my plea. Could I hold your gentle lady in my arms? For the first encounter, you turn me away. However, if I had a chance to date with the young lady, I will steal her fragrance like a bee. After our dating, it will make an attentive husband of me. Why does the lady need to be afraid of her strict mother?"

[Last Stanza but Four] "The old lady has worried so much and my dream is empty. Do young lady and me match each other well? I have talents and she has beauty. Zhang Chang will not be the only one to paint the eyebrows for his wife in the history. In such a beautiful spring, how I wish I was able to have the same fortune as Ruan Lang who met a fairy like lady in the dream, and latter became her husband. I am not boasting myself. Those lucky men in the history had moral, good manner, handsome looking and proper behavior, but I am gentle, swift and kind."

[Last Stanza but Three] "I am thinking of painting her eyebrows slightly by myself, and putting up the rouge on her face one day. The smell of powder would make me hungry. The lady wears a

却忘了辞长老。(见洁科)小生敢问长老:房舍何如?(洁云)塔院侧边西厢一间房,甚是潇洒,正可先生安下,见收拾下了,随先生早晚来。(末云)小生便回店中搬去。(洁云)既然如此,老僧准备下斋,先生是必便来。(下)(末云)若在店中人闹,到好消遣搬在寺中静处,怎么捱这凄凉也呵!

【二煞】院宇深,枕簟凉。一灯孤影摇书幌。纵然酬得今生志,著甚支吾此夜长!睡不著如翻掌,少可有一万声长吁短叹,五千遍倒枕槌床。

green dress and has a pair of small feet. Her red sleeves are long and fleeing; her fingers is long and slender. Those who do not think of the image of such a lady is rather hard-minded. If you want to avoid the most beautiful lady in the world, please allow me to pick up the seed of love sickness on the ground.

Oh. I forgot to say goodbye to the abbot."[Zhang Gong meets Fa Ben and says] "May I ask master whether my room has been prepared?"[Fa Ben says] "In the monastery yard, there is an empty room in the western chamber. It is quite lovely. Sir, you can settle down there. The room has been cleaned. You can come to stay at any time you want."

[Zhang Gong says] "Ok. I will return to the inn and bring my luggage here."

[Fa Ben says] "If so, I will prepare for the dinner. Sir, you must be sure to come back." [Exeunt Fa Ben and Fa Cong]

[Zhang Gong says] "If I stay in the noisy inn, time would pass by easily. If moved into this monastery, how am I able to endure such a loneliness without my lady as company?"

[Last Stanza but two] "The yard is deep, and the pillow is cold. The light from the lonely lamp casts shadows on the yellow paper of the book. Even if I realized my aspirations in this life, how could I kill such a long and lonely night? I can not sleep, but tossing on the bed for a long time. I sigh deeply many times, and beaten the

【尾】娇羞花解语，温柔玉有香。我和他乍相逢记不真娇模样，我则索手抵著牙儿慢慢的想。（下）

第三折

（正旦上云）老夫人著红娘问长老去了，这小贱人不来我行回话。（红上云）回夫人话了，去回小姐话去。（旦云）使你问长老，几时做好事？（红云）恰回夫人话也，正待回姐姐话。二月十五日请夫人、姐姐拈香。（红笑云）姐姐，你不知，我对你说一件好笑的勾当。咱前日寺里见的那秀才，今日也在方丈里。他先出门儿外，等著红娘，深深唱个喏道："小生姓张，名珙，字君瑞，本贯西洛人也，年二十三岁，正月十七日子时建生，并不曾娶妻。"姐姐，却是谁问他来？他又问："那壁小娘子，莫非莺莺小姐的侍妾乎？小姐常出来么？"被红娘抢白了一顿呵回来了。姐姐，我不知他想

pillows and the bed for five thousand times."

[Tune of Epilogue] "She is so beautiful that she puts flowers to shame. She is so gentle as if a jade with fragrance. I cannot remember her real looking at a brief glance, but I will put my hands under my cheek, and think of her grace slowly." [Exit]

Scene Three

[Ying Ying enters and says] "My mother sent Red Maid to the abbot and asked him when he is going to conduct a funeral, but she hasn't come back for a long time."

[Red Maid enters and says] "I have blready replied to the old lady, and now I am going tell my young lady."

[Ying Ying asks] "Have you asked the abbot when he is going to conduct funeral?"

[Red Maid said] "I have just replied to the old lady and now I am coming to you, my sister. On february 15th, the abbot will invite old lady and sister to burn incense."

[All of a sudden, Red Maid laughs and says] "Sister, you don't know. I have

甚么哩,世上有这等傻角!(旦笑云)红娘,休对夫人说。天色晚也,安排香案,咱花园内烧香去来。(下)(末上云)搬至寺中,正近西厢居址。我问和尚每来,小姐每夜花园内烧香。这个花园,和俺寺中合著。比及小姐出来,我先在太湖石畔墙角儿边等待,饱看一会。两廊僧众都睡著了,夜深人静,月朗风清,是好天气也呵!正是:闲寻方丈高僧语,闷对西厢皓月吟。

【越调】【斗鹌鹑】玉宇无尘,银河泻影,月色横空,花阴满庭。罗袂生寒,芳心自警。侧著耳朵儿听,蹑著脚步儿行:悄悄冥冥,潜潜等等。

something funny to tell you. The young scholar whom we met in the monastery several days ago was in abbot's room too. He was waiting for me outside. He made a deep bow to me and said,'My family name is Zhang, given name Gong, nickname Jun Rui. I was born in West Luo City. Twenty three years old this year. I was born on the 17th of the first moon. I have not married yet.'I said, 'Who asked you?'He asked again, 'Young sister, are you not the personal maid of lady Ying Ying? Will Miss Ying Ying often go out?'I scolded him to his face, and came back. Sister, I don't know what he was thinking then. It is amazing that he is such an idiot."[Ying Ying laughs] "Red Maid, don't tell my mother. It is late outside. Please set up for the incense burner table. Let's burn incense to the heaven in the garden." [Exeunt]

[Zhang Gong enters and says]"I have moved into the monastery, staying in the western chamber. I have asked the monk that the lady burns incense every day in the garden at night. This garden is near my room. When the lady comes out, I will wait for her at the foot of the wall near the stone side of the Tai lake, and have a feast view of her. The monks along the corridor are all sleeping. The night is deep, and the yard is quiet. The moon is bright, and the wind is soft. What a good weather it is! In such a loneliness, I will write poems chanting the moon in the western chamber."

[Tune of Fighting Quails Song] "There is no dust in the jade-like sky, and the Milk Way is casting shadows at night. The moon is

【紫花儿序】等待那齐齐整整,袅袅婷婷,姐姐莺莺。一更之后,万籁无声,直至莺庭。若是回廊下没揣的见俺可憎,将他来紧紧的搂定,则问你那会少离多,有影无形。

(旦引红娘上云)开了角门儿,将香桌出来者。(末唱)

【金蕉叶】猛听得角门儿呀的一声,风过处花香细生。蹑著脚尖儿仔细定睛:比我那初见时庞儿越整。

(旦云)红娘,移香桌儿,近太湖石畔放者。(末做看科云)料想春娇厌拘束,等闲飞出广寒宫。看

round and hanging on the sky. The shade of flowers is everywhere in the empty garden. Though in silk clothes, she still feels cold. The beautiful lady is in a hurry, knowing she is late tonight. She is walking stealthily, in light footsteps and listening carefully by the flower side."

[Tune of Violet Flower Song] "I am waiting for the elegant and graceful Ying Ying to come. After eight clock in the evening, it is quiet everywhere, till Ying Ying and Red Maid go to the garden together. If in the courtyard, with no one looking, I will hug Ying Ying directly in my arms. I will ask her why our meeting is so hard that I can only see her shadows."

[Ying Ying enters with Red Maid and says] "Open the side gate, and take the incense burner table out."

[Zhang Gong sings]

[Tune of Golden Banana Leaves Song] "Suddenly, I heard the opening sound of the side gate. The wind comes, carrying the fragrance of flowers. I stand up on my tiptoes, and open my eyes wildly. The image of the lady is more charming and elegant now than when I saw her at the first time."

[Ying Ying says] "Red Maid, move the incense burner table to the stone side near the Tai Hu Lake. [Zhang Gong is watching attentively] "I guess that beautiful lady is a goddess who is weary of her mother's restriction, so that she flies high into the moon palace. I saw her picking up an incense. The clothes on her bosom is half revealed. Silently, she burns the incense and her long sleeves are hanging on

他容分一捻,体露半襟,弹香袖以无言,垂罗裙而不语。似湘陵妃子,斜倚舜庙朱扉如月殿嫦娥,微现蟾宫素影。是好女子也呵!

【调笑令】我这里甫能见娉婷,比著那月殿嫦娥也不恁般撑。遮遮掩掩穿芳径,料应来小脚儿难行。可喜娘的脸儿百媚生,兀的不引了人魂灵!

(旦云)取香来。(末云)听小姐祝告甚么。(旦云)此一炷香,愿化去先人,早生天界,此一炷香,愿堂中老母,身安无事,此一炷香……(做不语科)(红云)姐姐不祝这一炷香,我替姐姐祝告:愿俺姐姐早寻一个姐夫,拖带红娘咱!(旦再拜云)心中无

the ground. She looks like Xiang Shui goddess, the wife of the first Emperor Shun. She leans on the banister, whose plain shadow is as elegant as Chang E (the Moon Goddess) in the moon palace. What a beautiful lady she is!"

[Tune of Song of Flirtation] "Here, I am able to see the graceful lady. She is even much more beautiful than Chang E in the moon palace. Half hiding herself, she walks pass the fragrant road. I guess that her small feet are too difficult to walk. Her lovely face is so enchanting and touching. How could I not be charmed by her!"

[Ying Ying says] "Please give me the incense."

[Zhang Gong says] "Let me hear what the lady is praying."

[Ying Ying says] "I burn the first stick of incense, wishing the dead soul of my decreased father can rise into heaven early. For the second, I wish my old mother in the house can live long. For the third..."[Ying Ying is silent]

[Red Maid says] "If sister do not pray for the third incense, I will pray for the sister. I wish my dear sister could find a good husband, and bring luck to me too."

[Ying Ying bows twice and says] "There are a thousand sorrows in my mind, which are all showed in these two bows." [She heaved a deep sigh]

[Zhang Gong says] "The lady is leaning on the banister and sighing so deeply. It seems that she is moved by something."

限伤心事,尽在深深两拜中。(长吁科)(末云)小姐倚栏长叹,似有动情之意。

【小桃红】夜深香霭散空庭,帘幕东风静。拜罢也斜将曲栏凭,长吁了两三声。剔团栾明月如悬镜,又不是轻云薄雾,都则是香烟人气,两般儿氤氲得不分明。我虽不及司马相如,我则看小姐颇有文君之意。我且高吟一绝,看他则甚:月色溶溶夜,花阴寂寂春。如何临皓魄,不见月中人?(旦云)有人墙角吟诗!(红云)这声音,便是那二十三岁不曾娶妻的那傻角。(旦云)好清新之诗!我依韵做一首。(红云)你两个是好做一首!(旦念诗云)兰闺久寂寞,无事度芳春。料得行吟者,应怜长叹人。(末云)好应酬得快也呵!

[Tune of Red Peach Blossoms Song] "The night is deep, and incense is burning. The smoke is meandering in the empty yard. The curtain is unmoved, as the east wind stops blowing. After bowing to the heaven, I lean on the banister and sigh deeply two or three times. The moon on the sky is as round as a hanging mirror, with neither mists, nor slight clouds surrounded. When the smoke is stronger, I can hardly see nowhere. Though I cannot be compared to Si Ma Xiangru, but I guess the lady share the same feeling with Zhuo Wenjun. I just made verses of four lines to see how she is going to respond to me.

The moon light is as soft as flowing water.

The shadows of flowers reflect the lonely spring night.

How to face such a beautiful moonlight?

Why can't I see the beloved one in such a sight?"

[Ying Ying says] "Someone is making verses at the corner of the wall!"

[Red Maid says] "Hearing from this voice, I guess it must be the idiot who is twenty three years old and still unmarried."

[Ying Ying says] "What a refreshing poem. I will compose one following his rhythm."

[Red Maid says] "Please compose one to hear."

[Ying Ying says] "The lady in the chamber is lonely for a long time.

【秃厮儿】早是那脸儿上扑堆著可憎,那堪那心儿里埋没著聪明。他把那新诗和得忒应声,一字字诉衷情,堪听。

【圣药王】那语句清,音律轻,小名儿不枉了唤做莺莺。他若是共小生、厮觑定,隔墙儿酬和到天明,方信道惺惺的自古惜惺惺。

我撞出去,看他说甚么。

【麻郎儿】我拽起罗衫欲行,(旦做见科)他陪著笑脸儿相迎。不做美的红娘忒浅情,便做道谨依来命。

(红云)姐姐,有人!咱家去来,怕夫人嗔著。
(莺回顾下)

Idling, she passes through the beautiful spring.

I guess the poem maker

Must have pity on the sighing maid!"

[Zhang Gong says] "How fast does she respond to my verses!"

[Tune of Bald Head Song] "Her charming appearance makes me more fascinated. What is more, she is so smart and clever, who composes verses following the same rhythm with mine so quickly. Each word reveals her true feeling. It is so pleasant to hear."

[Tune of Sovereign to the Medicine] "Her voice is so soft and clear. No wonder her nickname is Ying Ying. If she watched me with her pair of talking eyes, and making verses with me till the next morning, we are sure to appreciate with each other, as we are soul mates to one another.

I will run out and see what she is talking."

[Tune of Pockmarked Face Song] "I dragged my clothes and intended to go outside."

[Ying Ying sees Zhang Gong] "He is greeting me with a smile. Red maid is too unkind to ask me to leave, just following the order of my mother."

[Red Maid says] "Sister, somebody is here. Let's go away, in case the old lady will scold us."

[Ying Ying looks back and exits]

[Zhang Gong sings]

（末唱）

【幺篇】我忽听、一声、猛惊,元来是扑剌剌宿鸟飞腾,颤巍巍花梢弄影,乱纷纷落红满径。

小姐你去了呵,那里发付小生!

【络丝娘】空撇下碧澄澄苍苔露冷,明皎皎花筛月影。白日凄凉枉耽病,今夜把相思再整。

【东原乐】帘垂下,户已扃。却才个悄悄相问,他那里低低应。月朗风清恰二更,厮溪幸,他无缘,小生薄命。

【绵搭絮】恰寻归路,伫立空庭,竹梢风摆,斗柄云横。呀,今夜凄凉有四星,他不瞅人待怎生!虽然是眼角传情,咱两个口不言心自省。

今夜甚睡到得我眼里呵!

[Tune of Petty Song] "I suddenly heard some sound. As if being startled, I saw the birds returning home at night. Shaking in the shadows, the flowers petals falling on the ground.

My lady, you are going now. What shall I do to leave me alone!"

[Tune of Spinner Song] "The ladies are going, only leaving the empty stairs with cold dew glistening. The beautiful shade of flowers is shaking under the moonlight. It is so bleak that I am afraid to catch illness. Tonight, I have to sleep with love sickness again."

[Tune of Joy of Eastern Plain Song] "The curtains are drawn, and door is closed. Just then, I made verses with her secretly and she answered me fast in a low voice. The moon is bright and wind is clear. It has already reached nine o'clock at night. I am so lucky and yet unlucky. Maybe the lady and I are just passersby. What a feckless life I am living."

[Tune of Words of Cotton Song] "The ladies are walking way back home. I am standing in the empty room. The breeze stops blowing the top of bamboo trees, and big dipper stars appears on the sky. Tonight is so desolate that there are only four stars showing. Aren't the stars staring at human beings? Though she spoke only with her eyes to show the message of love and we two did not communicate too much, I am sure that we understand each other well in our mind.

Tonight, my dream is full of images of the lady!"

【拙鲁速】对著盏碧荧荧短檠灯,倚著扇冷清清旧帏屏。灯儿又不明,梦儿又不成窗儿外淅零零的风儿透疏棂,忒棱棱的纸条儿鸣枕头儿上孤零,被窝儿里寂静。你便是铁石人,铁石人也动情。

【幺篇】怨不能,恨不成,坐不安,睡不宁。有一日柳遮花映,雾障云屏,夜阑人静,海誓山盟——恁时节风流嘉庆,锦片也似前程美满恩情,咱两个画堂春自生。

【尾】一天好事从今定,一首诗分明照证。再不向青琐闼梦儿中寻,则去那碧桃花树儿下等。(下)

第四折

(洁引聪上云)今日二月十五日开启,众僧动法器者!请夫人小姐拈香。比及夫人未来,先请张生拈香,怕夫人问呵,则说道贫僧亲者。(末上云)

[Tune of Rush Speed Song] "Facing the glimmering light in the lamp, I leaned on the cold curtain. The light of the lamp is not bright, and I cannot fall into sleep. The slight wind is blowing the lattice window, and the window paper is making a sound, echoing in the room. The quilt is so quiet at night. Even if you are a stone-hearted man, you would be moved too."

[Tune of Petty Song] "I cannot blame, nor hate, nor sit, nor sleep. One day, the willows will shade the shadows of flowers, and the mist will tint the tent curtain. When the night is deep, we will make a solemn pledge of eternal love. After that, we can meet our parents, and the harmonious marriage is as sweet as flowers. Our painted walls are filled with the breath of spring."

[Tune of Epilogue] "From now on, good fortune will follow me. The verses exchanged is the witness of the love. I will not go for the imperial examinations, but wait for the beautiful lady beneath the peach flower trees."

Scene Four

[Fa Ben enters with Fa Cong. Fa Ben says] "Today is the 15th of the second moon. It is the time to conduct funeral service. Let's do a Buddhist mass. Please take out your musical instruments. Let's invite old

今日二月十五日,和尚请拈香,须索走一遭。

【双调】【新水令】梵王宫殿月轮高,碧琉璃瑞烟笼罩。香烟云盖结,讽咒海波潮。幡影飘飘,诸檀越尽来到。

【驻马听】法鼓金铎,二月春雷响殿角钟声佛号,半天风雨洒松梢。侯门不许老僧敲,纱窗外定有红娘报。害相思的馋眼脑,见他时须看个十分饱。

（末见洁科）（洁云）先生先拈香,恐夫人问呵,则说是老僧的亲。（末拈香科）

lady and young lady to burn incense. Now old lady hasn't arrived yet. We can ask Gentleman Zhang to burn the incense first. If the old lady asked, just say he is my relative."

[Zhang Gong enters and says] "Today is the 15th of the second moon. The abbot invites me to burn incense in the service. I have to take a walk there."

[Tune of Song of New Water] "The wall of Buddhist monastery is as high as a moon on the sky, and the smoke of incense surrounds its green-tinted roof, which turns into condensed clouds above the head. The magical words are spoken as if the tide waves of the sea which is raised by the wind. The banner is waving. The benefactors arrive successively."

[Tune of Halting the Horses Song] "The sacred drums and golden bells are ringing in every corner and all around. The Buddhist horn sounds like the thunder in the spring. The prayers to Buddha and the rings of bells sound like the wind and rain falling on the branches of loose trees. The noble men's door does not allow the monks to knock and Red Maid passes the news for the monks out of the window screen. Falling into love sickness, I am too eager to attend the ceremony, so that I may have the opportunity to meet her. I will glut my eyes to see her full."

[Zhang Gong meets Fa Ben] [Fa Ben says] "Sir, you can burn the incense first. If the old lady asked, you just say you are my relative." [Zhang Gong picks up an incense]

【沉醉东风】惟愿存在的人间寿高，亡化的天上逍遥。为曾祖父先灵，礼佛法僧三宝。焚名香暗中祷告：则愿得红娘休劣，夫人休焦，犬儿休恶。佛啰，早成就了幽期密约。

（夫人引旦上云）长老请拈香，小姐，咱走一遭。（末做见科）（觑聪云）为你志诚呵，神仙下降也。（聪云）这生却早两遭儿也。
（末唱）

【雁儿落】我则道这玉天仙离了碧霄，元来是可意种来清醮。小子多愁多病身，怎当他倾国倾城貌。

【得胜令】恰便似檀口点樱桃，粉鼻儿倚琼瑶。淡白梨花面，轻盈杨柳腰。妖娆，满面儿扑堆著俏苗条，一团儿衠是娇。

（洁云）贫僧一句话，夫人行敢道么？老僧有个

[Tune of Intoxicated to the East Wind Song] "I only hope those who are still alive in the world will have a long life, and those dead can be raised into heaven. I am praying for the dead soul of my ancestors in the Buddhist monastery. I burn a second incense, and pray secretly, 'I wish Red maid is not stubborn and stupid; the old lady is not strict and worried, and dogs will not bark at night. Buddha, please have pity for me and grant me a chance to have a secret date with the lady.'"

[The old lady enters with Ying Ying and Red Maid. The old lady says] "The abbot has asked us to burn incense today. Ying Ying, come with me."

[Zhang Gong looks at Fa Cong and says] "Moved by my sincerity, the goddess has condescended from heaven."

[Fa Cong says] "You have arrived too early."
[Zhang Gong sings]

[Tune of Falling Swam Song] "I have thought she is Chang E who leaves the cold palace in the sky, but it is my beloved lady who arrives to the alter. I am sick with longing, and she is so gorgeous looking."

[Tune of Triumphant Song] "Her lips is as red as cherry, and her nose is well curved like a white jade. Her face is like pear flower, and her waist is as slender as willow's blowing in the wind. She is so pretty and attractive; delicate and soft."

[Fa Ben says] "I have something to tell you, my old lady. I have a

敝亲,是个饱学的秀才,父母亡后,无可相报,对我说,央及带一分斋,追荐父母。贫僧一时应允了,恐夫人见责。(夫人云)长老的亲,便是我的亲,请来厮见咱。(末拜夫人科)(众僧见旦发科)

【乔牌儿】大师年纪老,法座上也凝眺举名的班首真呆僗,觑著法聪头做金磬敲。

【甜水令】老的小的,村的俏的,没颠没倒,胜似闹元宵。稔色人儿,可意冤家,怕人知道,看时节泪眼偷瞧。

【折桂令】著小生迷留没乱,心痒难挠。哭声儿似莺啭乔林,泪珠儿似露滴花梢。大师也难学,把一个发慈悲的脸儿来朦著。击磬的头陀懊恼,

relative, who is a well learned scholar on his way to the capital. His parents died, but he has nothing to show his gratitude to them. He told me to include him in the service. I have agreed. I hope my lady will not blame me."

[The Old Lady says] "If he is a relative of yours, so he is a relative of mine. Please call that gentleman to come and see me."

[Zhang Gong bows to the old lady] [Ying Ying carries a mischievous smile on her face]

[Tune of Pseudo-Melody Song] "The abbot has reached ages, and the head monk on the ceremony wears a dull expression. He is knocking Fa Cong's head with golden instrument, as if it was the drum."

[Tune of Sweet Water Song] "No matter old, young, rich or poor, they all greedily look at Ying Ying, and lost themselves as if nailed there. They were so enchanted by Ying Ying's beauty that they were befuddled, the scene of which looks like celebrating the noisy Lantern Festival. The lovely lady steals a look at Zhang Gong secretly, with a heart flustering like a rabbit, afraid of being noticed by other people."

[Tune of Picking Laurel Song] "I am bewildered, but not lost. The longings are overwhelming my mind. The young lady's crying is like warbler's warbling in the wood, and tears on her face fall down like dew on the pear flower petals. The abbot can cover his benevolent face with his sleeve. The monks in the rituals are totally flustered. The passerby who burn the incense are caught like a

添香的行者心焦。烛影风摇，香霭云飘，贪看莺莺，烛灭香消。

（洁云）风灭灯也。（末云）小生点灯烧香。（旦与红云）那生忙了一夜。

【锦上花】外像儿风流，青春年少，内性儿聪明，冠世才学。扭捏著身子儿百般做作，来往向人前卖弄俊俏。

（红云）我猜那生——

黄昏这一回，白日那一觉，窗儿外那会镢铎，到晚来向书帏里比及睡著，千万声长吁捱不到晓。

（末云）那小姐好生顾盼小子！

【碧玉箫】情引眉梢，心绪你知道愁种心苗，情思我猜著。畅懊恼，响铛铛云板敲，行者又嚎，沙弥又哨，怎须不夺人之好。

rabbit in the headlight. The shadows of candles are wavering, and the smoke in the monastery are floating above the roof. Everyone is so focused on looking at Ying Ying that they forget to lit the candles, or burn incense. "

[Fa Ben says] "The wind blow off the lamp."

[Zhang Gong says] "I will light the lamp and burn incense."

[Ying Ying says to the Red Maid] "This gentleman is so busy all night."

[Tune of Flower on the Brocade Song] "He looks dissolute on appearance, very young and handsome. He is wise and well learned. He pays much attention to his behavior, wishing to look extinguished in the crowds."

[Red Maid says] "I guess this gentleman—

He must have spent a very difficult time that evening, wishing the day to come sooner in order to meet you. He was talking to you at the window that night, and when he went back his room, he must have sighed all night till the day broke out."

[Zhang Gong says] "The lady is looking at me attentively."

[Tune of Green Flute Song] "The love sickness is revealed on the eyebrows. She must have shared the same feeling with me. In the monastery, the cloud-shaped iron plates are ringing, passersby are crying, and monks are whistling. It all disturbs my happiness."

（洁与众僧发科）（动法器了）（洁摇铃跪宣疏了，烧纸科）（洁云）天明了也，请夫人小姐回宅。（末云）再做一会也好，那里发付小生也呵！

【鸳鸯煞】有心争似无心好，多情却被无情恼。劳攘了一宵，月儿沉，钟儿响，鸡儿叫。唱道是玉人归去得疾，好事收拾得早。道场毕诸人散了，酩子里各归家，葫芦提闹到晓。（并下）

【络丝娘煞尾】则为你闭月羞花相貌，少不得蓊草除根大小。

题目　老夫人闭春院　　崔莺莺烧夜香
正名　小红娘传好事　　张君瑞闹道场

[Monks are moving their instruments.] [Fa Ben is ringing his bells, and burning the paper] "The day is bright now. My old lady and young lady, you can go back to the room."

[Zhang Gong says] "It is better to do the ceremony longer. Then you can dispatch me."

[Tune of Love birds' Epilogue Song] "It is better to fight for the love than do nothing. Those with ardent love is laughed at by those who have not. Tossing on the bed for the whole night, I find the moon falling from the sky, the bell ringing, and the roster cocking. If the beloved one left, I will suffer more love sickness. Good things should happen early. When the Buddhist rites finish, people have to leave. Everyone return home, and the next day arrive confusingly."

[Exeunt]

[Tune of Waggling Song] "For your beauty which outshines the moon and shames the flowers, I have to fight with other competitors."

Lady Cui comes to the monastery in the spring. Cui Yingying burns incense at night.

Red Maid comes with a good news. Zhang Gong performs religious rites.

五剧第二本

崔莺莺夜听琴杂剧

Act Two

楔　子

（夫人云）此事如何？（末云）小生有一计，先用著长老。（洁云）老僧不会厮杀，请秀才别换一个。（末云）休慌，不要你厮杀。你出去与贼汉说："夫人本待便将小姐出来，送与将军，奈有父丧在身。不争鸣锣击鼓，惊死小姐，也可惜了。将军若要做女婿呵，可按甲束兵，退一射之地。限三日功德圆满，脱了孝服，换上颜色衣服，倒陪房奁，定将小姐送与将军。不争便送来，一来父服在身，二来于军不利。"你去说来。（洁云）三日如何？（末云）有计在后。（洁朝鬼门道叫科）请将军打话。（飞虎卒上云）快送出莺莺来！（洁云）将军息怒。夫人使老僧来与将军说。（说如前了）（飞虎云）既然

Prologue

[The Old Lady asks] "What is your plan?"

[Zhang Gong says] "I indeed have a plan. But I have to ask for help from the abbot."

[Fa Ben says] "I am no fighter, so please change another one, sir."

[Zhang Gong says] "Don't worry. We don't need you to fight. Could you please just go out, and speak to the chief of rebels, 'The old lady had intended to give Ying Ying to the chief, however, her father died recently. She is till in mourning. If you continue beating gongs and drums, the lady will be terrified. You do not want to see such a result. If the chief wants to be a son-in-law, could you ask your soldiers not to move forward, but withdraw to the place where an arrow can shoot. After three days when the lady achieves perfect virtues and merits, she will take off mourning dress and change into a colorful one. Till that time, the old lady will send the lady to the chief as a gift. Wouldn't you feel happy if you don't lose a solider to bring the beauty back home? Firstly, the lady has to mourn for her father. Secondly, it will be unlucky for the general to marry her if she is still in mourning. Could you speak to him like this?" [Fa Ben asks] "What about in three days?" [Zhang Gong says] "I will tell you my plan latter."

[Fa Ben shouts to the chief of bandits] "General, could you please answer me?"

[Fei Hu enters and says] "Please give Ying Ying to me."

如此，限你三日后若不送来，我著你人人皆死，个个不存。你对夫人说去：恁的这般好性儿的女婿，教他招了者！（洁云）贼兵退了也，三日后不送出去，便都是死的。（末云）小子有一故人，姓杜，名确，号为白马将军，见统十万大兵，镇守著蒲关。一封书去，此人必来救我。此间离蒲关四十五里，写了书呵，怎得人送去？（洁云）若是白马将军肯来，何虑孙飞虎！俺这里有一个徒弟，唤做惠明，则是要吃酒厮打。若使央他去，定不肯去，须将言语激著他，他便去。（末唤云）有书寄与杜将军，谁敢去？谁敢去？

　　（惠明上云）我敢去！

[Fa Ben says] "Don't be hurry, general. The old lady asked me to answer you." [He speaks as it was planed before]

[Fei Hu says] "If it is so, I will give you three days. If you don't send Ying Ying to me within three days, I will punish all of you to die. No one is able to survive. You can reply to the old lady, 'He is such a good son-in-law. Please agree with the marriage between Ying Ying and me'."

[Fa Ben says] "Those bandits are retreating. He said if within three days, Ying Ying is not sent to him, all of us will die."

[Zhang Gong says] "I have a sworn brother, whose family name is Du, given name Que, nickname is Jun Shi, and he is the White Horse General. He has lead one hundred thousand soldiers, guarding the Pu Pass. If I write a letter to him, he is sure to come and save me. It is forty five miles from here to Pu Pass. If I wrote the letter, who is able to send it to him?"

[Fa Ben says] "If White Horse Genera is willing to come, why should we fear the thief Sun Feihu? I have a disciple here, whose name is Hui Ming. When he heard the news, he has intended to drink wine, and fight Sun Feihu with knife. If asked him to come and send the letter, I am not sure if he is willing, but if you can provoke him with words, he will be sure to come."

[Zhang Gong says to monks loudly.] "I have a letter to White Horse General. Who dares to send it to him? Who dares to send it to him?"

[Hui Ming enters and says] "I dare to go!"

【正宫】【端正好】不念《法华经》,不礼《梁皇忏》,甩了僧伽帽,袒下我这偏衫,杀人心逗起英雄胆,两只手将乌龙尾钢椽搦。

【滚绣球】非是我贪,不是我敢,知他怎生唤做打参,大踏步直杀出虎窟龙潭,非是我搀,不是我揽,这些时吃菜馒头委实口淡,五千人也不索炙煿煎熰。腔子里热血权消渴,肺腑内生心且解馋,有甚腌臜!

【叨叨令】浮沙羹宽片粉添些杂糁酸黄齑烂豆腐休调啖。万馀斤黑面从教暗,我将这五千人做一顿馒头馅。是必休误了也么哥,休误了也么哥!包残馀肉把青盐蘸。

　　(洁云)张秀才著你寄书去蒲关,你敢去么?(惠唱)

[Tune of Calm Dynasty Song] "I don't read scripture or pray. I throw my Sangha hat away and take off my robe. If anyone arouses my heroism to kill, I will hold steel hammer with house cleaning tail at the end in my hands."

[Tune of Rolling Embroidered Ball Song] "It's not because I am perverse, nor because I am bold, but it is because I am sitting in meditation all day. I wish I am able to kill out of tiger's lair and go into dragon's den. It's not because I love to fight, nor because I am eager to kill, it's because sometimes eating steamed bread and pickles everyday makes me feel tasteless in the mouth. There are five thousand monks in the monastery who don't want to eat fried food. The hot blood has quenched my thirst. The desire at the bottom of my heart satisfies my craving for delicious food. How filthy it is!"

[Tune of Nagging Song] "The thin gruel with wide strip of vermicelli, adding tiny grained Tofu does not satisfy my hunger. Just using ten thousands ponds black flour to make steamed breads is not enough for my stomach, and I will make these five thousand people turn into human meat buns. Don't miss the chance. Don't miss the chance. I will eat the meat human buns with salt."

[Fa Ben says] "Scholar Zhang asked you to send a letter to Pu Pass. Would you venture to go?"

[Hui Ming sings]

【倘秀才】你那里问小僧敢去也那不敢,我这里启大师用咱也不用咱。你道是飞虎将声名播斗南那厮能淫欲,会贪婪,诚何以堪!

(末云)你是出家人,却怎不看经礼忏,则厮打为何?
(惠唱)

【滚绣球】我经文也不会谈,逃禅也懒去参戒刀头近新来钢蘸,铁棒上无半星儿土渍尘缄。别的都僧不僧、俗不俗、女不女、男不男,则会斋的饱也则向那僧房中胡渰,那里怕焚烧了兜率伽蓝。则为那善文能武人千里,凭著这济困扶危书一缄,有勇无惭。

(末云)他倘不放你过去,如何?(惠云)他不放我呵,你放心。

【白鹤子】著几个小沙弥把幢幡宝盖擎,壮行者将捍棒镬叉担。你排阵脚将众僧安,我撞钉子把贼兵来探。

[Tune of Pseudo-scholar Song] "You are there to ask me whether I dare to go or not. I am asking my master whether he allows me to go or not. As Fei Hu is so greedy and lustful, how I dare reject!"

[Zhang Gong asks] "You are a monk. Why don't you read Buddhist text, but wish to fight?"

[Hui Ming sings]

[Tune of Rolling an Embroidered Ball Song] "I don't know how to read Buddhist text, or avoid mediation, but I am able to make the Buddhist monks' knives sharp and the iron bars cleaned from any dust. Other monks are neither monks, nor laymen, nor women, nor man. Those who fulfilled their stomach with tasteless food in the monastery shut themselves in the room from outside, not afraid of burning the monastery. I am willing to send this emergency letter to the general. I have courage, and will not regret."

[Zhang Gong asks] "If the chief of bandits will not allow you to pass through, ware you going to do?"

[Hui Ming says] "If he does not allow me to pass through, ha, that is easy."

[Tune of White Crane Song] "Please ask some young monks to carry Buddhist banners and parasols to go with me. I myself will carry stick and large iron pot. If you make plans to ease other monks' mind, I myself will meet the enemy boldly."

【二】远的破开步将铁棒飐,近的顺著手把戒刀钐,有小的提起来将脚尖忠跐,有大的扳下来把髑髅勘。

【一】瞅一瞅古都都翻了海波,滉一滉厮琅琅振动山岩,脚踏得赤力力地轴摇,手扳得忽剌剌天关撼。

【耍孩儿】我从来驳驳劣劣,世不曾忑忑忐忐,打熬成不厌天生敢。我从来斩钉截铁常居一,不似恁惹草拈花没掂三。劣性子人皆惨,舍著命提刀仗剑,更怕甚勒马停骖。

【二】我从来欺硬怕软,吃苦不甘,你休只因亲事胡扑俺。若是杜将军不把干戈退,张解元干将风月担,我将不志诚的言词赚。倘或纰缪,倒大羞惭。

（惠云）将书来,你等回音者。

【收尾】恁与我助威风擂几声鼓,仗佛力呐一

[Tune of a Second Stanza] "I will take big footsteps, and carry the iron bar in my hands. Those who are afar, I will sweep away with my iron bar. Those who are small, I would pick them up and kick them like a ball. Those who are tall, I will smash their heads."

[Tune of First Stanza] "Casting a glimpse of the old town, we found it as if as the sea turned over the waves. If I stomp, mountain rocks echo. The banners in the hands are waving heavily with my footsteps, and the sticks in the hands are shaking the heaven."

[Tune of Playing with the Child Song] "I am never crude or bloodthirsty, nor I am nervous or timid. I was born with courage of fighting. Since my childhood, I speak or act with determination and courage, never like you who are promiscuous in sex relations. Everyone is afraid of my fiery disposition. I am not afraid of death. Now, I pick up knife and sword for the uprightness. Who fears to stop the horse before the enemy?"

[Tune of a Second Stanza] "I was born to bully the strong and help the weak. I am not afraid of sufferings, but you should never worry about my courage because of your marriage. If White Horse General was unwilling to march his troops, it is not me but Gentleman Zhang whom should be blamed. You will not hear my kind words. What a shame if that's the case!"

[Hui Ming says] "Please give me the letter and wait for the reply."

[Tune of the Epilogue Song] "You beat the drummer for several times to cheer up my spirit. My blessed Buddha, I will utter a battle cry. Under the banner, I appear as a hero. I will make those five thousand bandits scared out of their wits."

声喊。绣旗下遥见英雄俺,我教那半万贼兵唬破胆。(下)

(末云)老夫人、长老都放心,此书到日,必有佳音。咱眼观旌节旗,耳听好消息。你看一封书札逡巡至,半万雄兵咫尺来。(并下)(杜将军引卒子上开)林下晒衣嫌日淡,池中濯足恨鱼腥,花根本艳公卿子,虎体原班将相孙。自家姓杜,名确,字君实,本贯西洛人也。自幼与君瑞同学儒业,后弃文就武,当年武举及第,官拜征西大将军,正授管军元帅,统领十万之众,镇守著蒲关。有人自河中来,听知君瑞兄弟在普救寺中,不来望我著人去请,亦不肯来,不知主甚意。今闻丁文雅失政,不守国法,剽掠黎民。我为不

[Zhang Gong says] "Old lady and abbot, you can ease your mind. If this letter arrives, there must come good news. Let's wait for the winning banners and good news. One letter from mine will be sure to invite five thousand strong soldiers to arrive here." [Exeunt]

[General Du enters with his soldiers.] "Usually, I dry my clothes in the woods and feel life so boring. I wash my feet in the ponds, but hate the smell of fish. The flowers should be appreciated by high rank officials, and the strong built body should belong to the grandchildren of Generals. My family name is Du, given name Que, and nickname Jun Shi. I was born in West Luo City. Zhang Junrui and I were classmates since we were children, and later, I gave up pen and picked up sword. In the same year, I won the first prize in the military imperial provincial examination and got the official position as West Expedition General, leading one hundred thousand troops, and guarding Pu Pass. Today, someone coming from He Zhong prefecture told me that my brother Jun Rui is staying in Pu Jiu monastery. Why doesn't he come to me? What is he thinking? I heard that recently Ding Wenya allowed his man to plunder and rob good people, instead of governing with good politics. I do not know whether this is true or not, so I dare not despatch the army to root out these thieves. Sun Zi said, 'In military operations, the general receives his commands from the sovereign, then he assembles soldiers to form units. In leading his troops, do not encamp or station where it is difficult for the army to pass through; ally with the local princes where the highway extends in all directions; do not linger where it is uninhabitable; venture into an enclosed region with shrewdness and stratagem; fight a desperate battle where there is no way to advance or retreat.

知虚实,未敢造次兴师。孙子曰:"凡用兵之法,将受命于君,合军聚众,圮地无舍,衢地交合,绝地无留围地则谋,死地则战途有所不由,军有所不击,城有所不攻,地有所不争,君命有所不受。故将通于九变之利者,知用兵矣。治兵不知九变之术,虽知五利,不能得人用矣。"吾之未疾进兵征讨者,为不知地利浅深出没之故也。昨日探听去,不见回报。今日升帐,看有甚军情,来报我知道者。(卒子引惠明和尚上开)(惠明云)我离了普救寺,一日至蒲关,见杜将军走一遭。(卒报科)(将军云)著他过来!(惠打问讯了云)贫僧是普救寺僧。今有孙飞虎作乱,将半万贼兵,围住寺门,欲劫故臣崔相国女为妻。有游客张君瑞奉书,令小僧拜投于麾下,欲求将军以解倒悬之危。(将军云)将过书来。(惠投书了)(将军拆书念曰)"珙顿首再拜大元

There are some roads which should not be followed; and some enemy troops which should not be attacked. There are some cities which should not be captured, some territories which should not be seized, and some orders from the sovereign which need not be obeyed. All the above are the tactical variables which a general or commander should thoroughly understand. Only if he knows them well can he know military operations. If he does not have a clear understanding of their real values, he cannot use a territory to his advantage though he is well acquainted with its topography. If a general does not know the tactical variables, he will not be able to bring the soldiers' fighting capacity into play, in spite of his knowing the five advantages. I have asked scouts to poke his nose into information, and has not get reply yet. Today, I will discuss military business in the tent to see whether there is any news."

[One soldier leads Monk Hui Ming, and enters] [Hui Ming says] "I left from Pu Jiu Monastery, and have reached Pu Pass in one day to meet General Du this time."

[The soldier reports to General] [General Du says], "Bring him in!"

[Monk Hui Ming bows to the General Du and says] "I am a monk in Pu Jiu Monastery. These days, Sun Feihu leads the five thousand rebels to besiege our monastery, trying to kidnap the daughter of former Prime Minister Cui as his wife. There is one guest called Zhang Junrui writing a letter to you, who asks me to bring the message to the general, wishing General could save us from danger as soon as possible."

[General Du says] "Give me the letter."

[Hui Ming presents the letter to General]

帅将军契兄蘁下：伏自洛中，拜违犀表，寒暄屡隔，积有岁月，仰德之私，铭刻如也。忆昔联床风雨，叹今彼各天涯客况复生于肺腑，离愁无慰于羁怀。念贫处十年藜藿，走困他乡羡威统百万貔貅，坐安边境。故知虎体食天禄，瞻天表，大德胜常使贱子慕台颜，仰台翰，寸心为慰。辄禀：小弟辞家，欲诣帐下，以叙数载间阔之情；奈至河中府普救寺，忽值采薪之忧。不期有贼将孙飞虎，领兵半万，欲劫故臣崔相国之女，实为迫切狼狈。小弟之命，亦在逡巡。万一朝廷知道，其罪何归？将军倘不弃旧交之情，兴一旅之师，上以报天子之恩，下以救苍生之急。使故相国虽在九泉，亦不泯将军之德。愿将军虎视去书，使小弟鹄观来旌。造次干渎，不胜惭愧。伏乞台照

[General Du opens the letter and reads] "Zhang Gong bowed to brother General once and twice again.

Since we were in the West Luo City, and I became the sworn brother to General, so many years have passed. I never forget the days that we exchange of pleasantries with each other, and I sincerely admire the good virtue from you. The days that I spent with you are deeply curved into my mind. I can not forget how we had a heart-to-heart talk with each other on the couch, and how deeply we sighed when we parted from each other. There are so much sorrows of parting that can not comfort me during the trip to other cities. I live in poverty for ten years, eating coarse food and vegetables, and travel to other cities, admiring you who leads one hundred thousand soldiers and protecting the frontier for the emperor. I know you are as healthy as a tiger, earning the salary of governmental official and able to meet the emperor in person. Your generosity always makes me show great respect to you. I have arrived at the Pu Jiu Monastery, intending to visit you, but suddenly I feel a slightly indisposed. At this time, the thief Sun Feihu took half thousand rebels, trying to kidnap the daughter of former Prime Minister Cui's family and force her to be his wife. All of us in the monastery now are in a dangerous situation. My life is in danger too. Just in case, if the emperor knows, how could you get away from guilt? If General doesn't forget our old friendship, I beg you to dispatch one brigade troops to the Pu Jiu Monastery, for one thing to reward the gratitude of the emperor, and for another to save the common people's life. Even if prime minister is rest in the grave, he will not forget the kindness of the general. I hope you will give this letter enough attention, and I am eagerly looking forward to your troops in the Pu Jiu Monastery. If I said something

不宣。张珙再拜。二月十六日书"(将军云)既然如此，和尚你行，我便来。(惠明云)将军是必疾来者。(将军云)虽无圣旨发兵，将在军，君命有所不受。大小三军，听吾将令：速点五千人马，人尽衔枚，马皆勒口，星夜起发，直至河中府普救寺，救张生走一遭。(飞虎引卒子上开)(将军引卒子骑竹马调阵拿绑下)(夫人洁同末上云)下书已两日，不见回音。(末云)山门外呐喊摇旗，莫不是俺哥哥军至了？(末见将军了)(引夫人拜了)(将军云)杜确有失防御，致令老夫人受惊，切勿见罪是幸。(末拜将军了)自别兄长台颜，一向有失听教。今得一见，如拨云睹日。(夫人云)老身子母，如将军所赐之命，将何

impetuous, I apologize here, since the matter is urgent. I believe that we have a tacit understanding with each other. Zhang Gong bows to you again. February 16th."

[General Du says] "Monk, you may go back ahead, and I will follow you this very night."

[Hui Ming says] "General, Please speed up."

[General Do says] "Though there is no imperial edict allowing me to dispatch troops, there is a saying ' When the general is in the army, the commands of the emperor may not be obeyed'. The three armies, follow my command: Please select five thousand soldiers. Each soldier should have a wooden gag in his mouth to ensure silence, and each horse should be flapped in its mouth. Let's start from this very starry night, and quickly match forward to the Pu Jiu Monastery to save my sworn brother's life."

[Sun Feihu enters with his soldiers] [The White Horse General enters. He deploys the troop and takes captive of the Sun Feihu]

[The Old Lady, Fa Ben, and Zhang Gong all enter] "It has been two days since you wrote the letter to the general, but there is no response yet."

[Zhang Gong says] "There is shouting and waving banners at the foot of the mountain outside. Has my brother arrived now?"

[Zhang Gong finally meets the General] [He introduces General to Du the Old Lady too.]

[General Du says] "This is the negligence of me in guarding the city, to make old lady scared. I wish you would not blame me."

补报？(将军云)不敢，此乃职分之所当为。敢问贤弟：因甚不至戎帐？(末云)小弟欲来，奈小疾偶作，不能动止，所以失敬。今见夫人受困，所言退得贼兵者，以小姐妻之，因此愚弟作书请吾兄。(将军云)既然有此姻缘，可贺，可贺！(夫人云)安排茶饭者。(将军云)不索。倘有馀党未尽，小官去捕了，却来望贤弟。左右那里，去斩孙飞虎去！(拿贼了)本欲斩首示众，具表奏闻，见丁文雅失守之罪。恐有未叛者，今将为首各杖一百，馀者尽归旧营去者！(孙飞虎谢了下)(将军云)张生建退贼之策，夫人面许结亲，若不违前言，淑女可配君

[Zhang Gong bows to the General] "I have not heard from you for a long time. Since parting with brother, I think our meeting is like a dream. Today, when I finally meet you, I feel like the clouds disappears, and the sun comes out."

[The Old Lady says] "My daughter's life and mine are saved by the general. How are we going to reward your kindness?"

[General Du says] "I dare not accept your gratitude. It is within my duty to protect you. I should be blamed for not taking precautions to make you alarmed. [To Zhang Gong] "I have something to ask you, my brother. Why don't you come to my troop?'"

[Zhang Gong says] "I should have come to pay a visit, but I suddenly caught a little illness. I should have gone with you today, but the old lady has promised a marriage between me and the young lady. When they were trapped, the old lady said anyone who is able to withdraw the bandits may marry the young lady. So, I wrote a letter to you and ask for help."

[General Du says] "There is such a lucky thing! Congratulation! Congratulation!"

[The Old Lady says] "General Du, please stay for the meal."

[General Du says] "Thank you, but I have something else to do. There is remaining confederates who haven't surrendered. I must arrest them. I will certainly pay a visit and show my congratulations latter. My soldiers, let's cut Sun Feihu's head!"

[Sun Feihu is caught] "I should have cut his head, and shown it to the public, but I will present a memorial to the emperor first, and

子也。(夫人云)恐小女有辱君子。(末云)请将军筵席者!(将军云)我不吃筵席了,我回营去,异日却来庆贺。(末云)不敢久留兄长,有劳台候。(将军望蒲关起发)(众念云)马离普救敲金镫,人望蒲关唱凯歌。(下)(夫人云)先生大恩,不敢忘也。自今先生休在寺里下,则著仆人寺内养马,足下来家内书院里安歇。我已收拾了,便搬来者。到明日略备草酌,著红娘来请你,是必来一会,别有商议。

accuse Ding Yawen's loosing duty of the guard. I am afraid that there is someone who did not take part in rebelling, so the leaders will get a punishment of flogging for one hundred times, and the left ones can return to where they were before!"

[Sun Feihu apologizes and Exeunt]

[General Du says] "Zhang Gong has the plan to withdraw the bandits. As the old lady has promised the marriage before, if you do not go back your words, the beauty is a well match to a gentleman."

[The Old Lady says] "I am afraid that my daughter is not worthy."

[Zhang Gong says] "Please have dinner with us, General."

[General Du says] "I will not eat dinner. I have to go back to the camp. I am sure to send my congratulation some other day."

[Zhang Gong says] "I dare not keep you long. Thank you again."

[General Du starts the journey to the Pu Pass][Everybody says] "The horsemen leave Pu Jiu Monastery kicking golden stirrups; the general heads forward to Pu Pass singing a song of victory."

[The Old Lady says] "I owe you great gratitude, Sir. I dare not forget your kindness of saving our lives. From now on, I wish you sir not to dwell in the monastery. Please ask servant to feed the horses inside the monastery, and you are able to rest in our study rooms. I have asked someone to clean the room, and you can just move in. Tomorrow, I will prepare for the meal, and ask Red Maid to invite you. Please be sure to come and we may have a chat as usual."

(末云)这事都在长老身上。(问洁云)小子亲事,未知何如?(洁云)莺莺亲事,拟定妻君。只因兵火至,引起雨云心。(下)(末云)小子收拾行李,去花园里去也!(下)

第一折

(净扮孙飞虎上开)自家姓孙,名彪,字飞虎。方今上德宗即位,天下扰攘。因主将丁文雅失政,俺分统五千人马,镇守河桥。近知先相公崔珏之女莺莺,眉黛青颦,莲脸生春,有倾国倾城之容,西子太真之颜,见在河中府普救寺借居。我心中想来,当今用武之际,主将尚然不正,我独廉何为?大小三军,听吾号令:人尽衔枚,马皆勒口,连夜进兵河中府,掳莺莺为妻,是我平生愿足!(法本慌上)谁想孙飞虎将半万贼兵,围住寺门,鸣锣击鼓,呐喊摇旗,欲掳莺莺

[Zhang Gong says] "It all depends on the abbot." [He asks Fa Ben and says] "What do you think of my marriage, abbot?"

[Fa Ben says] "About Ying Ying's marriage, she has a fiance before. However, because of this riots, she will rethink of whom to marry again."

[Zhang Gong says] "I will pack up my luggage, and remove into the garden which is madam Cui's headquarters!"

[Exeunt]

Scene One

[Sun Feihu enters] "My family name is Sun, given name is Biao, and nickname is Fei Hu. Now, De Zong emperor has just ascended on the throne, and the world is still in disorder. As my General Ding Wenya failed to discharge his duties, I have been allowed to command five thousand troops to guard the bridge of the river. Recently, I got to know the daughter of former Prime Minister Ying Ying has a pair of beautiful black eyebrows, and her face is as lovely as Lotus flower in the Spring. She has a beauty which can overthrow states and cities, with same fame as a beauty Xi Shi in the history. Now she has stayed in Pu Jiu Monastery for a few days. I am thinking that at the moment of using forces, my chief fails to

小姐为妻。我今不敢违误,即索报知夫人走一遭。(下)(夫人上慌云)如此却怎了?俺同到小姐卧房里商量去。(下)(旦引红上云)自见了张生,神魂荡漾,情思不快,茶饭少进。早是离人伤感,况值暮春天道,好烦恼人也呵!好句有情联夜月,落花无语怨东风。

【仙吕】【八声甘州】恹恹瘦损,早是伤神,那值残春。罗衣宽褪,能消几度黄昏?风袅篆烟不卷帘,雨打梨花深闭门,无语凭阑干,目断行云。

【混江龙】落红成阵,风飘万点正愁人。池塘梦晓,阑槛辞春。蝶粉轻沾飞絮雪,燕泥香惹落花尘。系春心情短柳丝长,隔花阴人远天涯近。香消了六朝金粉,清减了三楚精神。

(红云)姐姐情思不快,我将被儿熏得香香的,睡些儿。

discharge his duties, why should I keep my integrity? The three armies, listen to my command. Everyone put a wooden gag in the mouth to ensure silence, and use a rope to cover the mouth of horses to keep them quiet. Let's match forward to He Zhong Prefecture overnight, and kidnap Ying Ying as my wife. That is my lifelong wish!"

[Fa Ben enters in a panic and says] "No one knows that Sun Feihu has surrounded the monastery with five thousand rebel troops, beating drums, clanging gongs, waving the banners, and crying for a battle. They want to take captive of lady Ying Ying as bandit's wife. I dare not delay, but inform the old lady immediately."

[The Old Lady enters with a panic look] "What should we do now? I have to discuss with Ying Ying in her sleeping chamber."[Exeunt]

[Ying Ying enters with Red Maid and says] "Since I met Gentleman Zhang, my heart is flipping all the time. I barely eat these days. How sad the parting is! Not to mention it is late spring already, which always arouses sadness in people's mind, I can not forget the verses that we made that night. The falling petals is so silent that I cannot help blaming the East wind."

[Tune of Eight Beats in Gan Zhou Song] "Weak and weary through illness, people grow thin for love sickness. It upsets me, especially in the late spring. The garment of thin silk is too large for me to wear. How am I be able to pass through the lonely nights? The wind is curling upwards, and the smoke is hovering in the sky. The raindrops beat the peach blossom petals, and door of my room is deeply shut. I have nothing to say but lean on the

（旦唱）

【油葫芦】翠被生寒压绣裀，休将兰麝薰便将兰麝薰尽，则索自温存。昨宵个锦囊佳制明勾引，今日个玉堂人物难亲近。这些时坐又不安，睡又不稳，我欲待登临又不快，闲行又闷，每日价情思睡昏昏。

【天下乐】红娘呵，我则索搭伏定鲛绡枕头儿上盹，但出闺门，影儿般不离身。(红云)不干红娘事，老夫人著我跟著姐姐来。(旦云)俺娘也好没意思。

这些时直恁般堤防著人！小梅香伏侍的勤，老夫人拘系的紧，则怕俺女孩儿折了气分。

banisters. The tears fall from my check silently, as if dropping pearls."

[Tune of Dragon in the Troubled Water Song] "The petals fall on the ground successively, flying with the wind as if showers, which makes people sorrowful. Last night, my dream on the pool side is broken. Leaning on the banister, I said goodbye to the spring. The white butterflies are flying with floating catkins as if white snow, and swallows make nests with the dust of falling petals. My sorrows of spring is as long as the branches of willow trees, and the man whom I love is so near yet so far. How many beauties like me are waning in the history, and my spirit is weary."

[Red Maid says] "Sister, you are not happy these days. I will fume the quilt to make it comfortable to sleep."

[Ying Ying sings]

[Tune of Field cricket Song] "The Green quilt and silk mattress are cold. Even if you burn the sweet perfume out, you cannot make the lonely bed warm. Last night, he tries all his best to attract my attention, but today, it is hard for me to get close to him. These days, I feel it is difficult to sleep or sit. I wish to take a walk outside, but still feel weary and upset. So lost in lovesickness, I feel dozy all day."

[Tune of Everybody is joyful in the World Song] "Red Maid, I will take a nap on the silk pillow. But if I go out of the chamber, you may not follow me as my shadows."

[Red Maid says] "You can't blame me for following you. At this moment, old lady asked you and me to come to her."

（红云）姐姐往常不曾如此无情无绪，自曾见了那生，便却心事不宁，却是如何？

（旦唱）

【那吒令】往常但见个外人，氲的早嗔但见个客人，厌的倒褪从见了那人，兜的便亲。想著他昨夜诗，依前韵，酬和得清新。

【鹊踏枝】吟得句儿匀，念得字儿真，咏月新诗，煞强似织锦回文。谁肯把针儿将线引，向东邻通个殷勤。

【寄生草】想著文章士，旖旎人。他脸儿清秀身儿俊，性儿温克情儿顺，不由人口儿里作念心儿里印。学得来一天星斗焕文章，不枉了十年窗下无人问。

[Ying Ying says] "How boring my mother is!

I am always reminded not to meet strangers alone. The maid serves me attentively, and old lady disciplines me strictly, in case I do something indecently."

[Red Maid asks] "Sister, you are never so easily weary and angry. Since you met that Gentleman Zhang, you become so unsettled and restless. Why is it like this?"

[Ying Ying sings]

[Tune of Na Zha Song] "I have never seen a stranger in my life. I am always thinking that I should have a chance to meet a guest. Since that day I met Gentleman Zhang, I fall in love with him at first sight. Thinking of the verses that he made last night, I made new verses following his rhythm."

[Tune of Magpie on the Branch Song] "The verses are well made, and each word could be heard clearly. They are new fresh verses to quote the moon, much better than brocade palindromes. Who can be a match maker, to send messages of my true feelings?"

[Tune of Parasitic Grass Song] "I am thinking of the author of the verses. He has a handsome face. His figure is fine. His temper is mild and modest. I cannot help thinking of him constantly in mind. He is good at making well posed articles, not wasting his ten years' hard study under the window with hardships and loneliness."

(飞虎领兵上围寺科)(下)(卒子内高叫云)寺里人听者：限你每三日内，将莺莺献出来，与俺将军成亲，万事干休。三日之后不送出，伽蓝尽皆焚烧，僧俗寸斩，不留一个。(夫人洁同上，敲门了，红看了云)姐姐，夫人和长老都在房门前。(旦见了科)(夫人云)孩儿，你知道么，如今孙飞虎将半万贼兵，围住寺门，道你眉黛青颦，莲脸生春，似倾国倾城的太真，要掳你做压寨夫人。孩儿，怎生是了也？(旦唱)

【六幺序】听说罢魂离了壳，见放著祸灭身。将袖梢儿揾不住啼痕。好教我去住无因，进退无门。可著俺那埚儿里人急偎亲？孤孀子母无投奔，赤紧的先亡过了有福之人。耳边厢金鼓连

[Fei Hu leads the bandits to besiege the monastery] [A solider is shouting in a loud voice] "Listen, everyone in the monastery. Give you three days, and please send Ying Ying out. If she is married to our general, you will get peace in the monastery. If she is not sent out in three days, all the monastery buildings will be burnt and ruined. No matter you are a monk or a common man, your head will be cut off. No one has a chance to survive."

[The Old Lady enters with Fa Ben. She knocks the door of Ying Ying's chamber, and Red Maid says] "Sister, old lady and abbot are standing outside the door."

[Ying Ying salutes to her mother]

[The Old Lady asks] "My child, do you know what happened? Today, Sun Feihu led five thousand rebels to besiege the monastery. He said that he was amazed at your peerless beauty. They want to kidnap you to become the bandit's chief wife. My child, what shall we do now?"

[Ying Ying sings]

[Tune of Preclude to Green Wist Song] "After hearing this, I collapse there, with my soul leaving my body. Now, I am to blame myself. I wipe my tears with my sleeve. It makes me difficult either to stay or leave, in or out. Whom shall we rely upon? As an orphan and a widow, we have no one to go to shelter for help. Those who died first are lucky one. I hear the beating sound of drummer

天振,征云冉冉,土雨纷纷。

【幺篇】那厮每风闻,胡云,道我眉黛青颦,莲脸生春,恰便似倾国倾城的太真。兀的不送了他三百僧人!半万贼军,半霎儿敢翦草除根。这厮每于家为国无忠信,恣情的掳掠人民。更将那天宫般盖造焚烧尽,则没那诸葛孔明,便待要博望烧屯。

(夫人云)老身年六十岁,不为寿夭奈孩儿年少,未得从夫,却如之奈何?(旦云)孩儿有一计:想来则是将我与贼汉为妻,庶可免一家儿性命。(夫人哭云)俺家无犯法之男,再婚之女,怎舍得你献与贼汉,却不辱没了俺家谱?(洁云)俺同到法堂两廊下,问僧俗有高见者,俺一同商议个长便。

shaking the sky. There are numerous number of soldiers, rising the dust as if the falling rain."

[Tune of Petty Song] "The bandits said I have an impressive beauty with a pair of beautiful eyebrows and a face as lovely as a Lotus flower. What a nonsense he is talking. These bandits will make three hundred monks be killed in vain. Five thousand bandits will take a minute to kill us all. This guy is not loyal to the dynasty or to the family, and moreover, he plunders people recklessly. How can I endure him to burn the palace like monastery into ashes. If there is no military consultant Kong Ming Zhuge in the Three Kingdom, nobody will be able to burn the pathway in the Bo Wang Hillside to set traps for the enemy."

[The Old Lady says] "I am sixty years old this year. For me, I do not fear of death, but my child is still very young. She hasn't married yet. What should I do?"

[Ying Ying says] "I have an idea. Hand me over to the bandit and be wife, so that we are able to save other people's life."

[The Old Lady weeps] "We don't have men who commit crime nor women who marry again in our family tree. How could I send you to that bandit? Wouldn't it disgrace our family?"

[Fa Ben says] "Let's come to the corridors in the hall of the monastery, and ask whether other people may get some ideas. Let's discuss with them together."

[The Old Lady follows Fa Ben to the hall of the monastery]

(同到法堂科)(夫人云)小姐,却是怎生?(旦云)不如将我与贼人,其便有五。

【后庭花】第一来免摧残老太君,第二来免堂殿作灰烬,第三来诸僧无事得安存,第四来先君灵柩稳,第五来欢郎虽是未成人。

(欢云)俺呵,打甚么不紧。
(旦唱)

须是崔家后代孙。莺莺为惜己身,不行从著乱军,著僧众污血痕,将伽蓝火内焚,先灵为细尘,断绝了爱弟亲,割开了慈母恩。

【柳叶儿】呀,将俺一家儿不留一个龆龀。待从军又怕辱没了家门,我不如白练套头儿寻个自尽,将我尸榇,献与贼人,也须得个远害全身。

【青哥儿】母亲,都做了莺莺生忿,对傍人一言难尽。母亲,休爱惜莺莺这一身。

[The Old Lady asks] "My daughter, what do you think?"

[Ying Ying says] "It's better to send me to the bandits. Then everything is resolved."

[Tune of Backyard Flower Song] "For one thing, it will not worry my old mother, and for another it can avoid the ruins of the monastery. Thirdly, all the people in the monastery will be alive. Fourthly, my father's coffin will be unharmed. Fifthly, my brother Huan Er is still a young child."

[Huan Er says] "There is no need to concern about me."

[Ying Ying sings] "You are the descendant of the Cui Family. I am willing to sacrifice myself to marry that bandit, to avoid the bloodshed of the monks and ruins of the monastery. It is also for the protection of the coffin, the growth of my younger brother, and the safe of my old mother."

[Tune of Willow Leaves Song] "Sun Feihu will not allow a single child to be alive in our family. However, if I follow the bandit, I am afraid to disgrace our family. It is better to hang myself with a white silk and bring my corpse to the bandit. It can avoid injury to the family."

[Tune of Young Brother Song] "Mother, please forgive me for my infidelity. I bring disaster to others. Mother, please not have pity on Ying Ying. I have another idea. Whoever he is, if he can withdraw the bandits, and wish to become a live-son-in-law, I will marry to the hero."

恁孩儿别有一计:

不拣何人,建立功勋,杀退贼军,扫荡妖氛,倒陪家门,情愿与英雄结婚姻,成秦晋。

(夫人云)此计较可。虽然不是门当户对,也强如陷于贼中。长老,在法堂上高叫:两廊僧俗,但有退兵之策的,倒陪房奁,断送莺莺与他为妻。(洁叫了。住)(末鼓掌上云)我有退兵之策,何不问我?(见夫人了)(洁云)这秀才便是前日带追荐的秀才。(夫人云)计将安在?(末云)重赏之下,必有勇夫。赏罚若明,其计必成。(旦背云)只愿这生退了贼者。(夫人云)恰才与长老说下,但有退得贼兵的,将小姐与他为妻。(末云)既是恁的,休谎了我浑家,请人卧房里去,俺自有退兵之策。(夫人

[The Old Lady says] "That is a good idea. Though it is not well-matched marriage in social and economic status, it is better to be captive by the bandit. Abbot, please proclaim my proposal loudly in the hall of the monastery. Those monks and guests in the corridor, whoever has idea to withdraw the bandits and wish to become my live son in law, I am sure to marry Ying Ying to him."

[Fa Ben speaks loudly] [Zhang Gong enters, applauding his hands] "I have an idea to withdraw the bandits. Why don't you ask me?" [Zhang Gong meets Old Lady][Fa Ben says] "This is the gentleman whom I recommended to you on the fifteenth of the month."

[The Old Lady asks] "What is your plan?"

[Zhang Gong says] "Generous rewards will always rouse one to heroism. If you are strict and fair in meting out rewards and punishments, this plan must work."

[Ying Ying says secretly.] "I hope this man is able to withdraw the bandits."

[The Old Lady says] "I have spoken to the abbot just then. The people who standing in the corridor, whether you are a monk or a commoner, whoever can withdraw the bandits is able to marry my daughter."

[Zhang Gong says] "If that is so, this plan must work. Please let your daughter go back to the sleeping room. I will share you with my plan."

[The Old Lady says] "My daughter and Red Maid, you can go back to your room."

云)小姐和红娘回去者。(旦对红云)难得此生这一片好心。

【赚煞】诸僧众各逃生,众家眷谁偢问。这生不相识横枝儿着紧。非是书生多议论,也堤防著玉石俱焚。虽然是不关亲,可怜见命在逡巡。济不济权将秀才来尽。果若有出师表文,吓蛮书信,张生呵,则愿得笔尖儿横扫了五千人。(下)

[Ying Ying tells red Maid] "This gentleman is so kind-hearted."

[Tune of Winning Stanza] "The monks are escaping for their own lives. No one cares about the Cui's family. This young gentleman is a stranger, but he proposes to have a plan to save others. It is not that we are likely to criticize, but people should avoid jade and stone being burnt together. Though he is not a relative, he has pity on Ying Ying's family who are in danger. Whether his plan works or not, the young scholar distinguishes himself. In fact, if he really has an apprenticeship letter, he will make the five thousand bandits scared. Ha, this gentleman Zhang, wish your pen would sweep away the five thousand soldiers." [Exit]

第二折

（夫人上云）今日安排下小酌，单请张生酬劳。道与红娘，疾忙去书院中请张生，著他是必便来，休推故。（下）（末上云）夜来老夫人说，著红娘来请我，却怎生不见来？我打扮著等他，皂角也使过两个也，水也换了两桶也，乌纱帽擦得光挣挣的，怎么不见红娘来也呵？（红娘上云）老夫人使我请张生，我想若非张生妙计呵，俺一家儿性命难保也呵！

【中吕】【粉蝶儿】半万贼兵，卷浮云片时扫净，俺一家儿死里逃生。舒心的列山灵，陈水陆，张君瑞合当钦敬。当日所望无成，谁想一缄书到为了媒证。

【醉春风】今日个东阁玳筵开，煞强如西厢和月等。

Scene Two

[The Old Lady enters] "Today we will arrange a dinner with drinks and invite Gentleman Zhang alone to show our gratitude. Tell Red Maid to hurry up to the study room and invite Gentleman Zhang to dinner. He should not decline." [Exit]

[Zhang Gong enters and says] "Last night, the old lady told me that she was going to ask Red Maid to invite me to a feast, but where she is now? I have dressed up and waited for her. I have used two perfumed soaps, and cleaned myself with two bowls of water. My black gauze cap is cleaned shiny and bright. But where is Red Maid?"

[Red Maid enters and says] "The old lady asked me to invite Gentleman Zhang to have a feast. If it wasn't for his good plan, our whole family would have died."

[Tune of Pink Butterfly Song] "Five thousand rebels is wiped out like a floating clouds. Our family narrowly escapes with our death. The cheerful mountain god exhibits delicacies from land and sea in the feast. Gentleman Zhang should be respected. In the past, all his wish of marriage is nothing but an empty dream. Who knows a letter has turned into a certificate of marriage."

[Tune of Intoxicated to the Spring Wind Song] "Today the dinner

薄衾单枕有人温，早则不冷，受用足宝鼎香浓，绣帘风细，绿窗人静。

可早来到也。

【脱布衫】幽僻处可有人行？点苍苔白露泠泠。

隔窗儿咳嗽了一声。

（红敲门科）（末云）是谁来也？（红云）是我。

他启朱唇急来答应。

（末云）拜揖小娘子。

（红唱）

【小梁州】则见他叉手忙将礼数迎，我这里"万福，先生"。乌纱小帽耀人明，白襕净，角带傲黄鞓。

for entertaining the wise man is going to be held, which is much better than quoting verses for the moon in the western chamber. Today, my thin clothes, and single pillow will be warmed by the lady's body. In the morning, I will not feel cold any more. The tripod and thick smoke is good enough to bear. The embroidered curtain is lightly rolled up by the thin wind. The green windowed chamber is quiet."

"Please come early."

[Tune of Doffing off the Clothes Song] "Is there anyone walking on the incarcerate road? The moss is growing on the stairs, with cold white dew on the leaves."

Red Maid coughs out of the window.

[Red Maid knocks the door] [Zhang Gong asks] "Who is it?"

[Red Maid says] "It's me."

He hurries to answer the call.

[Zhang Gong says] "I bow to the sister."

[Red Maid sings]

[Tune of Small Laing Zhou Song] "I saw him standing in salute and greeting me with a bow. I said, 'Wish you all happiness, sir.' His black gauze cap is so shining that it can reflect people's face. His white shirt is very clean. Around his waist wears a yellow silk belt."

【幺篇】衣冠济楚庞儿整,可知道引动俺莺莺。据相貌,凭才性,我从来心硬,一见了也留情。

(末云)既来之,则安之。请书房内说话。小娘子此行为何?(红云)贱妾奉夫人严命,特请先生小酌数杯,勿却。(末云)便去,便去。敢问席上有莺莺姐姐么?

(红唱)

【上小楼】"请"字儿不曾出声,"去"字儿连忙答应可早莺莺跟前,"姐姐"呼之,喏喏连声。秀才每闻道"请",恰便似听将军严令,和他那五脏神愿随鞭镫。

(末云)今日夫人端的为甚么筵席?

(红唱)

【幺篇】第一来为压惊,第二来因谢承。不请街

[Tune of Petty Song] "He is decently dressed, and the outline of his body is neat. His looking is sure to touch lady Ying Ying's heart. Judging men according to his appearance and talents, I am always hard-minded. Now, when I saw him, I pay attention to him too."

[Zhang Gong says] "Since you are here, you may as well stay and make the best of it. Please have a talk in the study. What does sister come to visit me for?"

[Red Maid says] "I just follow the old lady's order, and invite you to have a cup of drinks. I hope you will not decline."

[Zhang Gong says] "I will come as soon as possible. Could I ask whether Sister Ying Ying will be present on the feast?"

[Red Maid sings]

[Tune of Ascending the Attic Song] "Before he utters a 'please', he hurried to say 'he is coming'. His soul is already flying by Ying Ying's side. He keeps saying 'Yes', and calling lady 'Ying Ting' as 'sister'. Whenever this scholar heard the word, 'please', he acts as if a soldier hearing the order from a general, and following him with his heart and soul."

[Zhang Gong asks] "What kind of feast is the old lady going to held?"

[Red Maid sings]

[Tune of Petty Song] "In the first place, it is to help us to give over the shocks. Secondly, it is to show our gratitude towards you. We

坊，不会亲邻，不受人情。避众僧，请老兄，和莺莺匹聘。

（末云）如此小生欢喜。（红）

则见他欢天喜地，谨依来命。

（末云）小生客中无镜，敢烦小娘子，看小生一看何如？
（红唱）

【满庭芳】来回顾影，文魔秀士，风欠酸丁。下工夫将额颅十分挣，迟和疾擦倒苍蝇，光油油耀花人眼睛，酸溜溜螫得人牙疼。

（末云）夫人办甚么请我？（红）

茶饭已安排定，淘下陈仓米数升，煤下七八碗软蔓青。

（末云）小生想来，自寺中一见了小姐之后，不想今日得成婚姻，岂不为前生分定？（红云）姻缘非人力所为，天意尔。

are not going to invite our neighbour, our relatives, or our friends, to avoid the gossips of the monks. We are going to make engagement between you and Ying Ying."

[Zhang Gong says] "I never feel so happy in my life."

[Red Maid sings] "He is overwhelmed with boundless joy, ready to obey my instructions."

[Zhang Gong says] "I have no mirror in my room. Could I bother sister to have a look at me. How do I look?"

[Red Maid sings]

[Tune of Courtyard full of Fragrance Song] "He is watching his image again and again. He is such a well learned scholar, but acting as a fool and poor man. He has taken great effort to clean his head, which could even make a housefly slip. His forehead is so shiny that it bewilders people's eyes. He is so prudish that it makes people's teeth ache."

[Zhang Gong asks] "What will be held in the feast?"

[Red Maid says] "All the food and drinks have been prepared. We have washed rice for several liters, and cooked vegetables into several dishes."

[Zhang Gong says] "When I think of the past, since the first glance of the lady Ying Ying, I have already fallen in love with her. I never expect that I have a chance to engage with her. Isn't it a predestined love between her and me?"

【快活三】咱人一事精,百事精。一无成,百无成。世间草木本无情。

自古云:地生连理木,水出并头莲,他犹有相兼并。

【朝天子】休道这生,年纪儿后生,恰学害相思病。天生聪俊,打扮素净,奈夜夜成孤零。才子多情,佳人薄幸,兀的不担阁了人性命。

(末云)你姐姐果有信行?(红)

谁无一个信行?谁无一个志诚?恁两个今夜亲折证。

我嘱付你咱:

【四边静】今宵欢庆,软弱莺莺,可曾惯经?你索款款轻轻,灯下交鸳颈。端详可憎,好煞人也无干净。

[Red Maid says] "It is the fate that brings lovers together, which is not controlled by man power."

[Tune of Happiness Three Song] "The man who is lucky in one thing will be lucky in everything. If he can't accomplish one thing, big or small, he is unable to accomplish everything. There is no feeling in the plants and trees in this world.

There is an old saying: There grows two trees, whose roots are interlocked with each other under the ground. There grows two lotus flowers on the same stem. He has the same luck with these lucky trees and lotus flowers."

[Tune of Homage to Emperor Song] "About this gentleman, at such a young age, he suffers from love sickness. He is naturally handsome, who dresses up neatly and cleanly. However, he feels lonely every night. The gifted scholar is amorous and the beautiful lady is fragile. What if does this love deprive of people's life?"

[Zhang Gong says] "Sister, do you really follow the order of the old lady?"

[Red Maid says] "Who can come without the order of the old lady? Who isn't sincere? You can see by yourself tonight. I will exhort to you again and again. Please remember:

[Tune of Four Sides Tranquility Song] "Tonight we will celebrate in happiness. Has the gentle Ying Ying experienced this before? You should behave tenderly and slowly. You may kiss each other gently under the lamp."

（末云）小娘子先行，小生收拾书房便来。敢问那里有甚么景致？

（红唱）

【耍孩儿】俺那里落红满地胭脂冷，休孤负了良辰媚景。夫人遣妾莫消停，请先生勿得推称。俺那里准备著鸳鸯夜月销金帐，孔雀春风软玉屏。乐奏合欢令，有凤箫象板，锦瑟鸾笙。

（末云）小生书剑飘零，无以为财礼，却是怎生？

（红唱）

【四煞】聘财断不争，婚姻事有成，新婚燕尔安排庆。你明博得跨凤乘鸾客，我到晚来卧看牵牛织女星。休僥幸，不要你半丝儿红线，成就了一世儿前程。

【三煞】凭著你灭寇功，举将能，两般儿功效如红定。为甚俺莺娘心下十分顺？都则为君瑞胸中百万兵。越显得文风盛，受用足珠围翠绕，结果了黄卷青灯。

[Zhang Gong says] "Sister, you can go first. I will come latter after I clean the room. Could I ask if there are any views in the feast?"

[Red Maid sings]

[Tune of Playing with the Child Song] "There are falling petals everywhere on the ground. Never miss the beautiful scenery. The old lady urged you not to decline. I will prepare for the golden silk canopy, and set up a peacock screen. We will play happy songs, with phoenix pipe and elephant plate. There are also brigt and beautiful 25-stringed plucked instruments and reed pipe with phoenix-like feature playing the good music."

[Zhang Gong says] "I am away from home in pursuit of scholarly honour for a long time. I'm so sorry that I have no money for betrothal gifts to lady Ying Ying. What shall I do?"

[Red Maid sings]

[Tune of Last Stanza but Four] "We will not ask for betrothal gifts, and the marriage is settled. We are just celebrating the marriage of the merry couple. Ying Ying and you will watch the Herd-boy and Weaving-girl stars at night together. Don't be restrained. How lucky to have an infinitely bright future, without asking you a single price of betrothal gifts."

[Tune of Last Stanza but Three] "As your plan works and recommends White Horse General, these two credits are more worthy than betrothal gifts. Why is my lady Ying Ying so happy at the moment? It is all because you have a million soldiers in your mind. It just shows your talents as well. You will be served by

【二煞】夫人只一家，老兄无伴等，为嫌繁冗寻幽静。

（末云）别有甚客人？

（红唱）

单请你个有恩有义闲中客，且回避了无是无非窗下僧。夫人的命，道足下莫教推托，和贱妾即便随行。

（末云）小娘子先行，小生随后便来。

（红唱）

【收尾】先生休作谦，夫人专意等。常言道"恭敬不如从命"，休使得梅香再来请。（下）（末云）红娘去了，小生拽上书房门者。我比及到得夫人那里，夫人道："张生，你来了也？饮几杯酒，去卧房内，和莺莺做亲去！"小生到得卧房内，和姐

pretty maids at waiting, and end the old life to read ancient classics under the oil lamp."

[Tune of Last Stanza but Two] "The old lady has only herself in her own family. Her brother has no wife now. She is tired of trivial details, and seeking for peaceful and quiet life."

[Zhang Gong asks] "Are there any other guests in the feast?"
[Red Maid sings] "No, only invite you, a free guest with grace and righteousness. My old lady urged again and again that you should not waste time and decline. Just follow with me."

[Zhang Gong says] " Sister, you go first. I will follow you later."
[Red Maid sings]

[Tune of Epilogue Song] "Sir, you should not be modest. My old lady is waiting for you purposely. There is an old saying that 'Obedience is better than politeness.' Don't allow me to invite you again." [Exit]

[Zhang Gong says] "The Red Maid is gone. I will close the door of the study room. I guess when I reach to the old lady, and the old lady will say, 'Gentleman Zhang, You finally arrived. Please drink a cup of wine, go to the bed room and marry lady Ying Ying tonight.' I will walk into the bedroom, take off lady's clothes, and wedlock with her. I hope our relationships is like fish and water. We will fly together as if a pair of love birds. I will peep at lady's looking at night. Her hair is hanging down on her head, and her starry eyes are half closed because of sleepiness. The quilt will be embroidered with green jade, and the stockings with lovebirds."

姐解带脱衣,颠鸾倒凤,同谐鱼水之欢,共效于飞之愿。觑他云鬟低坠,星眼微朦,被翻翡翠,袜绣鸳鸯。不知性命何如,且看下回分解。(笑云)单羡法本好和尚也:只凭说法口,遂却读书心。(下)

第三折

(夫人排桌子上云)红娘去请张生,如何不见来?(红见夫人云)张生著红娘先行,随后便来也。(末上见夫人施礼科)(夫人云)前日若非先生,焉得见今日。我一家之命,皆先生所活也。聊备小酌,非为报礼,勿嫌轻意。(末云)一人有庆,兆民赖之。此贼之败,皆夫人之福。万一杜将军不至,我辈皆无免死之术。此皆往事,不必挂齿。(夫人云)将酒来,先生满饮此杯。(末云)长者赐,少者不敢辞。(末做饮酒科)(末把夫人酒了)(夫人云)先生请坐。(末云)小子侍立座下,尚然越礼,焉敢与夫人对坐?(夫人云)道不得个"恭敬不如从命"。(末谢了,坐)(夫人

[Laughing and saying] "I am only jealous of good monk Fa Ben:only by preaching, he helps a scholarly man to fulfill his dream." [Exit]

Scene Three

[The Old Lady arranges the table and says] "Red Maid, I have asked you to invite Gentleman Zhang. Why I don't see him?"

[Red Maid greets the Old Lady and says] "Gentleman Zhang asked me to go first and he will follow at once."

[Zhang Gong enters and bows to The Old Lady]

[The Old Lady says] "Without your help, we are unable to survive until today. All our family's lives are saved by you. I just prepare for a few cups of drink to show our gratitude. These are not heavy gifts, but I hope you will not despise them."

[Zhang Gong says] "The reason why all of us is able to survive is up to the luck of my old lady. If General Du didn't arrive, all of us will die. What is bygones is all bygones. It is not worthy of mentioning it."

[The Old Lady says] "Have a toast. I will fill your cup with wine."

[Zhang Gong says] "To drink in honor of the elder, I dare not refuse."

云)红娘,去唤小姐来,与先生行礼者。(红朝鬼门道唤云)老夫人后堂待客,请小姐出来哩!(旦应云)我身子有些不停当,来不得。(红云)你道请谁哩?(旦云)请谁?(红云)请张生哩。(旦云)若请张生,扶病也索走一遭。(红发科了)(旦上)免除崔氏全家祸,尽在张生半纸书。

[Zhang Gong drinks his wine][Zhang Gong also pours out the wine for the old lady][The Old Lady says] "Sir, Please have seat."

[Zhang Gong says] "Out of rites, it's my honor to stand here and serve you. But how dare I sit with the elder together?"

[The Old Lady says] "There is a saying that 'It is better to obey me than to decline respectfully.'"

[The Zhang Gong says "Thank you" and takes a seat]

[Old Lady says] "Red Maid, call Ying Ying to come and ask her to give a salute to Gentleman Zhang."

[Red Maid calls] "The old lady is entertaining guests in the back hall. She asks sister to come and visit the guest too."

[Ying Ying replies] "I am not feeling very well. So I cannot come."

[Red Maid asks] "Do you know whom the old lady invites?"

[Ying Ying asks] "Whom?"

[Red Maid says] "Gentleman Zhang."

[Ying Ying says] "If it is Gentleman Zhang, I will come despite my illness."

[Red Maid starts to leave][Ying Ying enters] "It is all because of the letter that Gentleman Zhang writes that our family can avoid the disaster."

【双调】【五供养】若不是张解元识人多，别一个怎退干戈？排著酒果，列著笙歌。篆烟微，花香细，散满东风帘幕。救了咱全家祸，殷勤呵正礼，钦敬呵当合。

【新水令】恰才向碧纱窗下画了双蛾，拂拭了罗衣上粉香浮涴，则将指尖儿轻轻的贴了钿窝。若不是惊觉人呵，犹压著绣衾卧。

（红云）觑俺姐姐这个脸儿，吹弹得破，张生有福也呵！
（旦唱）

【幺篇】没查没利谎偻科，你道我宜梳妆的脸儿吹弹得破。

（红云）俺姐姐天生的一个夫人的样儿。

（旦唱）你那里休聒，不当一个信口开合。知他命福是如何，我做一个夫人也做得过。

（红云）往常两个都害，今日早则喜也。

[Tune of Provision Song] "If Gentleman Zhang didn't know a lot of people, how can these rebels retreat? We arrange the drinks and fruits, and sing the pipe song for him. The smoke of incense coil is thin, and the fragments of flowers can be scented slightly. It meanders with the east wind which is blowing the curtain slightly. Thanks Gentleman Zhang for saving our whole family. It is proper discipline rite to show great respect to Gentleman Zhang."

[Tune of New Water Song] "Just then I painted my eyebrows under the window, scent my clothes with fragrance, painted my fingertips, and adjusted the hairpin. If not to meet Gentleman Zhang, I would rather lay on the embroidered pillow."

[Red Maid said] "Look at your face, my sister. It will amaze all the performance. How lucky Gentleman Zhang is!"

[Ying Ying sings]

[Tune of Petty song] "Don't talk nonsense. How could I amaze all the performance!"

[Red Maid says] "My sister has the good looking to be a good wife of a lord."

[Ying Ying sings] "Don't wag your tongue too freely. Who knows whether he has a good fortune or not, but I am qualified to be a good wife of this gentleman."

[Red Maid says] "Usually, two people both suffer from love sickness. Today it is happy wedding for the both."

（旦唱）

【乔木查】我相思为他,他相思为我,从今后两下里相思都较可。酬贺间礼当酬贺,俺母亲也好心多。

（红云）敢著小姐和张生结亲呵,怎生不做大筵席,会亲戚朋友,安排小酌为何?（旦云）红娘,你不知夫人意。

【搅筝琶】他怕我是陪钱货,两当一便成合。据著他举将除贼,也消得家缘过活。费了甚一股那,便待要结丝萝!休波,省人情的奶奶忒虑过,恐怕张罗。

（末云）小子更衣咱。（做撞见旦科）
（旦唱）

【庆宣和】门儿外,帘儿前,将小脚儿那。我恰待目转秋波,谁想那识空便的灵心儿早瞧破,就得我倒趄,倒趄。

[Tune of Brushwood Song] "I feel love sickness for his sake, and he for mine. Since today, both of us will be free from this sickness. To show our gratitude towards Gentleman Zhang, my mother has such a good heart."

[Red Maid says] "If it is a wedding party between sister and Gentleman Zhang, why doesn't the old lady prepare for a larger banquet, and invite friends and relatives to come?"

[Ying Ying says] "Red Maid, you don't know my mother's meaning."

[Tune of Playing Pipa Song] "She is afraid that I am a depreciating asset. At one meeting, I will be married Gentleman Zhang willingly. Even if he proposed the general to withdraw the rebels, he should have a fortune to support the family. Why should I marry him just because of his heroic behavior? Don't worry. About the ways of the world, my mother has think carefully about it. She is planing it for me."

[Zhang Gong says] "I will change my clothes." [He meets Ying Ying] [Ying Ying sings]

[Tune of Celebrating of Harmony Song] "Out of the door and in front of the curtain, I move my small feet. I take a few furtive glances to explore and meet his eyes, which makes me take a few steps back out of shyness."

[Zhang Gong is looking at Ying Ying]

（末见旦科）（夫人云）小姐近前，拜了哥哥者！（末背云）呀，声息不好了也！（旦云）呀，俺娘变了卦也！（红云）这相思又索害也！

（旦唱）

【雁儿落】荆棘剌怎动那，死没腾无回豁，措支剌不对答，软兀剌难存坐！

【得胜令】谁承望这即即世世老婆婆，著莺莺做妹妹拜哥哥。白茫茫溢起蓝桥水，不邓邓点着袄庙火。碧澄澄清波，扑剌剌将比目鱼分破。急攘攘因何，吃搭地把双眉锁纳合。

（夫人云）红娘看热酒，小姐与哥哥把盏者！
（旦唱）

【甜水令】我这里粉颈低垂，蛾眉频蹙，芳心无那。俺可甚"相见话偏多"！星眼朦胧，檀口嗟

[The Old Lady says] "My daughter, please come forward, and bow to your brother Gentleman Zhang."

[Zhang Gong says secretly] "This is not a good sign."

[Ying Ying says] "Ah, my mother has changed her mind!"

[Red Maid says] "That love sickness is coming again."

[Ying Ying sings]

[Tune of Falling Swan Song] "He is so surprised that he cannot move. I am silent, too. In a confusion and panic, I am just standing there. It seems as if there is a thorn on my seat so that I can barely move."

[Tune of Triumphant Song] "Who knows my mother asked me to call Gentleman Zhang as bother. In a vast of whiteness, the water overwhelmed the blue bridge; and in an impulsive mood, the Xian Monastery is burnt. The clear blue waves break the company of flatfish. How should I not be worried about it? I have to knot my eyebrows."

[The Old Lady says] "Red Maid, please fill the cup with hot wine. Let Ying Ying give a toast to her brother."

[Ying Ying sings]

[Tune of Sweet Water Song] "Here, I lower down my head, and knot my eyebrows. There is no mood to drink any more. Why would I say to him when I meet him in face! I half open my eyes and sigh deeply, though I try my best not to be heard. Everything

咨,撧窨不过。这席面儿畅好是乌合!

(旦把酒科)(夫人央科)(末云)小生量窄。(旦云)红娘,接了台盏者!

【折桂令】他其实咽不下玉液金波。谁承望月底西厢,变做了梦里南柯。泪眼偷淹,酪子里揾湿香罗。他那里眼倦开软瘫做一垛,我这里手难抬称不起肩窝。病染沉疴,断然难活。则被你送了人呵,当甚么喽啰!

(夫人云)再把一盏者。(红递盏了)(红背与旦云)姐姐,这烦恼怎生是了?
(旦唱)

【月上海棠】而今烦恼犹闲可,久后思量怎奈何?有意诉衷肠,争奈母亲侧坐。成抛趓,咫尺间如间阔。

is so wrong!"

[Ying Ying fills the cup][The Old Lady urges Zhang Gong to drink][Zhang Gong says] "Sorry, I can drink no more."

[Ying Ying says] "Red Maid, Please remove the cup."

[Tune of Plucking Laurel Song] "He cannot swallow the jade liquid. Who knows the delights of chanting the love verses each other in the western chamber under the moonlight has turned into an empty dream? He tries hard to stop tears from rolling down, wiping them with his silk sleeves. He feels so weary, and almost collapses there. Here, I am unable to raise my hands. He shrugs his shoulders. He is hopelessly ill with lovesickness. Mother, his life is nearly killed by you. Why do you arrange this banquet?"

[The Old Lady says] "Please drink another cup of wine."

[Red Maid fills the cup] [Red Maid asks Ying Ying secretly behind] "Sister, where are your sorrows coming from?"

[Ying Ying sings]

[Tune of Moon over Malus Spectabilis Song] "Today this worries can still be bearable. What to do with it in the future? I have intended to tell my true feeling to you, however, my mother is sitting there and watching. There is no hope for this marriage. Though we are so near to each other, the distance between us is still far."

【幺篇】一杯闷酒尊前过,低首无言自摧挫。不甚醉颜酡,却早嫌玻璃盏大,从因我,酒上心来觉可。

(夫人云)红娘,送小姐卧房里去者。(旦辞末出科)(旦云)俺娘好口不应心也呵!

【乔牌儿】老夫人转关儿没定夺,哑谜儿怎猜破黑阁落甜话儿将人和,请将来著人不快活。

【江儿水】佳人自来多命薄,秀才每从来懦。闷杀没头鹅,撇下陪钱货,下场头那答儿发付我!

【殿前欢】恰才个笑呵呵,都做了江州司马泪痕多。若不是一封书将半万贼兵破,俺一家儿怎得存活。他不想结姻缘想甚么?到如今难著莫。老夫人谎到天来大,当日成也是恁个母亲,今日败也是恁个萧何。

【离亭宴带歇拍煞】从今后玉容寂寞梨花朵,胭脂浅淡樱桃颗,这相思何时是可?昏邓邓黑海来

[Tune of Petty Song] "When I give you a toast, you lower down your head and sigh alone. You cannot intoxicated with the wine, but why not scotch the big cup all at once. You will feel better if you were drunk."

[The Old Lady says] "Red maid, please send the lady to her room."

[Ying Ying bows and Zhang Gong gets up]

[Ying Ying says] "Why does my mother say yes, but mean no!"

[Tune of Pseudo-Melody Song] "The old lady changes her idea. She plays a guessing riddle game and lies with sweet words, making everyone unhappy."

[Tune of Clear Water Song] "Since the ancient time, the beautiful ladies always have a bad fate, and talented scholars are born weak. Flurried, the young man abandons the beautiful wife as if she was a distressed goods. How are you going to plan for me next!"

[Tune of before the Palace Song] "Several moments ago, everyone is laughing. However, at this moment, failed scholars' tears are overflowing. Without his letter to withdraw the five thousand rebels, how we are going to survive? Didn't he want to marry me before? Now it is hard to guess. My mother tells a big lie. She was my mother that day, but today, she changed her mind so quickly. It is so unlike her."

[Tune of Farewell Feast and Epilogue Song] "Since then, my face will be as pale as pear flowers. The lips will not be cherry red. When will this love sickness come to an end? So gloomy the day, it

深,白茫茫陆地来厚,碧悠悠青天来阔。太行山般高仰望,东洋海般深思渴。毒害的恁么!俺娘呵,将颤巍巍双头花蕊搓,香馥馥同心缕带割,长搀搀连理琼枝挫。白头娘不负荷,青春女成担阁,将俺那锦片也似前程蹬脱。俺娘把甜句儿落空了他,虚名儿误赚了我。(下)

(末云)小生醉也,告退。夫人跟前,欲一言以尽意,未知可否。前者,贼寇相迫,夫人所言,能退贼者,以莺莺妻之。小生挺身而出,作书与杜将军,庶几得免夫人之祸,今日命小生赴宴,将谓有喜庆之期不知夫人何见,以兄妹之礼相待?小生非图哺啜而来,此事果若不谐,小生

is as deep as dark sea. A vast expanse of whiteness, the land is as endless as blue sky. I am looking forward to seeing you as if looking up to the top of Tai Hang Mountain. I am longing to meeting you, as if too thirsty to drink up the water in the East sea. All of these makes me sick! My mother, why do you use you hands to break the double headed flowers? Why do you cut the love's knot which is thick with fragrant scent? Why do you break the branches of two trees whose roots interlock with each other? I will wait for my love to come lonely till my hair grows white. The lovely youth is delayed by you. My glorious future is broken by you. My mother uses sweet words to flatter him, and trick me by empty titles." [Exeunt Ying Ying and Red Maid]

[Zhang Gong says] "I am so drunk, so I have to leave. I have something to say before I leave, which I don't know whether it is proper or not. When we were trapped by the thieves before, the old lady said whoever was able to withdraw the thief would marry Ying Ying. So I recommend myself, and write to General Du, to avoid the misfortune of us. Today, the old lady asked me to attend the banquet, and I wondered when the marriage would be settled. However, you just allow me to treat Ying Ying as my sister. I don't come here to have something to eat or drink. The things shouldn't go on like this. So I have to leave first."

[The Old Lady says] "Gentleman Zhang, I own you the gratitude for saving our lives. However, when my husband was alive, he has made an engagement between Ying Ying and my nephew Zheng Heng. Several days ago, I wrote a letter to him, but he has not

即当告退。(夫人云)先生纵有活我之恩,奈小姐先相国在日,曾许下老身侄儿郑恒。即日有书赴京,唤去了,未见来。如若此子至,其事将如之何?莫若多以金帛相酬,先生拣豪门贵宅之女,别为之求,先生台意若何?(末云)既然夫人不与,小生何慕金帛之色!却不道"书中有女颜如玉"?则今日便索告辞。(夫人云)你且住者,今日有酒也。红娘,扶将哥哥去书房中歇息,到明日咱别有话说。(下)(红扶末科)(末念)有分只熬萧寺夜,无缘难遇洞房春。(红云)张生,少吃一盏却不好?(末云)我吃甚么来?(末跪红科)小生为小姐,昼夜忘餐废寝,魂劳梦断,常忽忽如有所失。自寺中一

replied yet. If Zheng Heng arrives, what shall we do? How about choosing some gold and silver to show our gratitude towards you? I will recommend you to the daughter of good families? What do you think?"

[Zhang Gong says] "If my old lady does not agree with marriage between me and Ying Ying, I have no mood of admiring golden silk and other beautiful girls. Haven't you heard of the saying that there is a beautiful woman in the books? I will bid farewell to you today."

[The Old Lady says] "Just stay for a moment. You are drunk today. Red Maid, please support brother to take a rest in the study room. Tomorrow, we will have another talk." [Exit]

[The Red Maid supports Zhang Gong.] [Zhang Gong mummers] "We just have the lot to spend the same night in the monastery, however, we are not allowed to enjoy the pleasure of bridal chamber."

[Red Maid says] "Gentleman Zhang, would it be better if you drink less cup of wine?"

[Zhang Gong says] "How much do you think I have been drinking?"

[Zhang Gong suddenly kneels down to the Red Maid] "Red Maid, you don't know. For lady's sake, I forget eating the meal and have difficulty in sleeping. In the day time, I am always in a daze, as if something is lost. Since the last meeting with your lady in the monastery, when we made verses in partition walls, I have experienced thousands of lovesicknesss in my mind. At that night, we face the wind, and quot the moon. I have thought I was lucky, for I got the

见，隔墙酬和，迎风带月，受无限之苦楚。甫能得成就婚姻，夫人变了卦，使小生智竭思穷，此事几时是了？小娘子，怎生可怜见小生，将此意申与小姐，知小生之心。就小娘子前解下腰间之带，寻个自尽。(末念)可怜刺股悬梁志，险作离乡背井魂。(红云)街上好贱柴，烧你个傻角！你休慌，妾当与君谋之。(末云)计将安在？小生当筑坛拜将。(红云)妾见先生有囊琴一张，必善于此。俺小姐深慕于琴。今夕妾与小姐同至花园内烧夜香，但听咳嗽为令，先生动操。看小姐听得时，说甚么言语，却将先生之言达知。若有话说，明日妾来回报。这早晚怕夫人寻，我回去也。(下)

promise of marriage, however, the old lady has changed her mind. It exhausts me. When should this come to an end? Sister, if you had pity for me, could you tell your lady my heart? If not, I will unloose my girdle, and hang myself in front of your face."

[Zhang Gong murmurs] "What a pity for my poor aspiration to get fame in the imperial exam! I will commit suicide in a strange town."

[Red Maid says] "It is better to pick up the cheap firewood and burn you this idiot! Don't be in a rush. Can I scheme with you together?"

[Zhang Gong says] "May I ask what your plan is? I will be grateful to you all my life. I will build a monastery to worship you."

[Red Maid says] "I saw there is a ancient zither in your baggage, and I guess that you shoud be good at playing it. My lady is also a favorite of the ancient zither music. Tonight, my lady and I will burn incense in the garden. You will hear my coughing as a sign, so you can play the music. When my lady heard the music and asked who is playing, I will tell her about your affections to her. If she says anything, tomorrow I will tell you. Now, it's late. I am afraid that old lady may call me. I have to go now." [Exit]

第四折

（末上云）红娘之言，深有意趣。天色晚也，月儿，你早些出来么！（焚香了）呀，却早发擂也。呀，却早撞钟也。（做理琴科）琴呵，小生与足下湖海相随数年，今夜这一场大功，都在你这神品——金徽、玉轸、蛇腹、断纹、峄阳、焦尾、冰弦之上。天那，却怎生借得一阵顺风，将小生这琴声，吹入俺那小姐玉琢成、粉捏就知音的耳朵里去者！（旦引红上）（红云）小姐，烧香去来，好明月也呵！（旦云）事已无成，烧香何济？

月儿，你团圆呵，咱却怎生！

【越调】【斗鹌鹑】云敛晴空，冰轮乍涌风扫残红，香阶乱拥离恨千端，闲愁万种。夫人那，"靡不有初，鲜克有终。"他做了个影儿里的情郎，我做了个画儿里的爱宠。

Scene Four

[Zhang Gong enters and says] "What Red Maid was talking is interesting. It is getting late. My beautiful moon, could you come out earlier today?" [It's the time to burn incense.] "Ah, I have heard the drum of time beating early today. Early today." [Putting out the ancient zither] "Ah, ancient zither, you have traveled with me for a dozens of years, and tonight you should do me a great favor. Everything depends on you—holy thing. Look, you are made from fortune paulownia wood on the Yi Yang Mountain, with inlaid metallic sound marks, jade string, the transverse scales, broken lines, burning tail, and ice silk strings. Oh, my heaven! How to borrow a slight of wind to make my music come to lady's jade-made ears! I know she is my soul mate just at the first glance. [Ying Ying enters with Red Maid]

[Red Maid says] "My lady, let's burn incense. What a bright moon it is tonight!"

[Ying Ying says] "Everything is settled. What is the use of burning incense? Big bright moon, how round you look tonight, but how lonely I am now!"

[Tune of Fighting Quails Song] "The thick clouds cover the bright sky. A blast of wind blows away the falling petals on the ground. On the fragment stairs, a thousand partings and sorrows happened. My mother can not keep her kindness till the end. He has become a lover in the shadow, and I have become someone in the painting."

【紫花儿序】则落得心儿里念想,口儿里闲题,则索向梦儿里相逢。俺娘昨日个大开东阁,我则道怎生般炮凤烹龙。朦胧!可教我"翠袖殷勤捧玉钟",却不道"主人情重"?则为那兄妹排连,因此上鱼水难同。

(红云)姐姐,你看月阑,明日敢有风也。(旦云)风月天边有,人间好事无。

【小桃红】人间看波:玉容深锁绣帏中,怕有人搬弄。想嫦娥西没东生有谁共?怨天公,裴航不作游仙梦。这云似我罗帏数重,只恐怕嫦娥心动,因此上围住广寒宫。

(红做咳嗽科)(末云)来了。(做理琴科)(旦云)这甚么响?(红发科)

[Tune of Violet Flower Song] "I keep thinking of his images in my mind and mentioning his name whenever I am free. I have to seek reunion with him in the dream. Yesterday my mother held really a big banquet. I had thought she intended to show our gratitude. But how ambiguous she is! She has asked me to serve the drink to him, but doesn't she know how deeply we love each other? Why in hell does she name us as brother and sister?"

[Red Maid says] "Sister, look there is a halo around the moon. I wonder whether it will be windy tomorrow."

[Ying Ying says] "There is a halo around the moon on the sky, but there is no happiness in this world."

[Tune of Red Peach Blossoms Song] "Looking at the mundane world: The beautiful lady locks herself in the deep chamber, afraid to be cheated by others. She is wondering if Chang E would feel lonely in the moon palace. She is blaming the heaven for not giving her a dreamy pillow which may allow her to dream of her lover. These clouds around the moon are as thick as clothes and wefts in the lady's chamber. Maybe Chang E's heart is palpitating for love, so that these clouds surround the moon palace and blindfold her eyes."

[Red Maid coughs] [Zhang Gong says] "Yes."

[He starts playing an ancient zither]

[Ying Ying asks] "Where does this music come from?"

[Red Maid makes a face]

[Ying Ying sings]

（旦唱）

【天净沙】莫不是步摇得宝髻玲珑？莫不是裙拖得环珮玎玲？莫不是铁马儿檐前骤风？莫不是金钩双控，吉丁当敲响帘栊？

【调笑令】莫不是梵王宫，夜撞钟？莫不是疏竹潇潇曲槛中？莫不是牙尺剪刀声相送？莫不是漏声长滴响壶铜？潜身再听在墙角东，元来是近西厢理结丝桐。

【秃厮儿】其声壮，似铁骑刀枪冗冗其声幽，似落花流水溶溶其声高，似风清月朗鹤唳空其声低，似听儿女语，小窗中，喁喁。

【圣药王】他那里思不穷，我这里意已通，娇鸾雏凤失雌雄。他曲未终，我意转浓，争奈伯劳飞燕各西东，尽在不言中。

[Tune of Clear Sky over the Sand Song] "Is it the sound of shaking the jade hairpins while lady is walking? or, is it the tinkling sound of jade that women's skirts wear? or, is it the clip-cop sound of horse's hoof in the strong wind? or, is it the sound of sword and golden hooks, or, the knocking against the curtained window?"

[Tune of Flirting Song] "Is it the sound of the king of Brahma's palace ringing bells at night? or, is it the sound of the sparse bamboo branches waving in the banister? or, is it the sound of scissors and irony foot measure around? or, is it the sound of dropping water from the copper dipper? Listening carefully, I find the sound coming from the eastern corner of the wall. Oh, it should have come from the man who live in the western chamber."

[Tune of Bald Head Song] "When the music strain is strong, it is like the movement of mighty and powerful armies with swords and guns. When the music strain is high, it seems like petals falling into the ponds. When the music strain is slow, it sounds like the crane crying in the clear wind and bright moon night. When the music strain is low, it sounds like two lovers whispering below the window."

[Tune of Sovereign of Medicine Song] "He is thinking of me all the time, and I understand his true feeling now. We look like a pair of lover birds, who los the company of the other. He doesn't stop playing, and my love to him is deeper than before. However, the shrike and the shallow fly in different directions, and the separation is inevitable. Though he says nothing, what he expressed is more than words."

我近书窗听咱。(红云)姐姐,你这里听,我瞧夫人,一会便来。(末云)窗外是有人,已定是小姐。我将弦改过,弹一曲,就歌一篇,名曰《凤求凰》。昔日司马相如,得此曲成事,我虽不及相如,愿小姐有文君之意。(歌曰)有美人兮,见之不忘。一日不见兮,思之如狂。凤飞翱翱兮,四海求凰。无奈佳人兮,不在东墙。张弦代语兮,欲诉衷肠。何时见许兮,慰我彷徨?愿言配德兮,携手相将。不得于飞兮,使我沦亡。(旦云)是弹得好也呵!其词哀,其意切,凄凄然如鹤唳天。故使妾闻之,不觉泪下。

【麻郎儿】这的是令他人耳聪,诉自己情衷。知音者芳心自懂,感怀者断肠悲痛。

【幺篇】这一篇与本宫始终不同。又不是《清夜

"I will come nearer to the window, and listen to the music."

[Red Maid says] "Sister, you can listen to the music here. I will go to the old lady, in case she will call me, and come back later."

[Zhang Gong says] "There is a shadow outside the widow. It must be the lady. I will change the tune, and play the music called 'Seeking for phoenix love'. Before, Si Ma Xiangru has engaged with Zhuo Wenjun because of this song. Though I can not be compared with him, I wish my lady shares the same feeling as Wen Jun."

[Zhang Gong starts to sing] "There is but one beauty in the world. Since my first sight of you, your image will never be dispelled from my mind. Not seeing you would drive me insane. I am like a male phoenix, seeking my soul mate. Are my words worthy of your love? Oh, to fly with you, hand in hand. Without you, I have no wings. Before encountering you, I knew not where to go. A beautiful lady, so near, yet far, Love sickness punishes my heart. Let's fly high together, shoulder to shoulder. Each for the other. Let's open our wings, otherwise, I will die."

[Ying Ying says] "What a touching song it is! The lyrics are full of grief, and the feelings are sincere. It sounds as miserable as crane crying in the sky. So, when I hear it, I cannot help shedding my tears."

[Tune of Pockmarked Face Song] "His wonderful music makes my ears sharp, and I understand his true feelings in the heart. Being a soul mate to him, I understand his music and sighing for myself, I cannot help feeling grief stricken."

[Tune of Petty Songs] "This music is different than what he played

闻钟》，又不是《黄鹤》《醉翁》，又不是《泣麟》《悲凤》。

【络丝娘】一字字更长漏永，一声声衣宽带松。别恨离愁，变做一弄。张生啊，越教人知重。

（末云）夫人且做忘恩，小姐，你也说谎也呵！（旦云）你差怨了我。

【东原乐】这的是俺娘的机变，非干是妾身脱空。若由得我呵，乞求得效鸾凤。俺娘无夜无明并女工，我若得些儿闲空，张生啊，怎教你无人处把妾身作诵。

【绵搭絮】疏帘风细，幽室灯清，都则是一层儿红纸，几棍儿疏棂，兀的不是隔著云山几万重！怎得个人来信息通？便做道十二巫峰，他也曾赋高唐来梦中。

（红云）夫人寻小姐哩，咱家去来。
（旦唱）

【拙鲁速】则见他走将来气冲冲，怎不教人恨匆

before. It's unlike listening to the bell ringing in the still night, nor yellow Crane howling, nor a old drunk man murmuring, nor unicorns sobbing and nor phoenix crying."

[Tune of Spinner Song] "His every word lingers in the air long and forever, as if dropping water. His every sound makes my belt no longer tight. The grief of parting has all melt into one song. The listener is full of heartbroken grief. Gentleman Zhang, you make me value you so much in my mind."

[Zhang Gong says] "The old lady forgets my kindness. My lady, you are lying too."

[Ying Ying says] "Don't blame me."

[Tune of the joy of Eastern Plain Song] "This is all because of the ingratitude of my mother, not my lying. If I am able to control my fate, I would beg to be a pair of love birds with you. My mother asks me to do the needlework day and night. If I am free, Gentleman Zhang, why shouldn't I allow you to talk with me when no one is here?"

[Tune of Cotton Wool Song] "The wind is blowing the curtain, and lamp is dim in the quiet room. There is just a thin red paper and few scattered wood between us, but it makes me feel there are a thousand mountains between us. How are we able to send messages? Even if the difficulties are as high as twelve peaks in the Wu Mountain, the lovers can still overcome it."

[Red Maid says] "The old lady is looking for sister. I will come to them."

[Ying Ying sings]

匆,就得人来怕恐。早是不曾转动,女孩儿家直恁响喉咙。紧摩弄,索将他拦纵,则恐怕夫人行把我来厮葬送。

(红云)姐姐,则管里听琴怎么?张生著我对姐姐说,他回去也。(旦云)好姐姐呵,是必再著住一程儿。(红云)再说甚么?(旦云)你去呵,

【尾】则说道夫人时下有人唧哝,好共歹不著你落空。不问俺口不应的狠毒娘,怎肯著别离了志诚种。(并下)

【络丝娘煞尾】不争惹恨牵情斗引,少不得废寝忘餐病症。

　　题目　张君瑞破贼计　莽和尚生杀心
　　正名　小红娘昼请客　崔莺莺夜听琴

[Tune of Rush Speed Song] "I see my maid coming with hurried footsteps. I realized the separation is close. I have to go to my strict mother immediately. However, I feel myself unable to move, and can only respond my maid in a loud voice. Is it in a hurry? It is better to stop her from calling so loud, less my mother knows and kills the gentleman."

[Red Maid says] "Sister, do you like the music? Gentleman Zhang asked me to tell you he was going to leave."

[Ying Ying says] "Good sister, could you tell him to stay longer?"

[Red Maid says] "What else do you want me to say?"

[Ying Ying says] "You can tell him like this."

[Tune of Epilogue] "At the moment, there is someone speaking ill of him in my mother's ears, so that she disagrees with the marriage at the moment, but I will not disappoint him. I will not wait for my vicious mother's proposal. How am I able to separate with the man whom I love dearly heart and soul?"

[Tune of Epilogue of Weaving Girl Song] "Why doesn't this make people ticklish? The lovers fall into love sickness, which will add symptom of illness of forgetting the meal and sleeping."

Zhang Gong comes with a good strategy to drive the bandits away. The bold monk takes actions in the interest of the oppressed.

The Red Maid invites the guest in the daytime. Cui Yingying listens to the Gu Qing at night.

五剧第三本

张君瑞害相思杂剧

Act Three

楔　子

　　(旦上云)自那夜听琴后,闻说张生有病,我如今著红娘去书院里,看他说甚么。(叫红科)(红上云)姐姐唤我,不知有甚事,须索走一遭。(旦云)这般身子不快呵,你怎么不来看我?(红云)你想张……(旦云)张甚么?(红云)我张着著姐姐哩。(旦云)我有一件事,央及你咱。(红云)甚么事?(旦云)你与我望张生去走一遭,看他说甚么,你来回我话者。(红云)我不去,夫人知道不是耍。(旦云)好姐姐,我拜你两拜,你便与我走一遭。(红云)

Prologue

[Ying Ying enters and says] "Since listening to Gentleman Zhang playing the ancient zither music that night, I heard him seriously ill. Today, I have sent Red Maid to go to his study room, to see how everything is going."

[Ying Ying calls Red Maid.]

[Red Maid enters and says] "Sister is calling me. I don't know what she is asking me for."

[Ying Ying says] "How slows you are walking. Why don't you come to see me as soon as possible?"

[Red Maid says] "You are missing Zhang……"

[Ying Ying says] "Which Zhang?"

[Red Maid says] "I am opening (as same as 'zhang' in Chinese) my eyes and looking to sister ."

[Ying Ying says] "I need your help with one thing."

[Red Maid asks] "What's the thing?"

[Ying Ying says] "Would you help me to go and visit Gentleman Zhang? To hear what he is going to talk to me?"

[Red Maid says] "I will not go there. If the old lady knows, I will get punished."

[Ying Ying says] "Good sister, I bow to you twice. Could you go for

侍长请起,我去则便了。说道:"张生,你好生病重,则俺姐姐也不弱。"只因午夜调琴手,引起春闺爱月心。

【仙吕】【赏花时】俺姐姐针钱无心不待拈,脂粉香消懒去添,春恨压眉尖。若得灵犀一点,敢医可了病恹恹。(下)

(旦云)红娘去了,看他回来说甚话,我自有主意。(下)

第一折

(末上云)害杀小生也。自那夜听琴之后,再不能够见俺那小姐。我著长老说将去,道:"张生好生病重!"却怎生不见人来看我?却思量上

me this time?"

[Red Maid says] "Please get up, sister. I will go now. I will speak to him like this, 'Gentleman Zhang, how much do you suffer from love sickness? My sister does not look better.' Just because of hearing the ancient zither music in the night, my lady has fallen into deep love sickness."

[Tune of Company of Fairy Song] "My sister has no mood to do the needle works, nor she has spirit to put power on her face. She is grief for the spring, with her eyebrows knitting all the time. If two lovers are able to connect with each other for a while, would this love sickness be cured?" [Exit]

[Ying Ying says] "Red Maid has gone. Let's see what she is going to tell me after meeting Gentleman Zhang. Then, I will decide for myself." [Exit]

Scene One

[Zhang Gong enters.] "How it would kill me that night! Since playing the musical instrument that night, I can see my lady no more. I speak to the abbot that I will leave immediately. The abbot stopped me and said, 'Gentleman Zhang, how ill you look!' Why didn't anybody come to see me? Now, I feel a little sleepy and take a little nap."

来，我睡些儿咱。(红上云)奉小姐言语，著我看张生，须索走一遭。我想咱每一家，若非张生，怎存俺一家儿性命也！

【仙吕】【点绛唇】相国行祠，寄居萧寺。因丧事，幼女孤儿，将欲从军死。

【混江龙】谢张生伸志，一封书到便兴师。显得文章有用，足见天地无私。若不是剪草除根半万贼，险些儿灭门绝户了俺一家儿。莺莺君瑞，许配雄雌，夫人失信，推托别词将婚姻打灭，以兄妹为之。如今都废却成亲事。一个价糊突了胸中锦绣，一个价泪揾湿了脸上胭脂。

【油葫芦】樵悴潘郎鬓有丝，杜韦娘不似旧时，带围宽清减了瘦腰肢。一个睡昏昏不待观经史，一个意悬悬懒去拈针指，一个丝桐上调弄出离恨谱，一个花笺上删抹成断肠诗，一个笔下写幽情，一个弦上传心事：两下里都一样害相思。

[Red Maid enters and says] "I follow the order of my lady to go and see Gentleman Zhang. I am always thinking that without him, our whole family will not be able to survive. He has saved our life!"

[Tune of Rouge Lip of Fairy Song] "The former prime minister is dead, and his coffin stayed in the monastery. Suddenly, there came a calamity. The bandits asked lady Ying Ying to be their chief's wife."

[Tune of Dragon in the Troubled Water Song] "Thanks for Gentleman Zhang, one letter arrives, and five thousand soldiers of General Du comes. The letter is worthy, and the heaven and earth is selflessness. If not for withdrawal the five thousand rebels, all our family will not survive. Ying Ying should have married to Gentleman Zhang forever, but why did my old lady break her words? To make Ying Ying and Gentleman Zhang treat each other as brother and sister. Now, because of this, one suffers from love sickness and wastes his talents; one weeps day and night and wets the rouge on her face."

[Tune of Field Cricket Song] "Haggard looking, handsome gentleman grows white hair on his temples. The beautiful lady does not look like what she was before. The clothes has become larger, and the waist more slender. One is so sleepy everyday, so that he has no mean to read classics and history, another one is too lazy that she has no mood to do the needle work. One plays an ancient zither music song to reveal the grief in the heart, and another one writes poems with a broken heart. One expresses her

【天下乐】方信道才子佳人信有之,红娘看时,有些乖性儿,则怕有情人不遂心也似此。他害的有些抹媚,我遭著没三思,一纳头安排著憔悴死。

却早来到书院里,我把唾津儿润破窗纸,看他在书房里做甚么。

【村里迓鼓】我将这纸窗儿湿破,悄声儿窥视。多管是和衣儿睡起,罗衫上前襟褶裎。孤眠况味,凄凉情绪,无人伏侍。觑了他涩滞气色,听了他微弱声息,看了他黄瘦脸儿。张生呵,你若不闷死,多应是害死。

【元和令】金钗敲门扇儿。

(末云)是谁?

(红唱)

我是个散相思的五瘟使。俺小姐想著风清月朗夜深时,使红娘来探尔。

(末云)既然小娘子来,小姐必有言语。

love in poems; and another one shows his feeling in the string. Two people with same heart both suffer deeply from lovesickness."

[Tune of Universal Joy Song] "There is a message to be delivered between the lady and the man. When I look at the message, I feel it is a bit strange. I am afraid the lover will not be satisfied. He looks so enchanted. I blame myself for no good idea, finally, make him so haggard.

I have arrived to the study room earlier. I poked the window paper, to see what he is doing inside."

[Tune of Village Drum Song] "I poke the window paper, and peer at him secretly from outside. He is sleeping with his clothes, with forepart of his silk clothes creased. Gentleman Zhang, if you will not die for gloominess, you will die for lovesickness."

[Tune of Song of Peace] "I use my gold hairpin to knock the door."

[Zhang Gong says] "Who is it?"

[Red Maid sings] "I am one of the five chief demons of folklore personifying pestilence. My lady is thinking of the beautiful night with clear moon and slight wind these days, so she asks me to come."

[Zhang Gong says] "Since sister has come, the lady must have something to say."

[Red Maid sings] "My lady has not had the mood to make up by now. She keeps repeating your name all day."

（红唱）

俺小姐至今脂粉未曾施,念到有一千番张殿试。

（末云）小姐既有见怜之心,小生有一简,敢烦小娘子达知肺腑咱。（红云）只恐他番了面皮。

【上马娇】他若是见了这诗,看了这词,他敢颠倒费神思。

他拽扎起面皮来:"查得谁的言语你将来,这妮子怎敢胡行事!"他可敢嗤、嗤的扯做了纸条儿。

（末云）小生久后多以金帛拜酬小娘子。
（红唱）

【胜葫芦】哎,你个馋穷酸俫没意儿,卖弄你有家私,莫不图谋你东西来到此?先生的钱物,与红娘做赏赐,是我爱你的金赀?

【幺篇】你看人似桃李春风墙外枝,卖俏倚门儿。我虽是个婆娘有气志,则说道:"可怜见小子,只身独自!"恁的呵,颠倒有个寻思。

（末云）依著姐姐:"可怜见小子,只身独自!"

[Zhang Gong says] "Since the lady has pity on me, I have a letter for her. Could I bother you to send the letter to your lady to express my true heart feelings?"

[Red Maid says] "I am afraid that he will turn against me if I didn't send the letter for him."

[Tune of Charming on the Horse Song] "If she read this verses, she will be wasting out again.

She will wear a cold face and speak to me, 'Who asks you to do this? Little bitch.' She will tear up the letter into pieces."

[Zhang Gong says] "I will definitely reward sister with heavy gold in the future."

[Red Maid sings]

[Tune of Better than Guard Song] "How boring you are, Mr gentleman. You are going to show off your treasure in the family. Did I come here just for the sake of your money? Who wants your reward?"

[Tune of Petty Song] "You regard us as branches of peach or plum trees growing outside of the wall, living a whore's life. Though I am a girl, I am spirited. I want to say 'Have pity on that young man. How lonely he is!' Just for this sake, I am willing to help you."

[Zhang Gong says] "Thank you for having pity on me. Just as sister

（红云）兀的不是也。你写来，咱与你将去。（末写科）（红云）写得好呵，读与我听咱。（末读云）"珙百拜，奉书芳卿可人妆次：自别颜范，鸿稀鳞绝，悲怆不胜。孰料夫人以恩成怨，变易前姻，岂得不为失信乎？使小生目视东墙，恨不得腋翅于妆台左右患成思渴，垂命有日。因红娘至，聊奉数字，以表寸心。万一有见怜之意，书以掷下，庶几尚可保养。造次不谨，伏乞情恕。后成五言诗一首，就书录呈：相思恨转添，谩把瑶琴弄。乐事又逢春，芳心尔亦动。此情不可违，虚誉何须奉。莫负月华明，且怜花影重。"

said, 'Have pity on that young man. How lonely he is!'"

[Red maid says] "Of course it is. Please write, and I will send the message for you."

[Zhang Gong starts writing]

[Red Maid says] "How nice your handwriting looks. What are you writing? Could you read it for me?"

[Zhang Gong starts to read.] "Zhang Gong bows to the lady for a hundred times. I am writing to the beloved one: Since parting with you that night, I cannot hear from you any more. Deep sorrows have overwhelmed my mind. I didn't expect that your mother changed her mind, and broken her promises. I am watching to the east wall day and night, hating for myself not having a pair of wings to fly into your dressing chamber. My longings for you has caused me deep love sickness. My life is just near its end. Now Red Maid has come, so I just write a few words, to express my true sorrows. If you had pity on me, could you reply the message? If so, I am still able to survive for a few days. If I have said something improper, I apologize here. I cannot betray this love feeling. There is no need to follow the empty reputation. Don't fail to live up to the bright moon, but have pity for the thick shade of flowers under the moonlight."

(红唱)

【后庭花】我则道拂花笺打稿儿,元来他染霜毫不勾思。先写下几句寒温序,后题著五言八句诗。不移时,把花笺锦字,叠做个同心方胜儿。忒聪明,忒敬思,忒风流,忒浪子。虽然是假意儿,小可的难到此。

【青哥儿】颠倒写鸳鸯两字,方信道"在心为志"。

(末云)姐姐将去,是必在意者!

(红唱)

看喜怒其间觑个意儿。放心波学士!我愿为之,并不推辞,自有言词。则说道:"昨夜弹琴的那人儿,教传示。"

这简帖儿我与你将去,先生当以功名为念,休堕了志气者!

【寄生草】你将那偷香手,准备著折桂枝。休教那淫词儿污了龙蛇字,藕丝儿缚定鹍鹏翅,黄莺儿夺了鸿鹄志;休为这翠帏锦帐一佳人,误了你玉堂金马三学士。

[Red Maid sings]

[Tune of Backyard Flower Song] "I had thought he would start with a draft on the fancy stationery paper, but I don't expect that he took no second thought when holding the writing brush pen. He just wrote a few greetings in the beginning, and a poem of eight lines at the end. When he finished, he just folded the paper into the shape of heart. He is so clever, so thoughtful, so romantic, and so understanding. Even if he is pretending, it is enough to show his feelings."

[Tune of Young Brother Song] "Writing with 'Bird love' instead of 'love bird', Gentleman Zhang urges me to say that 'The letter shows his true feelings'."

[Zhang Gong says] "Sister, Please keep this in the mind!"

[Red Maid sings] "I will give the message to Ying Ying when she is happy. Please take it easy, my scholar. I am willing to do this for you, not to refuse you, out of pity for you. I know what I should say. I will say, 'The man who played an ancient zither that night asked me to send a message to you'.

Keep it in the mind, Gentleman Zhang. I will send the message for you, but you should not give up your learning and break your backbone."

[Tune of Parasitic Grass Song] "You wish to marry the fair lady, but you must pick up the laurel crown. Don't write amorous words with the writing brush everyday. The tender feeling is tied tightly on the wings of roc. The love from Ying Ying should not deprive your ambition and never allow love sickness to plough under

(末云)姐姐在意者!(红云)放心,放心。

【煞尾】沈约病多般,宋玉愁无二,清减了相思样子。则你那眉眼传情未了时,我中心日夜藏之。怎敢因而,"有美玉于斯",我须教有发落归著这张纸。凭著我舌尖儿上说词,更和这简帖儿里心事,管教那人儿来探你一遭儿。(下)

(末云)小娘子将简帖儿去了,不是小生说口,则是一道会亲的符箓。他明日回话,必有个次第。且放下心,须索好音来也。且将宋玉风流策,寄与蒲东窈窕娘。(下)

第二折

(旦上云)红娘伏侍老夫人,不得空,偌早晚敢待来也。困思上来,再睡些儿咱。(睡科)(红上云)奉小姐言语,去看张生,因伏侍老夫人,未曾回小姐话去。不听得声音,敢又睡哩。我入去看

your scholarly talents. You are able to ride golden horses and enter the jade hall."

[Zhang Gong says] "Sister, please keep this in the mind."

[Red Maid says] "Of course. Of course."

[Tune of Pseudo-Epilogue Song] "Just like scholar Sheng Yue in the Liang dynasty, Gentleman Zhang easily gets sick. He is as handsome as Song Yu, but full of worries. He grows lean and haggard out of love sickness. I have noticed how you and my lady would pass the love message with the corner of your eyes. Now I hold this jade like letter with care. I will speak out the love between you with my tongue, and pass the love sickness through the message. I am sure to ask my lady to go and see you for once." [Exit]

[Zhang Sheng says] "The Red Maid has already gone and sent the message. I am not talking big, but this message must provide me a chance of a good marriage. I will wait for her response. There must be good news coming, so I will just easy my mind. I will be a next Song Yu who secretly pass the love message to his romantic lover." [Exit]

Scene Two

[Ying Ying enters and says] "Red Maid is serving my mother, so she has no time to come to me. She will come here sooner and later. Now I feel sleepy, so I will take a nap."

一遭。

【中吕】【粉蝶儿】风静帘闲,透纱窗麝兰香散,启朱扉摇响双环。绛台高,金荷小,银釭犹灿。比及将暖帐轻弹,先揭起这梅红罗软帘偷看。

【醉春风】则见他钗嚲玉横斜,髻偏云乱挽。日高犹自不明眸,畅好是懒,懒。(旦做起身长叹科)(红唱)半晌抬身,几回摇耳,一声长叹。

我待便将简帖儿与他,恐俺小姐有许多假处哩。我则将这简帖儿放在妆盒儿上,看他见了说甚么。
(旦做照镜科,见帖看科)
(红唱)

【普天乐】晚妆残,乌云嚲,轻匀了粉脸,乱挽起云鬟。将简帖儿拈,把妆盒儿按,开拆封皮孜孜看,颠来倒去不害心烦。

   (旦怒叫)红娘!(红做意云)呀,决撒了也!

   厌的早扢皱了黛眉。

   (旦云)小贱人,不来怎么!

(红唱)

   忽的波低垂了粉颈,氲的呵改变了朱颜。

180

[Ying Ying is sleeping]

[Red Maid enters and says] "My lady asked me to go and see Gentleman Zhang. I was about to reply, but delayed to reply out of serving the old lady. I don't hear any sound in the room. Maybe she is sleeping again. I will go inside and have a look."

[Tune of Pink Butterfly Song] "The wind is still, and the curtain is closed. The fragrance disappears from the screen window. I open the red door, and my earrings ring. The stage for the lamp is high, and candles are dim. The sparkles are still shinning. I will flick the warm bed curtain, and open the light red bed curtain to peep at my lady."

[Tune of Intoxicated Vernal Wind Song] "The jade on her hair is slanting and her beautiful hair is rolled up leisurely on the head. The sun is bright in the sky, but she is still sleepy on the bed. How lazy she is!"

[Ying Ying gets up and sighs deeply]

[Red Maid says] "After a long time, she gets up, scratches her cheek, and utters a deep sigh.

I will give her the letter, but I am afraid that my lady would pretend as if she didn't care. I just put the letter on her making up box, to see what she is going to say."

[Ying Ying looks at herself in the mirror, and suddenly she sees the letter. She starts to read]

[Red Maid sings]

[Tune of Universal Joy Song] "There is less making ups on her face. Her hair is rolled leisurely on the head. She picks up the letter, closes

（旦云）小贱人，这东西那里将来的？我是相国的小姐，谁敢将这简帖来戏弄我？我几曾惯看这等东西？告过夫人，打下你个小贱人下截来。（红云）小姐使将我去，他著我将来，我不识字，知他写著甚么？

【快活三】分明是你过犯，没来由把我摧残使别人颠倒恶心烦。你不"惯"，谁曾"惯"？

姐姐休闹，比及你对夫人说呵，我将这简帖儿，去夫人行出首去来！（旦做揪住科）我逗你耍来。（红云）放手，看打下下截来！（旦云）张生两日如何？（红云）我则不说。（旦云）好姐姐，你说与我听咱！（红唱）

the making up box, tears up the cover, and starts to read attentively. She keeps reading it over and over again, not annoyed at all."

[Ying Ying calls Red Maid angrily] "Red Maid!"

[Red Maid understands] "I spoil the things. She is so angry that she keeps knitting her eyebrows."

[Ying Ying says] "Your little bitch, what does this thing come from? I am the lady of the prime minister prefecture. Who dares to write such a letter to ridicule me? When have I read such things before? I will tell my mother, and see how she is going punish you."

[Red Maid says] "My lady, it is you who asked me to go and see Gentleman Zhang, and he asked me to take the letter back. I don't learn to read. Who knows what he wrote?"

[Tune of Happiness Three song] "It is you who made mistakes, but you put the blames on me. How annoying it is to turn the truth upside down? If you are not, who is used to reading such a letter?"

"Sister, don't be angry. If you are going to tell the old lady, I will present the letter to the old lady myself."

[Ying Ying clutches Red Maid's sleeves] "Good sister, I am kidding."

[Red Maid says] "Please release me. What if I was beating by the old lady?"

[Ying Ying asks] "How is Gentleman Zhang these days?"

[Red Maid says] "I will not tell you."

[Ying Ying says] "Good sister, please tell me."

[Red Maid sings]

【朝天子】张生近间、面颜，瘦得来实难看。不思量茶饭，怕见动弹晓夜将佳期盼，废寝忘餐。黄昏清旦，望东墙淹泪眼。

（旦云）请个好太医看他证候咱。（红云）他证候吃药不济。病患、要安，则除是出几点风流汗。

（旦云）红娘，不看你面时，我将与老夫人看，看他有何面目见夫人！虽然我家亏他，只是兄妹之情，焉有外事。红娘，早是你口稳哩，若别人知呵，甚么模样！（红云）你哄著谁哩！你把这个饿鬼，弄的他七死八活，却要怎么？

【四边静】怕人家调犯，"早共晚夫人见些破绽，你我何安。"问甚么他遭危难？撺断、得上竿，掇了梯儿看。

（旦云）将描笔儿过来，我写将去回他，著他

[Tune of Homage to the Emperor Song] "Recently, Gentleman Zhang looks too sallow and emaciated. He doesn't eat or sleep, or reluctant to move, but pray for the lovely night to arrive soon. When the evening comes, his eyes will be full of tears."

[Ying Ying says] "Please get a doctor for Gentleman Zhang."

[Red Maid says] "No medicine in the world will work for his symptom. If he is sick in the body, after a little rest and a little sweat, he will be recovered. But he is not."

[Ying Ying says] "Red Maid, if not for your sake, I will show the letter to my mother. See how he is going to face my mother? Though our family owes him gratitude, the relationship between him and me are just sister and brother. What else can happen? Red Maid, you are trustful. What if to change others? I can't imagine the consequence!"

[Red Maid says] "What are you kidding? You make this hungry man more dead than alive. What are you going to do?"

[Tune of Four Side Tranquility Song] "You are afraid that he is flirting with you. 'What should we do if the old lady finds out?' If you don't care for him, why do you allow him to climb the tree first, and remove the ladder latter? Whom are you showing?"

[Ying Ying says] "Please hand me a writing brush, and I may write him all answers. Warn him not to do this next time."

[Ying Ying is writing a letter][She looks up and says to the Red Maid] "Could you please tell him like this, 'My sister pays her deep respect to you

下次休是这般!(旦做写科)(起身科云)红娘,你将去说:"小姐看望先生,相待兄妹之礼如此,非有他意。再一遭儿是这般呵,必告夫人知道。"和你个小贱人都有说话!(旦掷书下)

(红唱)

【脱布衫】小孩儿家口没遮拦,一迷的将言语摧残。把似你使性子,休思量秀才,做多少好人家风范。(红做拾书科)

【小梁州】他为你梦里成双觉后单,废寝忘餐。罗衣不奈五更寒,愁无限,寂寞泪阑干。

【幺篇】似这等辰勾空把佳期盼,我将这角门儿世不曾牢拴,则愿你做夫妻无危难。我向这筵席头上整扮,做一个缝了口的撮合山。

(红云)我若不去来,道我违拗他,那生又等我回报,我须索走一遭。(下)(末上云)那书倩红娘将去,未见回话。我这封书去,必定成事。这

and treats you as a brother. There is no other meanings. If you write another letter like this, she is sure to tell the old lady.' I am warning him as well as warning you, little bitch." [Ying Ying throws the letter on the ground and leaves.]

[Red Maid sings.]

[Tune of Doffing the Clothes Song] "As a child, I don't know how to restrain my tongue, and being enchanted, I speak rushingly wrong. If you get into a huff, you should not think of that scholar again, so that you can be the good daughter of the big family."

[Red Maid picks up the letter]

[Tune of Small Liang Zhou Song] "For your sake, he dreams nothing but you, however, when he wakes up, he is alone. He forgets eating or drinking. His thin clothes can not stand the coldness in the midnight. There are unbounded sorrows, and his tears will be dried up for you."

[Tune of Petty song] "It is an ordeal to wait for the beloved one. I am never against the love between you, and wish you to be the husband and wife. I am just a match maker to bring you together."

[Red Maid speaks to herself] "If I didn't go, that man would have thought I didn't send the message. He is waiting for my reply, so I have to go and have a look." [Exit]

[Zhang Gong enters and says] "Red Maid hasn't replied me the message. I believe the moment my letter is sent, the marriage will be completed. She will come sooner."

早晚敢待来也。(红上)须索回张生话去。小姐,你性儿忒惯得娇了!有前日的心,那得今日的心来?

【石榴花】当日个晚妆楼上杏花残,犹自怯衣单!那一片听琴心清露月明间。昨日个向晚,不怕春寒,几乎险被先生馈。那其间岂不胡颜?为一个不酸不醋风魔汉,隔墙儿险化做了望夫山。

【斗鹌鹑】你用心儿拨雨撩云,我好意儿传书寄简。不肯搜自己狂为,则待要觅别人破绽。受艾焙权时忍这番,畅好是奸!

"张生是兄妹之礼,焉敢如此!"

对人前巧语花言,没人处便想张生,背地里愁眉泪眼。

(红见末科)(末云)小娘子来了,擎天柱,大事如何了也?(红云)不济事了,先生休傻。(末云)小生简帖儿,是一道会亲的符箓,则是小娘子不用

[Red Maid says] "I need to reply to that Gentleman. My lady, you are too spoiled. If you had the mood to listen to the music, why should you send such a letter?"

[Tune of Pomegranate Flower Song] "That night, you had a late make-up. The few apricot blossoms were still lingering on the branches. You wore thin clothes, afraid it would not protect you from cold. However, you were still standing there and listening to ancient zither music under the bright moon and clear wind. At that time, didn't you feel ashamed for yourself? For the sake of a poor scholar, you have nearly frozen into a mountain which looks in the direction of your lover forever."

[Tune of Fighting of Quails Song] "You have planted the seed of love, and I have the good heart to pass the message of love. I don't think that I am doing the madness, but I am looking for the signs of this love. You are suffering deeply for his sake. How happy it will be if you acknowledge it!

'I just treat Gentleman Zhang as brother.' How could it be like this?

In front of others, my lady pretends not to care. But in private, she is wiping tears sorrowfully."

[Red Maid meets Zhang Gong] [Zhang Gong says] "My good sister, you finally come. You are the pillar that supports the heaven. How is everything going?"

[Red Maid says] "There is no use any more. Gentleman Zhang, don't be silly."

[Zhang Gong says] "The letter that I wrote to the lady is a talisman for

心,故意如此。(红云)我不用心?有天哩!你那简帖儿好听!

【上小楼】这的是先生命悭,须不是红娘违慢。那简帖儿到做了你的招状,他的勾头,我的公案。若不是觑面颜,厮顾盼,担饶轻慢。

先生受罪,礼之当然。贱妾何辜?

争些儿把你娘拖犯!

【幺篇】从今后相会少,见面难。月暗西厢,凤去秦楼,云敛巫山。你也赸,我也赸,请先生休讪,早寻个酒阑人散。

(红云)只此再不必申诉足下肺腑,怕夫人寻,我回去也。(末云)小娘子此一遭去,再著谁与小生分剖?必索做一个道理,方可救得小生一命。(末跪下揪住红科)(红云)张先生是读书人,岂不知此

love. It must be you, my sister, who is not serious about it, so that it does not work."

[Red Maid says] "Am I not serious? My goodness! How well you are talking!"

[Tune of Ascending an Attic Song] "This is your fate, not because of my laziness. The letter that you wrote to my lady has become the evidence of your guilt. I may even be punished by it. If it wasn't for my sister to save my face, I will bear the blame.

If you get punished, it is just and fair. But how innocent I am!

You nearly encumber me."

[Tune of Petty Song] "Since then, our meeting will be rare. The moon is casting shadows on the western chamber; the phoenix is flying to the whore house, and the clouds is covering the Wu Mountain. Gentleman Zhang, don't accost my lady. It is better to drink wine and forget her earlier."

[Red Maid says] "There is no need to write your true feeling on the letter and ask me to send. I am afraid that my old lady is seeking for me, so I have to go now."

[Zhang Gong says] "If sister goes away now, who is going to share with me my sorrows? I will ask for only a reason. Only by this can save my life."

[Zhang Gong kneels down to Red Maid and clutches her sleeve]

[Red Maid says] "Gentleman Zhang, you are a well learned scholar. Why don't you know my lady's meaning? It looks so easy."

意,其事可知矣。

【满庭芳】你休要呆里撒奸。你待要恩情美满,却教我骨肉摧残。老夫人手执著棍儿摩娑看,粗麻线怎透得针关?直待我拄著拐帮闲钻懒,缝合唇送暖偷寒。

待去呵,小姐性儿撮盐入火,消息儿踏著泛。

待不去呵,(末跪哭云)小生这一个性命,都在小娘子身上。

(红唱)

禁不得你甜话儿热趋。好著我两下里做人难。

我没来由分说,小姐回与你的书,你自看者。(末接科,开读科)呀,有这场喜事!撮土焚香,三拜礼毕。早知小姐简至,理合远接接待不及,勿令见罪。小娘子,和你也欢喜。(红云)怎么?(末云)小姐骂我都是假,书中之意,著我今夜花园里

[Tune of Courtyard Full of Fragrance Song] "Don't be a rouge there. While you are wishing for love, why not think of the torture that she has? The old lady is holding the stick, how could the deep rope go through the needle's eye? While I am wasting my time to help the lazy and the weak, my lips are sealed forever, so how can I continue acting as a match maker?

I am going now. The young lady is very annoyed. I am afraid that the news will be spread."

[Zhang Gong kneels down with his tears and snivels streaming down] "Don't go. It's up to you, my dear sister, whether I live or die."

[Red Maid sings] "I can not bear your sweet words. It makes me too difficult to do one thing, but say another.

All I said has a reason. This is the letter that my lady sent to you. You can read it by yourself."

[Zhang Gong holds the letter in the hands, and starts to read] "Aha, I never expect that such a good thing will happen to me. I will burn incense, and bow down to you three times. If I should have known lady is so considerate and thoughtful, I will not offend you. My sister, you should be happy for me too."

[Red Maid asks] "What did she say?"

[Zhang Gong says] "On the appearance, the lady looked angry. However, what she writes in the letter is to ask me to meet her in the garden tonight and spend a lovely night with her."

[Red Maid asks] "Could you read the letter for me?"

来,和他"哩也波,哩也啰"哩!(红云)你读书我听。(末云)"待月西厢下,迎风户半开。隔墙花影动,疑是玉人来。"(红云)怎见得他著你来?你解与我听咱。(末云)"待月西厢下",著我月上来,"迎风户半开",他开门待我,"隔墙花影动,疑是玉人来",著我跳过墙来。(红笑云)他著你跳过墙来,你做下来。端的有此说么?(末云)俺是个猜诗谜的社家,风流隋何,浪子陆贾。我那里有差的勾当?(红云)你看我姐姐,在我行也使这般道儿。

【耍孩儿】几曾见寄书的颠倒瞒著鱼雁,小则小心肠儿转关。写著道西厢待月等得更阑,著你跳东墙"女"字边"干"。元来那诗句儿里包笼著三更枣,简帖儿里埋伏著九里山。他著紧处将人慢。恁会云雨闹中取静,我寄音书忙里偷闲。

[Zhang Gong says] "The moonlight falls on the western chamber; the winds blows the door open. A shadow moves in the next wall, wondering if it is the shadow of the beloved one coming."

[Red Maid asks] "How do you know she is waiting for you? Could you explain it to me?"

[Zhang Gong explains] "The moonlight falls on the western chamber, which means that she asks me to wait for her when the moon climbs up to the sky. 'The winds blows the door open' means that she is going to open the door and meet me. 'A shadow moves in the next wall. Wondering if the beloved one is coming.' means she asks me to jump over the wall, and come to her. [Red Maid laughs and says] "She asks you to jump over the wall, and have an affair with her. Does she really mean this?"

[Zhang Gong says] "I am an expert of guessing the furor poetics, as easy as Sui He, and as libertine as Lu Jia. How can I be wrong?"

[Red Maid says] "Look at my sister. She is deceiving me too here."

[Tune of Playing with the Child Song] "When have you ever seen that the messenger is cheated by the sender? She is really so clever and cautious all the time. She is writing to allow you to come when the moonlight shines on the western chamber, and ask you to jump the wall, and have a happy time with her. Oh, no one expects that the lines in the verses means the happy time at night. One letter has hided a secret as large as havens. For such an important matter, I suffered slight. You will wedlock with each other, and I am fooling myself by sending such a letter."

【四煞】纸光明玉板,字香喷麝兰,行儿边湮透非春汗?一缄情泪红犹湿,满纸春愁墨未干。从今后休疑难,放心波玉堂学士,稳情取金雀鸦鬟。

【三煞】他人行别样的亲,俺跟前取次看,更做道孟光接了梁鸿案。别人行甜言美语三冬暖,我跟前恶语伤人六月寒。我为头儿看:看你个离魂倩女,怎发付掷果潘安。

（末云）小生读书人,怎跳得那花园过也。（红唱）

【二煞】隔墙花又低,迎风户半拴,偷香手段今番按。怕墙高怎把龙门跳?嫌花密难将仙桂攀。放心去,休辞惮。你若不去呵,望穿他盈盈秋水,蹙损了淡淡春山。

[Tune of Last Stanza but Four] "The light of the paper is as bright as the jade plate. Every word has the smell of fragrance. Each line is written with her sweat. The tears are still leaving lines on the paper and the ink is not dried. You will not be worried in the future. Take it easy, my well learned scholar. You are sure to marry a beauty this night."

[Tune of Last Stanza but Three], "Those lovers are extremely sweet to each other, and I observe them in my leisure time. It seems as if Meng Guang holds the tray level with brows from his wife Liang Hong. She is scolding me before, which makes the June as cold as winter. When rereading the letter from beginning, the cold winter warms. Let's take a look at your beautiful lady, how are you going to deal with man as handsome as Pan An?"

[Zhang Gong says] "I am a scholar. How am I able to jump over the wall to the garden?"

[Red Maid sings]

[Tune of Last Stanza but Two] "Below the next wall, the flowers are low. Facing the wind, the door is closed. It is a test for you to see whether you are sincere. If you are afraid of the hall wall, how are you able to jump the dragon wall? If you dislike the densely growing flowers, you are unable to climb the fairy vine. Take it easy. Don't be afraid. If you didn't come, you are never going to wait for Ying Ying again, despite that you keep gazing anxiously as

（末云）小生曾到那花园里，已经两遭，不见那好处。这一遭，知他又怎么？（红云）如今不比往常。

【煞尾】你虽是去了两遭，我敢道不如这番。你那隔墙酬和都胡侃，证果的是今番这一简。（红下）

（末云）万事自有分定，谁想小姐有此一场好处。小生是猜诗谜的社家，风流隋何，浪子陆贾，到那里扢扎帮便倒地。今日颓天百般的难得晚。天，你有万物于人，何故争此一日？疾下去波！读书继晷怕黄昏，不觉西沉强掩门。欲赴海棠花下约，太阳何苦又生根？（看天云）呀，才晌

if to gaze the vast autumn water, and keep frowning as if to break the spring mountainside."

[Zhang Gong says] "I have been to the garden twice, but those goods things never happen. If I come again, who knows what will happen this time?"

[Red Maid says] "This time is different than before."

[Tune of Epilogue Song] "Though you have been there twice, I trust they will never be as fun as this time. Those talking through the walls are all nonsense. You will see what is going to happen this time." [Exit]

[Zhang Gong says] "Everything is settled by destiny. Who knows my lady will give me such a chance? I am an expert of furor poetics, as easy as Sui He, and as libertine as Lu Jia. I will guess the meaning of verses as soon as it is made. Why is it so difficult to be dark today? The light of the sunshine, you give everything to the human world, why do you still fight for daylight in a day! Please get darker quickly. When I was reading the book, I follow the daytime, afraid that the evening would arrive early. When I talk with a friend, the sun is setting down too soon to the west, so I am reluctant to close the door. Today, I am about to date under the Malus spectabilis flowers. Why does the sun still hang on the sky?"

[Looking at the clouds in the sky.] "Ah, it just passes the moon. I have to wait longer."

午也,再等一等。(又看科)今日万般的难得下去也呵!碧天万里无云,空劳倦客身心。恨杀鲁阳贪战,不教红日西沉。呀,却早倒西也,再等一等咱。无端三足乌,团团光烁烁。安得后羿弓,射此一轮落!谢天地,却早日下去也。呀,却早发擂也!呀,却早撞钟也!拽上书房门,到得那里,手挽著垂杨,滴流扑跳过墙去。(下)

第三折

(红上云)今日小姐著我寄书与张生,当面假多般意儿,元来诗内暗约著他来。小姐也不对我说,我也不瞧破他,则请他烧香。今夜晚妆处比每日较别,我看他到其间怎的瞒我?(红唤科)姐姐,咱烧香去来。(旦上云)花阴重叠香风细,庭

[Looking at the clouds in the sky again.] "Why is it so difficult to wait for the sunset today? The sky is bright and cloudless, which only exhausts people's body and mind. I hate the Old Lu Yang greedy for the war with the sun, not allowing the sun to set down earlier. Ah, it finally sets down to the west. I have to wait for a while. There is no reason why the sun is so round and burning. If I am able to shoot an arrow, I will shoot this sun down from the sky. Thank goodness. It sets down early today. Please beat the drum to report the night early. I will close the door of the study room, and walk towards the wall. I climb the willow branch, and jump over the wall." [Exit]

Scene Three

[Red Maid says] "Today, my lady asked me to send the message to Gentleman Zhang. She scolded that Gentleman in my presence, however, she wrote in the poem to date with him secretly. My lady did not tell me. I will not expose her. I just invite her to burn the incense. Tonight, her making up is different from what she was before. I will see how she is going to deceive me?"

[Red Maid calls Ying Ying] "Sister, let's burn incense."

[Ying Ying enters and says] "The shadows of flowers overlap with each other and the fragment wind blows slowly and softly. The yard is dark and deep, but the moon is hanging brightly in the sky."

院深沉淡月明。(红云)今夜月明风清,好一派景致也呵!

【双调】【新水令】晚风寒峭透窗纱,控金钩绣帘不挂。门阑凝暮霭,楼角敛残霞。恰对菱花,楼上晚妆罢。

【驻马听】不近喧哗,嫩绿池塘藏睡鸭自然幽雅,淡黄杨柳带栖鸦。金莲蹴损牡丹芽,玉簪抓住荼蘼架。夜凉苔径滑,露珠儿湿透了凌波袜。

我看那生和俺小姐巴不得到晚。

【乔牌儿】自从那日初时想月华,捱一刻似一夏。见柳梢斜日迟迟下,早道"好教贤圣打"。

【搅筝琶】打扮的身子儿诈,准备著云雨会巫峡。只为这燕侣莺俦,锁不住心猿意马。

不则俺那小姐害,那生呵——

[Red Maid says] "Tonight the moon is bright and the wind is clear. What a beautiful scene it is!"

[Double tune of New Water Song] "The night wind is cold, blowing through the window screen. The golden hook is not hanging the curtain. The threshold of the door coagulates evening haze, and the corner of the building holds back the sunsets clouds. Just looking herself in the mirror, Ying Ying carefully makes herself up in the chamber upstairs."

[Tune of Halting the Horses Song] "Not noisy at all, the green pond with sleeping ducks is naturally elegant. On the light yellow willow branches perches the ravens. The small feet treads the buds of peony flowers, and jade hairpin entwines the shrub. At night, the stairs with moss are slippery, and the dew wets the beautiful socks of a beautiful lady.

I think Gentleman Zhang and my lady both cannot wait for the nightfall."

[Tune of Pesto-melody Song] "Since she thinks of the meeting under the moonlight, one moment is as long as a whole summer. The sun is slowly descending from the tree branches, which they wish it could be buried by the saint."

[Tune of Playing Pipa Song] "After carefully making ups, she looks extremely beautiful. She is going for the date with beloved one latter. Just for a moment of sweetness, she is so absent-minded now.

Not only my lady suffers the love sickness, but also that Gentleman

二三日来水米不粘牙。因姐姐闭月羞花,真假,这其间性儿难按纳,一地里胡拿。

姐姐这湖山下立地,我开了寺里角门儿。怕有人听俺说话,我且看一看。(做意了)偌早晚,傻角却不来"赫赫赤赤"来?(末云)这其间正好去也,赫赫赤赤。(红云)那鸟来了。

【沉醉东风】我则道槐影风摇暮鸦,元来是玉人帽侧乌纱。一个潜身在曲槛边,一个背立在湖山下。那里叙寒温?并不曾打话。

(红云)赫赫赤赤,那鸟来了。(末云)小姐,你来也。(搂住红科)(红云)禽兽!(末云)是我。(红云)你看得好仔细著!若是夫人怎了?(末云)小生害得眼花,

Zhang—

In two or three days, he never eats or drinks. Just because my sister is bewitchingly beautiful. True or not, he is too eager to meet with my sister. He is playing a fool in front of us.

Sister, stay below the poolside rock. I open the side door of the monastery. I am afraid that someone will hear us talking, I will go and have a look."

[Red Maid opens the side door] "It is so late. Why hasn't that fool come yet?"

[Zhang Gong says] "It's the right time to come. Hirsch…"

[Red Maid says] "That bird is coming."

[Tune of Intoxicated to the East Wind Song] "I have thought it was the sound of wind blowing the raven perched branches, and shadows of locust trees waving in the breeze, but it is the handsome man's black gauze cap. One hides himself behind the winding banister, and one stands with her back below the poolside rock. Why don't they say hello to each other? They don't interchange with each other."

[Red Maid says] "Hirsch. That bird is coming."

[Zhang Gong says] "My lady, you have come." [He hugs the Red Maid]
[Red Maid says] "Amorist."

[Zhang Gong says] "It's me."

搂得慌了些儿，不知是谁。望乞恕罪。

（红唱）

便做道搂得慌呵，你也索觑咱，多管是饿得你个穷神眼花。

（末云）小姐在那里？（红云）在湖山下。我问你咱：真个著你来哩？（末云）小生猜诗谜社家，风流隋何，浪子陆贾，准定扢扎帮便倒地。（红云）你休从门里去，则道我使你来。你跳过这墙去，今夜这一弄儿助你两个成亲。我说与你，依著我者。

【乔牌儿】你看那淡云笼月华，似红纸护银蜡，柳丝花朵垂帘下，绿莎茵铺著绣榻。

【甜水令】良夜迢迢，闲庭寂静，花枝低亚。他

[Red Maid says] "Please look carefully! What if it was the old lady herself?"

[Zhang Gong says] "I am bewildered. Sorry that I was too hurry to hug, before knowing whom I was hugging. I beg for apologize."

[Red Maid sings] "He said it was because he was bewildered. You should look carefully at who is standing in front of you. You must be too hungry to be dazed."

[Zhang Gong asks] "Where is the lady?"

[Red Maid says] "Standing below the poolside rock. I ask you again whether my lady really asked you to come or not."

[Zhang Gong says] "I am an expert of furor poetics, as easy as Sui He, and as libertine as Lu Jia. It can not be wrong."

[Red Maid say] "Please don't come inside of the door, in case my lady would think I allow you to come. You should climb over the wall, and she will marry you at this night. I will nag you, and you should follow me."

[Tune of Pseudo-Melody Song] "The slight clouds cover the bright moon, and the red paper covers the light from silver candles. The willow branches hang down on the flowers, and the green grass is the embroidered silk mattress."

[Tune of Sweet Water Song] "The beautiful night is long, and the empty yard is quiet. The flower branches are hanging low. She is such a beautiful and gentle girl. Please hide your eagerness and talk

是个女孩儿家,你索将性儿温存,话儿摩弄,意儿谦洽。休猜做败柳残花。

【折桂令】他是个娇滴滴美玉无瑕,粉脸生春,云鬓堆鸦。恁的般受怕担惊,又不图甚浪酒闲茶。则你那夹被儿时当奋发,指头儿告了消乏。打叠起嗟呀,毕罢了牵挂,收拾了忧愁,准备著撑达。

　　(末作跳墙搂旦科)(旦云)是谁?(末云)是小生。(旦怒云)张生,你是何等之人!我在这里烧香,你无故至此。若夫人闻知,有何理说?(末云)呀,变了卦也!

(红唱)

【锦上花】为甚媒人,心无惊怕?赤紧的夫妻每、意不争差。我这里蹑足潜踪,悄地听咱:一个羞惭,一个怒发。

to her gently, so that you are able to understand each other well. Don't make her a prostitute no longer young."

[Tune of Picking Laurel Song] "She is as beautiful as a jade without a spot, whose face is like spring, and whose hair is rolled like raven. You are in worries and fears all day, but I am helping you, not wishing to drink your wine and tea. When you are excited in the quilt, your fingers may stick to her sweat. Take up your courage, and stop concerning. Say goodbye to your sorrows and wait for the happiness."

[Zhang Gong jumps off the wall, and hugs Ying Ying.][Ying Ying asks] "Who is it?"

[Zhang Gong says] "It's me."

[Ying Ying bursts out anger and says] "Gentleman Zhang, what kind of person you are? I am burning incense here, but you enter the garden without a reason. What if the old lady hears it?"

[Zhang Gong says] "Ah, she changes her mind."

[Red Maid sings]

[Tune of flower on the Brocade Song] "As a matchmaker, why am I not afraid? It's just like husband and wife, who always quarrel with each other. I am here walking slowly and listening to what they are talking. One is ashamed of himself, and another one is so angry."

【幺篇】张生无一言,呀,莺莺变了卦。一个悄悄冥冥,一个絮絮答答。却早禁住隋何,进住陆贾,叉手躬身,装聋作哑。

张生背地里嘴那里去了?向前搂住丢番,告到官司,怕羞了你?

【清江引】没人处则会闲嗑牙,就里空奸诈。怎想湖山边,不记"西厢下"。香美娘处分破花木瓜。

(旦云)红娘,有贼!(红云)是谁?(末云)是小生。(红云)张生,你来这里有甚么勾当?(旦云)扯到夫人那里去。(红云)到夫人那里,恐坏了他行止。我与姐姐处分他一场。张生,你过来,跪著!(生

[Tune of Petty Song] "Gentleman Zhang did not utter a word. Ha, Ying Ying has changed her mind. One is sneaking, and the other is scolding. The former Sui He and Lu Jia stays there silently, pretending to be dumb and deaf.

What is Gentleman Zhang's reason? Just then, he hugged you. Is he afraid that he will be sued to jail, or is he afraid that he will bring shame to you?"

[Tune of Clear River Song] "You wag your tongue when no one is there. You have fallen into a trap now. You only think of rocks by the poolside, but forget of the western chamber. Ying Ying is blaming the handsome looking gentleman."

[Ying Ying says] "Red Maid, there is a thief."

[Red Maid asks] "Who is it?"

[Zhang Gong says] "It's me."

[Red Maid says] "What are you doing here?"

[Ying Ying says] "Let's go to my mother."

[Red Maid says] "If we go to the old lady, I am afraid it will break his future. Let me punish him for sister. Gentleman Zhang, come here and kneel down."

[Zhang Gong kneels down]

[Red Maid says] "You have well read classics, so you must know the etiquette of Zhou Gong. Why do you come here at this time of the night?"

跪科)(红云)你既读孔圣之书,必达周公之礼。夤夜来此何干?

【雁儿落】不是俺一家儿乔作衙,说几句衷肠话:我则道你文学海样深,谁知你色胆有天来大。

（红云）你知罪么?（末云）小生不知罪。

（红唱）

【得胜令】谁著你夤夜入人家?非奸做贼拿。你本是个折桂客,做了偷花汉不想去跳龙门,学骗马。

姐姐,且看红娘面,饶过这生者。(旦云)若不看红娘面,扯你到夫人那里去,看你有何面目见

[Tune of Falling of Swan Song] "It's not our family who wants to punish you, but please allow me to say something sincere. I know your learning is as profound as ocean, however, your lust is as boundless as high sky."

[Red Maid asks] "Do you know what you are guilty for?"

[Zhang Gong says] "I don't know."

[Red Maid sings]

[Tune of Triumphant Song] "Who asks you to come to the garden so late? You must be either a thief or rapist. You should be a well learned scholar. However, you just want to be a philanderer who don't long for jumping out of the dragon gate, but to deceive horse.

Sister, please forgive this gentleman, for Red Maid's sake."

[Ying Ying says] "If not Red Maid intercedes for you, I will drag you to my mother, and see how dare you have face to meet the folks of your hometown? Get up!"

[Red Maid sings] "Thank you for sister's kindness, and forgiving this man for my sake. If this case is brought into the court, they must say 'You are just a scholar, so you should read classic under the cold window. Who asks you to sneak into other's garden? You are either a thief or rapist.' My gentleman, a good whipping on your delicate skin will be waiting for you!"

[Ying Ying says] "Gentleman Zhang, though we owe you gratitude of saving our lives, we will be sure to repay your kindness. However, as long as we are brother and sister, how can you have other

江东父老！起来。(红唱)谢小姐贤达，看我面遂情罢。若到官司详察，"你既是秀才，只合苦志于寒窗之下，谁教你贪夜辄入人家花园？做得个非奸即盗。"先生呵，整备著精皮肤吃顿打。

（旦云）先生虽有活人之恩，恩则当报。既为兄妹，何生此心？万一夫人知之，先生何以自安？今后再勿如此。若更为之，与足下决无干休！(下)(末朝鬼门道云)你著我来，却怎么有偌多说话？(红扳过末云)羞也，羞也！却不"风流隋何，浪子陆贾"？(末云)得罪波"社家"，今日便早则死心塌地。(红唱)

【离亭宴带歇拍煞】再休题春宵一刻千金价，准备著寒窗更守十年寡。猜诗谜的社家，你拍了"迎风户半开"，山障了"隔墙花影动"，绿惨了"待月西厢下"。你将何郎粉面搽，他自把张敞眉儿画。强风情措大。晴干了尤云殢雨心，悔过了窃玉偷香胆，删抹了倚翠偎红话。

feelings towards me? What if my mother knows? Will you have an easy life in the future? Please do not do this again. If you do this again, I will not forgive you for the second time."[Exit]

[Zhang Gong shouts at Ying Ying's back] "You asked me to come, but why do you say such things to me?"

[Red Maid turns Zhang Gong over and says] "What a shame! What a shame! Why shouldn't you call yourself as easy as Sui He, and as libertine as Lu Jia any more?"

[Zhang Gong says] "Having offended an expert, I am dead set on this."

[Red Maid sings]

[Tune of Farewell Feast and Epilogue Song] "Never mention one minute in a spring night is worthy of a thousand taels of gold, but you should preserve ten years in your studies in spite of hardships. The expert of furor poetry says that it is mountains not the barred door stand in your way. You do not have the chance of seeing the shadows of flowers on the next wall. It brings shame when you say she wants you to 'Wait under the moonlight in the western chamber.' You rub your face with powder, and she has painted her eyebrows with grace. You want a love affair with her, but now you should regret for your audacity, and and forget the honey sweet words to her."

[Zhang Gong says] "I will write another letter, and have to bother sister to send it to her again. Could I just show my heart felt feeling?"

（末云）小生再写一简，烦小娘子将去，以尽衷情如何？（红唱）淫词儿早则休，简帖儿从今罢。犹古自参不透风流调法。从今后悔罪也卓文君，你与我学去波汉司马。（下）

（末云）你这小姐送了人也！此一念小生再不敢举。奈有病体日笃，将如之奈何？夜来得简方喜，今日强扶至此，又值这一场怨气，眼见休也。则索回书房中纳闷去。桂子闲中落，槐花病里看。（下）

第四折

（夫人上云）早间长老使人来，说张生病重。我着长老使人请个太医去看了，一壁道与红娘，看哥哥行问汤药去者。问太医下甚么药，证候如何，便来回话。（下）（红上云）老夫人才说张生病沉重，昨夜吃我那一场气，越重了。莺莺呵，你送了他人。（下）（旦上云）我写一简，则说道药方，着

[Red Maid says] "If it were love words, please stop writing. You should not write letter since now. Since the ancient time, no one can thoroughly understand methods of flirtation from men. You have wronged Zhuo Wenjun, and should have learned more from Si Ma Xiangru in the Han dynasty." [Exeunt]

[Zhang Gong says] "Your lady has already made engagement with others. Since then, I dare not act ruthlessly again. However, my health is declining day by day. What should I do now? I just felt a little happier when I read the letter from Ying Ying in the morning, so I dragged my sick body to come here. But unexpectedly, I suffered from this rebuff. I think my life is coming to an end. It is better to return to the study room, and solve the puzzle myself. I only have the chance to look at the falling flower in the spring at leisure time." [Exit]

Scene Four

[The Old Lady enters and says] "In the morning, abbot asked somebody to come and tell me that Gentleman Zhang is seriously ill. I asked abbot to try to find a doctor for him and tell me the prescription. [Exit]

[Red Maid enters and says] "The old lady just said that Gentleman

红娘将去与他，证候便可。(旦唤红科)(红云)姐姐，唤红娘怎么？(旦云)张生病重，我有一个好药方儿，与我将去咱。(红云)又来也。娘呵，休送了他人！(旦云)好姐姐，救人一命，将去咱。(红云)不是你，一世也救他不得！如今老夫人使我去哩，我就与你将去走一遭。(下)(旦云)红娘去了，我绣房里等他回话。(下)(末上云)自从昨夜花园中吃了这一场气，投著旧证候，眼见得休了也。老夫人说，著长老唤太医来看我，我这颓证候，非是太医所治的。则除是那小姐美甘甘、香喷喷、

Zhang is serious ill. After the rebuff that he suffered last night, he is more ill than ever. He said desperately, 'Ying Ying, you are given to other man'." [Exit]

[Ying Ying enters and says] "Gentleman Zhang is seriously ill. I will write him a letter with the prescription. I will ask Red Maid to send it to him, and I am sure he will feel better."

[Ying Ying calls Red Maid] [Red Maid says] "Sister is calling me. What can I do for you?"

[Ying Ying says] "Gentleman Zhang is seriously ill. I have written a good prescription, and please send it to him."

[Red Maid says] "Again, my God, please not send him letter any more."

[Ying Ying says] "Good sister, please save that man's life."

[Red Maid says] "Except you, no one can save his life. Okay. Today, the old lady asked me to go and visit him, so I will send your message to him at the same time." [Exit]

[Ying Ying says] "Red Maid has gone. I am waiting for her in the chamber." [Exit]

[Zhang Gong enters and says] "Since last night, I suffered the rebuff, my symptom is more serious. I think I am waning and dying. The Old Lady said she would ask a doctor to make prescription to me, however, my illness can not be healed by doctors, except I am able to swallow the lady's tasty, aromatic, affectedly sweet saliva."

凉渗渗、娇滴滴一点唾津儿咽下去，这席病便可。（洁引太医上，"双斗医"科范了）（下）（洁云）下了药了，我回夫人话去，少刻再来相望。（下）（红上云）俺小姐送得人如此，又著我去动问，送药方儿去，越著他病沉了也。我索走一遭。异乡易得离愁病，妙药难医断肠人！

【越调】【斗鹌鹑】则为你彩笔题诗，回文织锦送得人卧枕著床，忘餐废寝折倒得鬓似愁潘，腰如病沈。恨已深，病已沉，昨夜个热脸儿对面抢白，今日个冷句儿将人厮侵。

昨夜这般抢白他呵！

【紫花儿序】把似你休倚著桄门儿待月，依著韵脚儿联诗，侧著耳朵儿听琴。

见了他撇假佯多话："张生，我与你兄妹之礼，甚么勾当！"怒时节把一个书生来迭噷。

欢时节："红娘，好姐姐，去望他一遭！"将一个侍妾来逼临。难禁，好著我似线脚儿般殷勤不离了针。从今后教他一任。

这的是俺老夫人的不是——将人的义海恩

[Fa Ben enters with the doctor. The doctor feels Zhang Gong's impulse. Then he exits]

[Fa Ben says] "The doctor has prescribed the medicine. I will respond to the old lady, and call on you later."[Exit]

[Red Maid enters] "My sister has made Gentleman seriously ill, and asked me to go to Gentleman Zhang again now. She said to send him the prescription. I think it will make him sicker. However, I had better to come, and call a visit to him. It is easy for a stranger to suffer from sadness in a strange place. The good medicine will never heal the heartbreaking people."

[Tune of Fighting Quail Song] "You are the first to write the verses for the one who is lying on the bed. For your sake, he forgets eating the meal and sleeping. The sorrows even make him grow white hair on the temples and lose his weight. The lovesickness is strong and the illness is serious. Last night, you irritated him with hot words, and today you hurt him again with cold words.

Last night, how she rebuffed him off!"

[Tune of Violet Flower Song] "You leaned on the door alone, waiting for the moon climbing up in the dark night. You wrote the verses following his rhythm and listened to the ancient zither music attentively.

When you met him, you pretend to be angry. 'Gentleman Zhang, we are just brother and sister. What are you saying!'

When you are angry, you blame the scholar. When you are happy,

山，都做了远水遥岑。

（红见末问云）哥哥病体若何？（末云）害杀小生也！我若是死呵，小娘子，阎王殿前少不得你做个干连人。（红叹云）普天下害相思的，不似你这个傻角。

【天净沙】心不存学海文林，梦不离柳影花阴，则去那窃玉偷香上用心。又不曾得甚，自从海棠开想到如今。

因甚的便病得这般了？（末云）都因你行——怕说的谎——因小侍长上来！当夜书房一气一个死。小生救了人，反被害了。自古人云："痴心女子负心汉"，今日反其事了。

you said, 'Red Maid, my good sister, please take a look at him.' She asked a maid to call on Gentleman Zhang. I am as busy as a threading a needle who passes the messages. From now on, I will allow the things to go as it is.

This is all due to my old lady's fault. She makes that gentleman's tremendous favor turn into the distant water and far away mountain."

[Red Maid enters and asks Zhang Gong] "Brother, how do you feel today?"

[Zhang Gong says] "It nearly kills me. If I died, my sister, you can not escape from the responsibility."

[Red Maid sighs] "Of all those who suffer love sickness in this world, no one is like you, this idiot."

[Tune of Clear Sky Over the Sand] "You think of nothing but your dream in the shadows of willows and flowers. You just want to steal flowers. But so far you have not succeeded."

"Why are you seriously ill today?"

[Zhang Gong says] "It's all because of you—telling lies—and your lady! That night, in the study room, I am too angry to die. I have saved people, but on the other hand, I am nearly hurt by others. There is an old saying, 'Infatuated girl and unfaithful man'. Today, it is totally the other way around."

[Tune of Song of flirtation] "Thinking carefully myself, I think

（红唱）

【调笑令】我这里自审，这病为邪淫，尸骨岩岩鬼病侵。更做道秀才每从来恁。似这般干相思的好撒唔。功名上早则不遂心，婚姻上更返吟复吟。

（红云）老夫人著我来，看哥哥要甚么汤药。小姐再三伸敬，有一药方，送来与先生。（末做慌科）在那里？（红云）用著几般儿生药，各有制度，我说与你：

【小桃红】"桂花"摇影夜深沉，酸醋"当归"浸。（末云）桂花性温，当归活血，怎生制度？（红唱）面靠著湖山背阴里窨。这方儿最难寻，一服两服令人恁。

this illness is caused by lechery. The skeleton of corpse is as high as a mountain, and love sickness invades my whole body. Not to mention a scholar is always like this. Such a love sickess is not easy to swallow, is it? I have long lost the will for the scholarly honor of official rank, but cry heartbrokenly for the loss of my love."

[Red Maid says] "The old lady asks me to come and inquire brother what kind of medicine that you want. My young lady has showed her respect to you again, and send you a prescription."

[Zhang Gong stands up immediately and asks] "Where is it?"

[Red Maid says] "Taking use of these several medicines, you have to obey the rule. I am telling you:

[Tune of Red Peach Flowers] "Under the shadows of osmanthus flowers waving at deep night, you should put Chinese angelica in the soar vinegar."

[Zhang Gong says] "Osmanthus flowers are warm in nature, but Chinese angelica invigorates blood circulation. Why should I take these two medicine?"

[Red Maid sings] "Standing at the rock by poolside, young lady feel the smell of Osmanthus flowers tinting on the clothes. This prescription is hard to find. After taking it one or two times, you will soon recover."

[Zhang Gong asks] "What should I avoid?"

（末云）忌甚么物？

（红唱）

忌的是"知母"未寝，怕的是"红娘"撒沁。吃了呵，稳情取"使君子"一星儿"参"。

这药方儿，小姐亲笔写的。（末看药方大笑科）（末云）早知姐姐书来，只合远接，小娘子……（红云）又怎么？却早两遭儿也。（末云）不知这首诗意，小姐待和小生"里也波"哩。（红云）不少了一些儿？

【鬼三台】足下其实咛，休妆唔。笑你个风魔的翰林，无处问佳音，向简帖儿上计禀。得了个纸条儿恁般绵里针，若见玉天仙怎生软厮禁？俺那小姐忘恩，赤紧的偻人负心。

书上如何说？你读与我听咱。（末念云）"休将闲事苦萦怀，取次摧残天赋才。不意当时完妾命，岂防今日作君灾？仰图厚德难从礼，谨奉新诗可当媒。寄与高唐休咏赋，今宵端的雨云来。"此韵非前日之比，小姐必来。（红云）他来呵，怎生？

[Red Maid sings] "You should avoid "the knowing old lady" not sleeping, and fear Red Maid for acting shamelessly. Take this medicine, you can read by yourself.

This prescription is written by the young lady."

[Zhang Gong reads the prescription and laughs] [Zhang Gong says] "If I had known sister was sending lady's letter, I should have greeted you earlier. Sister…"

[Red Maid asks] "What's the matter? Why do you change your face?"

[Zhang Gong says] "I don't know the meaning of the letter. Lady said she was waiting to have sex with me tonight."

[Red Maid asks] "Is there something wrong?"

[Tune of Three Terrace] "You are really a fool, who tries to look wise. I laugh at you, such a enchanted member of imperial academy. There is no way to ask for good news, but to find answers on the paper. Just getting a letter, you look so excited. If you met another celestial beauty, you are sure to forget yourself. No wonder my lady will forget your kindness.

What does it write in the letter? Please read it for me."

[Zhang Gong starts to read] "Never bother about the trivial things in the past, it is rather a ravage to the talented man. If you listened to me last time, how can it become a disaster to you? There is no way to repay your kindness. This new poem can be the match maker. 'Sending the letter to Gao Tang who dreams of goddess, a happy marriage will tie between us tonight.' This poem is different from previous one. Tonight, your lady must have come."

【秃厮儿】身卧著一条布衾，头枕著三尺瑶琴，他来时怎生和你一处寝？冻得来战兢兢，说甚知音？

【圣药王】果若你有心，他有心，昨日秋千院宇夜深沉花有阴，月有阴，"春宵一刻抵千金"，何须"诗对会家吟"？

（末云）小生有花银十两，有铺盖赁与小生一付。
（红唱）

【东原乐】俺那鸳鸯枕，翡翠衾，便遂杀了人心，如何肯赁？至如你不脱解和衣儿更怕甚？不强如手执定指尖儿恁？倘或成亲，到大来福荫。

（末云）小生为小姐如此容色，莫不小姐为小生也减动丰韵么？
（红唱）

【绵搭絮】他眉弯远山不翠，眼横秋水无光，体

[Red Maid says] "If she comes, what will happen?"

[Tune of Bold Head Song] "You are lying on cloth mattress and resting your head on the cheap pillow. How can she lie with you when she comes? It will be too cold at night, so how can you have a love talk with each other?"

[The saint king of drug medicine] "If you really take it seriously, and she takes it seriously, she will come for sure. Last night, in the deep courtyard, when the night is deep, and the moonlight is wane, we should have already joined a lovely wedding night. Why were we reciting poems to each other on the other hand?"

[Zhang Gong says] " I have ten tasels of silver. Could you please buy me some sheets and coverlets?"

[Tune of Joy of Eastern Plain Song] " I have a pillow with embroidered mandarin ducks in pairs and a jade green coverlet, but how can I borrow you to satisfy your lewd desire? If you sleep with your clothes on the body, what else do you fear? Isn't better to doff of her clothes with your fingertips? If you are sincere in love, heaven will bless you life long happiness."

[Zhang Gong says] "I have suffered so much love sickness for lady's sake. How about my lady?

[Red Maid sings]

[Tune of Cotton Wool Song] "Her eyebrows is like far away mountains which no longer black, and her eyesight is like autumn water, which no

若凝酥,腰如弱柳,俊的是庞儿俏的是心,体态温柔性格儿沉。虽不会法灸神针,更胜似救苦难观世音。

(末云)今夜成了事,小生不敢有忘。
(红唱)

【幺篇】你口儿里谩沉吟,梦儿里苦追寻。往事已沉,只言目今,今夜相逢管教恁。不图你甚白璧黄金,则要你满头花,拖地锦。

(末云)怕夫人拘系,不能勾出来。(红云)则怕小姐不肯。果有意呵。

【煞尾】虽然是老夫人晓夜将门禁,好共歹须教你称心。

(末云)休似昨夜不肯。(红云)你挣揣咱。来时节肯不肯尽由他,见时节亲不亲在于恁。(并下)

longer shines. Her body is as white as snow in the winter, and her waist is as slender as the weak willow in the breeze. She looks lovely, but her character is gentle, tender, and sure. Though she doesn't know how to do acupuncture and moxibustion, she is better than Guanyin to save people from sufferings."

[Zhang Gong says] "If I am married tonight, I will remember your kindness forever."

[Red Maid sings]

[Tune of Petty Song] "You keep murmuring in your mouth, and looking for your lover in the dream. The past is in the past. What matters is today. Tonight, you will meet. I am helping you, not for your room covered with gold, nor flowers on your head, nor carpet of brocade."

[Zhang Gong says] "I am afraid that old lady is too strict to allow the lady to slip."

[Red Maid says] "You should not be concerned for that, but you should fear whether my lady is unwilling to come or not. But I guess that she really has such intentions."

[Tune of Epilogue Song] "Though my lady closed the door at night, she was eager to satisfy you for one night."

[Zhang Gong says] "I am afraid it would be like yesterday."

[Red Maid says] "For this, you can decide by yourself. Whether she comes or not tonight is up to her, but whether you will kiss her or not is up to you."

【络丝娘煞尾】因今宵传言送语,看明日携云握雨。

  题目 老夫人命医士 崔莺莺寄情诗
  正名 小红娘问汤药 张君瑞害相思

[Tune of Epilogue of Weaving Girl Song] "Today, Red Maid sends the message and tomorrow it will come a good marriage."

The old lady Cui asks for the health of Zhang Gong. Cui Yingying sends a love letter.

The Red Maid tries to cure Zhang Gong's loversickness Zhang Gong suffers more.

五剧第四本

草桥店梦莺莺杂剧

Act Four

楔　子

（旦上云）昨夜红娘传简去与张生，约今夕和他相见，等红娘来做个商量。（红上云）姐姐著我传简儿与张生，约他今宵赴约。俺那小姐，我怕又有说谎。送了他性命，不是耍处。我见小姐，看他说甚么。（旦云）红娘，收拾卧房，我睡去。（红云）不争你要睡呵，那里发付那生？（旦云）甚么那生？（红云）姐姐，你又来也，送了人性命，不是耍处！你若又番悔，我出首与夫人：你著我将简帖儿约下他来。（旦云）这小贱人倒会放刁。羞人答答的，怎生去！（红云）有甚的羞？到那里则合著眼者！（红催莺云）去来，去来！老夫人睡了也。（旦走科）（红云）俺姐姐语言虽是强，脚步儿早先行也。

Prologue

[Ying Ying enters and says] "I asked Red Maid to send a letter to Gentleman Zhang, and proposed a date with him tonight. I will wait for the Red Maid to be back, and discuss this with her."

[Red Maid enters and says] "My sister asked me to send a letter to Gentleman Zhang, and proposed to have a date tonight. I am afraid my sister is lying again. If that is the case, it would damage him. That is no funny at all. I will meet my sister, and see what she is going to say."

[Ying Ying says] "Red Maid, please clean the chamber. I am going to sleep."

[Red Maid says] "I will not stop you from sleeping, but how are you going to deal with that gentleman?"

[Ying Ying says] "What gentleman?"

[Red Maid says] "Sister, here you are again. If you torment over that man, it is no funny at all. If you regret, I will confess to the old lady that you sent me to send a message to him and date him."

[Ying Ying says] "Your little cat! How crafty you are. I feel so shy myself! How can I go like this?"

【仙吕】【端正好】因姐姐玉精神，花模样，无倒断晓夜思量。著一片志诚心，盖抹了漫天谎。出画阁，向书房，离楚岫，赴高唐，学窃玉，试偷香，巫娥女，楚襄王。楚襄王敢先在阳台上。（下）

[Red Maid says] "There is no need to feel shy. I just close my eyes when you arrive there."

[Red Maid urges Ying Ying again] "Please go. Please go! The old lady is sleeping now."

[Ying Ying walks away.] [Red Maid says] "Though my sister is stubborn in the mouth, she is walking very fast."

[Tune of Calm Dignity Song] "Because of the jade spirit and flower-like looking of my lady, Gentleman Zhang is thinking of her day and night. With a true heart for going date, Ying Ying's behavior is much better than the lies of the old lady. Walking out of the chamber towards the study room, and leaving the Chu Mountain and meeting the Gao Tang in the dream, my lady and Gentleman Zhang secretly made love with each other. One is the goddess of Wu Er, and the other is the husband Chu Xiang King. Chu Xiang King is still standing on the porch." [Exeunt]

第一折

（末上云）昨夜红娘所遗之简，约小生今夜成就。这早晚初更尽也，不见来呵，小姐休说谎咱！人间良夜静复静，天上美人来不来？

【仙吕】【点绛唇】伫立闲阶，夜深香霭、横金界。潇洒书斋，闷杀读书客。

【混江龙】彩云何在？月明如水浸楼台。僧居禅室，鸦噪庭槐。风弄竹声、则道似金佩响，月移花影、疑是玉人来。意悬悬业眼，急攘攘情怀，身心一片，无处安排，则索呆答孩倚定门儿待。越越的青鸾信杳，黄犬音乖。

小生一日十二时，无一刻放下小姐。你那里知道呵！

Scene One

[Zhang Gong enters and says] "The letter that Red Maid left me last night will make my dream come true tonight. It is the first of the five night watch periods now, but the lady hasn't come. My lady, don't lie to me again. The beautiful night is deep and quiet. The beauty in the heaven, will you come or not?"

[Tune of Rouged Lips of a Fairy Song] "Standing on the stairs leisurely, I see the night going deeper slowly, and the fragrance of flowers is thicker in the monastery. Waiting in the free and lonely study room, I will be killed by suffocation."

[Tune of Dragon in the Troubled Water Song] "Where are colorful clouds? The moonlight is as bright as water shining on the tower. The monks return to the meditation room, and ravens are cracking on the pagoda tree in the yard. The wind blows the sparse bamboo trees, as if the tinkling of the gold and jade which is worn by lady as ornaments on the waist. The moon moves, and shadows of flowers overlap with each other. I am suspected that the beautiful lady has arrived. I am looking at the door anxiously in my mind, feeling too worried to sit or stand. My whole body and mind are blank, just leaning on the door and waiting for her coming as if a child. Quietly, there is no message from my beloved one. The yellow dog is silent at night.

For me, I spend every minute of the day thinking of my lady. But my lady how could you know about it?"

【油葫芦】情思昏昏眼倦开,单枕侧,梦魂飞入楚阳台。早知道无明无夜因他害,想当初不如不遇倾城色。人有过,必自责,勿惮改。我却待"贤贤易色"将心戒,怎禁他兜的上心来。

【天下乐】我则索倚定门儿手托腮,好著我难猜:来也那不来?夫人行料应难离侧。望得人眼欲穿,想得人心越窄,多管是冤家不自在。

偌早晚不来,莫不又是谎么?

【那吒令】他若是肯来,早身离贵宅,他若是到来,便春生敝斋,他若是不来,似石沉大海。数著他脚步儿行,倚定窗棂儿待。寄语多才:

【鹊踏枝】恁的般恶抢白,并不曾记心怀拨得个

[Tune of Field Cricket Song] "With so much love sickness in my mind, I half open my eyes. Lying on the single pillow, my dream has already flied to the balcony. If I have known that I suffer love sickness day and night for her sake before, I would rather never meet peerless beauty on that day. If someone makes mistakes, he must examine himself, not afraid to correct them. I should have chosen a wife based on her virtue rather than her look, however, why does lady Ying Ying's face appear in my mind again?"

[Tune of Universal Joy Song] "I had better lean on the door and rest my cheek on my hands. It is difficult to guess whether she comes or not? Maybe she is difficult to leave her mother's side. I keep gazing anxiously till my eyes are strained. The more I think, the more narrow-minded I become. It is for her sake that I am seriously ill.

If she doesn't come tonight, is she lying to me again?"

[Tune of Na Zha Song] "If she wants to come, she should have left her room early. If she has come, we must spend a good night in my shabby house. If she doesn't come, it will be like a stone sinking into the deep sea without causing ripples. I am counting her footsteps, and waiting for her anxiously under the window. I want to speak to her like this—"

[Tune of Magpie on the Branch Song] "Last time, you satirized me to my face, but I do not bear it in my mind, waiting for you to change your mind, to come here this night and leave next morning. For half a year, we just flash amorous glances with the

意转心回,夜去明来。空调眼色经今半载,这其间委实难捱。

小姐这一遭若不来呵——

【寄生草】安排著害,准备著抬。想著这异乡身强把茶汤捱,则为这可憎才熬得心肠耐,办一片志诚心留得形骸在。试著那司天台打算半年愁,端的是太平车约有十馀载。

(红上云)姐姐,我过去,你在这里。(红敲科)(末问云)是谁?(红云)是你前世的娘。(末云)小姐来么?(红云)你接了衾枕者,小姐入来也。张生,你怎么谢我?(末拜云)小生一言难尽。寸心相报,惟天可表!(红云)你放轻者,休就了他。(红推旦入云)

corner of our eyes. It is so difficult to spend time without you by my side.

My lady, if you don't come this time—"

[Tune of Parasitic Grass Song] "I am ready to die. Who knows I have to struggle for drinking tea and soup in the strange town to keep alive. It is because of you that life become unbearable. If you also love me, my life will be saved. If I am doomed to have half year of grief, this sorrows will be loaded in my mind for more than ten years."

[Red Maid enters and says] "Sister, I will go to the gentleman first, and you should wait for me here."

[Red Maid knocks the door] [Zhang Gong asks] "Who is it?"

[Red Maid says] "It is your mother in your prelife."

[Zhang Gong asks] "Has the lady come?"

[Red Maid says] "Take the pillow. The lady has come. Gentleman Zhang, how are you going to thank me for?"

[Zhang Gong bows and says] "I can not express my gratitude to you in words. Heaven can be my witness. I am willing to pay back your kindness with all my heart."

[Red Maid says] "Put the pillow lightly. Don't spoil it."

[Red Maid pushes Ying Ying into the room] "Sister, you can go inside. I am waiting for you outside."

姐姐,你入去,我在门儿外等你。(末见旦跪云)张生有何德能,敢劳神仙下降,知他是睡里梦里?

【村里迓鼓】猛见他可憎模样,小生那里得病来?

早医可九分不快。先前见责,谁承望今宵欢爱!著小姐这般用心,不才张珙,合当跪拜。小生无宋玉般容,潘安般貌,子建般才。姐姐,你则是可怜见为人在客。

【元和令】绣鞋儿刚半拆,柳腰儿勾一搦。羞答答不肯把头抬,只将鸳枕捱。云鬟仿佛坠金钗,偏宜鬏髻儿歪。

【上马娇】我将这纽扣儿松,把搂带儿解,兰麝散幽斋。不良会把人禁害,哈,怎不肯回过脸儿来?

【胜葫芦】我这里软玉温香抱满怀。呀,阮肇到天台。看至人间花弄色,将柳腰款摆,花心轻拆,露滴牡丹开。

【幺篇】但蘸著些儿麻上来,鱼水得和谐,嫩

[Zhang Gong kneels down to Ying Ying and says] "What have I done to deserve this? Am I in the dream or not?"

[Tune of Village Drums Song] "She suddenly saw his haggard face. Gentleman Zhang, where does your illness come from?"

"It's only you who are able to heal me. Since you have arrived, my illness has been almost healed. Before you rebuffed me, so I never expected that I had the fortune to have such a happiness tonight! For your consideration, the unlearned Zhang Gong kneels down to you with my heart and soul. I have no Song Yu's look, Pan An's figure, or Zi Jian's talent. Sister, you must have pity on me."

[Tune of Peace Song] "The embroidered shoes are half taken off, and the willow-like waist are half leaning in Genlteman Zhang's arms. She feels so shy that she is unable to look up her head, but lie on the loverbirds pillow. The golden pin falls from the head, and her hair bun is slanting down."

[Tune of Charming on the Horse Song] "I loose the button of your clothes, and untie the belt on your waist. The fragrance from your body meanders in the room. If people love over the rules, it will destroy their lives. Ha, why don't you turn your face to me?"

[Tune of Better than Gourd Song] "I am holding the nephrite in my arms. Ah, I am so lucky. Spring comes on earth and beautiful flowers spurts. I am hugging her willow slim waist. I tear carefully the heart of flowers, and make the dew drip on her peony flower."

[Tune of Petty Song] "Her peony sips with open lips. We are as harmony as fish and water. The beautiful butterflies sips the pistil

蕊娇香蝶恣采。半推半就,又惊又爱,檀口韫香腮。

(末跪云)谢小姐不弃,张珙今夕得就枕席,异日犬马之报。(旦云)妾千金之躯,一旦弃之。此身皆托于足下,勿以他日见弃,使妾有白头之叹。(末云)小生焉敢如此!(末看手帕科)

【后庭花】春罗元莹白,早见红香点嫩色。

(旦云)羞人答答的,看甚么。(末唱)灯下偷睛觑,胸前著肉揣。畅奇哉!浑身通泰,不知春从何处来。无能的张秀才,孤身西洛客,自从逢稔色,思量的不下怀。忧愁因间隔,相思无摆划。谢芳卿不见责。

of the fragment flowers. The lady yields with a show of reluctance. Surprised and exhilarated, two lips kiss each other."

[Zhang Gong kneels down and says] "Thanks you for no dislike and avoid. Tonight Zhang Gong had a chance to sleep with you on the same pillow and next day, I would be willing to be your horses and dogs."

[Ying Ying says] "I am a respected girl, but today I have devoted to you by myself. I hope you will not forsake me in the future, and make me a lifetime regret."

[Zhang Gong says] "How dare I do this?"

[Zhang Gong gazes at the handkerchief]

[Tune of Flowers in the Backyard Song] "Chunluo silk is very white, with slight fragment red spots on it."

[Ying Ying says] "How bashful you are staring at me! What are you looking at?"

[Zhang Gong sings] "Under the lamp, I secretly peer at the beautiful lady. Her bosoms are very plump. How strange it is! I feel refreshed all over my body, not knowing where does this health come from? Incapable scholar Zhang, coming from West Luo City alone, thinks of the lady with peerless beauty day and night since my first meeting with her. I am full of sorrows, because I cannot meet you, and unable to deal with love sickness in my mind. Thanks for my lady not blaming me for saying this."

【柳叶儿】我将你做心肝儿般看待,点污了小姐清白。忘餐废寝舒心害,若不是真心耐,志诚捱,怎能勾这相思苦尽甘来?

【青哥儿】成就了今宵欢爱,魂飞在九霄云外。投至得见你多情小奶奶,憔悴形骸,瘦似麻秸。今夜和谐,犹自疑猜。露滴香埃,风静闲阶,月射书斋,云锁阳台。审问明白,只疑是昨夜梦中来,愁无奈。

(旦云)我回去也,怕夫人觉来寻我。(末云)我送小姐出来。

【寄生草】多丰韵,忒稔色。乍时相见教人害,霎时不见教人怪,些时得见教人爱。今宵同会

[Tune of Willow Leaves Song] "I treat you as my precious darling, and defiled the innocence of your virgin body. It is all because of this love sickness making me sleepless and forgetting the meal. If not for my sincerity and stubbornness, how could I wait for this day to come when the bitterness ends and happiness begins."

[Tune of Blue Song] "I have completed the happy marriage tonight, and my soul has already flied into the ninth heaven. I try my best to make you feel my love, though I become thin and wane as if husked hemp stalk in your eyes. Tonight we are in a harmony, however, I still doubt if I was in a dream. The dew falls on the fragment ground. The wind is quiet and the stairs are empty. The moonlight ray shines through the window of my study, and the place where we made love is just as sweet as a shower. I feel as if I just wake up from the sleep last night, still feeling helplessness in my mind."

[Ying Ying says] "I have to go now. I am afraid that my mother has woken up and sought for me."

[Zhang Gong says] "I will send my lady to go out."

[Tune of Parasitic Grass Song] "Walking with an elegance, the lady is so beautiful. The sudden meeting of her makes me suffer from love sickness, and sudden disappearance of her makes me blame for her coldness. The short dating with her makes me love her forever. Tonight, we meet under the green window curtain,

碧纱厨,何时重解香罗带?

(红云)来拜你娘!张生,你喜也!姐姐,咱家去来。

(末唱)

【赚煞】春意透酥胸,春色横眉黛,贱却人间玉帛。杏脸桃腮,乘著月色,娇滴滴越显得红白。下香阶,懒步苍苔,动人处弓鞋凤头窄。叹鲰生不才,谢多娇错爱。

若小姐不弃小生,此情一心者,你是必破工夫明夜早些来。(下)

第二折

(夫人引保上云)这几日窃见莺莺语言恍惚,神思加倍,腰肢体态,比向日不同。莫不做下来了么?(俫云)前日晚夕,奶奶睡了,我见姐姐和红娘

and when shall I have a chance to untie her fragment belt again?"

[Red Maid says] "Please bow to your mother. Gentleman Zhang, congratulation! Sister, let's go back."

[Zhang Gong sings] "The love is penetrating through her snow white bosoms. The scenery of spring is painting her black eyebrows, whose light overshadows all the jade and money in the world. Her face is as fair as apricot flowers and cheek as rosy as peach flowers, which is more beautiful under the moonlight. She slackens her pace, tramping on the moss lazily. Her small feet is so lovely and charming. I have to sigh for being an incapable scholar and thank for the pity of the beloved one."

"If my lady doesn't forsake me, and love me as I love you, Please come earlier tomorrow night." [Exit]

Scene Two

[The Old Lady enters with Huan Er and says] "Recently, Ying Ying seems to be absent-minded and worried. Her figure and manner are different than before. Does she do something immorally?"

[Huan Er says] "At the night of the day before yesterday, when mamma was asleep, I saw my sister and Red Maid coming to the garden and burning incense, but they hadn't come back for a long time. So I went to sleep at my room."

烧香，半晌不回来，我家去睡了。(夫人云)这桩事都在红娘身上。唤红娘来！(俫唤红科)(红云)哥哥唤我怎么？(俫云)奶奶知道你和姐姐去花园里去，如今要打你哩！(红云)呀，小姐，你带累我也！小哥哥你先去，我便来也。(红唤旦科)(红云)姐姐，事发了也。老夫人唤我哩，却怎了？(旦云)好姐姐，遮盖咱！(红云)娘呵，你做的稳秀者——我道你做下来也！(旦念)月圆便有阴云蔽，花发须教急雨催。(红唱)

【越调】【斗鹌鹑】则著你夜去明来，到有个天长地久不争你握雨携云，常使我提心在口。则合带月披星，谁著你停眠整宿？老夫人心数多，情性岁，使不著我巧语花言，将没做有。

[The Old Lady says] "All of this should be blamed on the Red Maid. Call Red Maid here!"

[Huan Er calls the Red Maid] [Red Maid asks] "Brother, what do you call me for?"

[Huan Er says] "Mama knows you and sister have been to the garden. She is going to beat you."

[Red Maid calls on Ying Ying and says] "Sister, the old lady knows. She asked me to come to her. What shall I do?"

[Ying Ying says] "My good sister, please cover the shame for me!"

[Red Maid says] "My mother, how secretive you did your affairs—I have thought you will not be known by the old lady."

[Ying Ying says] "When the moon is round, there will be dark clouds to cover it. When flowers come out, they will wait for the falling of rain eagerly."

[Tune of Fight Quails Song] "You had gone by night, and come back in the next day. I don't argue with you for your everlasting and unchanging love, but I am standing there, gnawed by anxiety. You should go before dawn and come home when the moon is up, but who asks you to sleep there all night? The old lady is very suspicious and unkind. Her temper is fierce. She doesn't allow me to lie to her, making yes to no."

【紫花儿序】老夫人猜那穷酸做了新婿,小姐做了娇妻,"这小贱人做了牵头"。俺小姐这些时春山低翠,秋水凝眸。别样的都休,试把你裙带儿拴,纽门儿扣,比著你旧时肥瘦,出落得精神,别样的风流。

(旦云)红娘,你到那里,小心回话者。(红云)我到夫人处,必问:"这小贱人!

【金蕉叶】我著你但去处行监坐守,谁著你迤逗的胡行乱走?若问著此一节呵如何诉休?你便索与他个知情的犯由。

姐姐,你受责理当,我图甚么来?

【调笑令】你绣帏里效绸缪,倒凤颠鸾百事有。我在窗儿外几曾轻咳嗽,立苍苔将绣鞋儿冰透。今日个嫩皮肤倒将粗棍抽,姐姐呵,俺这通殷勤的著甚来由?

[Tune of Violet flower Song] "The old lady guess that poor scholar has become the bridegroom, and her daughter has become his wife. It must be me who is the match maker. Recently, your eyebrows is as black as greenery mountain, and your eyesight gazes with affectionate like. Not to mention other changes, please untie the belt of your dress and unbutton your clothes, compared with the thinness in the old time, your become more spirited and refined."

[Ying Ying says] "Red Maid, when you answer to the old lady, please be careful."

[Red Maid says] "When I comes to the old lady, she must say, 'your little bitch.'

[Tune of Golden Banana Leaves Song] 'I have told you to watch on your lady's behavior, but who asked you to lead her astray?' If I was asked like this, I should have told her the reason. Sister, you should be blamed, but what is my attempt?"

[Tune of Song of Flirtation] "You have sexual love between each other under the embroidered curtain, and enjoyed the extremely happiness of this love affair. How many times do I cough lightly out of the window? My feet is too cold to stand on the moss-grown stairs. Today, my tender skin will be whipped by the thick stick. What can I gain by so eagerly passing the message between you and him?

姐姐在这里等著,我过去。说过呵,休欢喜,说不过,休烦恼。(红见夫人科)(夫人云)小贱人,为甚么不跪下!你知罪么?(红跪云)红娘不知罪。(夫人云)你故自口强哩。若实说呵,饶你,若不实说呵,我直打死你这个贱人!谁著你和小姐花园里去来?(红云)不曾去,谁见来?(夫人云)欢郎见你去来,尚故自推哩!(打科)(红云)夫人,休闪了手。且息怒停嗔,听红娘说。

【鬼三台】夜坐时停了针绣,共姐姐闲穷究,说张生哥哥病久,咱两个背著夫人向书房问候。

(夫人云)问候呵,他说甚么?(红云)他说来,

Sister, please wait for me here. I am going to the old lady. If I have convinced the old lady, you should not be too excited. If I haven't, don't be worried."

[Red Maid meets The Old Lady] [The Old Lady says] "Your little bitch, kneel down. Would you confess your guilt?"

[Red Maid kneels down and says] "Red Maid doesn't know what I am guilty for."

[The Old Lady says] "You are still tough and reluctant to confess. If you tell the truth, I will forgive you. If not, I will beat your little bitch to death. Who asked you and lady to go to the garden?"

[Red Maid says] "We have never been there. Who saw us?"

[The Old Lady says] "Huan Er saw you go. Don't tell lies."

[The Old Lady is going to beat the Red Maid]

[Red Maid says] "Old lady, please wait for a moment. Could you listen to my explanation?"

[Tune of Three Terraces Song] "Last night when my lady finished needling, I told my sister that brother Zhang has been sick for a long time. So we go and see him."

[The Old Lady asks] "When you visit him, what did he say?"

[Red Maid says] "He said that the old lady did not know how to charge human affairs. She returned my kindness with ingratitude. My happy life is full of worries now. He says, 'Red Maid, please go

道:"老夫人事已休,将恩变为仇,著小生半途喜变做忧。"他道:"红娘你且先行,教小姐权时落后。"

(夫人云)他是个女孩儿家,著他落后怎么?(红唱)

【秃厮儿】我则道神针法灸,谁承望燕侣莺俦。他两个经今月馀则是一处宿,何须你一一问缘由?

【圣药王】他每不识忧,不识愁,一双心意两相投。夫人得好休,便好休,这其间何必苦追求?常言道"女大不中留"。

(夫人云)这端事,都是你个贱人!(红云)非是张生、小姐、红娘之罪,乃夫人之过也。(夫人云)这贱人到指下我来,怎么是我之过?(红云)信者,人之根本,"人而无信,不知其可也。大车无輗,小车无軏,其何以行之哉?"当日军围普救,夫

first. I have something to talk to the lady'."

[The Old Lady asks] "She is a lady. Why does he ask her to go later?"

[Red Maid sings]

[Tune of Bald Men Song] "I have thought he will be cured by acupuncture and moxibustion, but who knows it is lovesickness that brought his illness unrecovered. That night, they stay together in one room. Why do you need to go details one by one?"

[Tune of Sovereign of Medicine Song] "They don't know sorrows, but they both love each other whole heartedly. My old lady, you should stop obstructing, if you know the advantages and disadvantages. Why should you go into details? There is an old saying that 'A grown girl can't be kept at home'."

[The Old Lady says] "It is because of you to make such a scandal happen!"

[Red Maid says] "The fault is not about Zhang, lady or Red Maid. It is your fault, my old lady."

[The Old Lady says] "This little bitch turns the blame on me. I will hear where my fault is?"

[Red Maid says] "Faith is the basic of human's virtue. Confucius says, 'If human has no faith, no one knows what he is going to do. Just like the two ends of the crossbar of the cart missing the buttons, how can it be driven?' That day, Gentleman Zhang invited the soldiers to save the monastery. The old lady had promised that those who was able to withdraw the rebels can marry your daughter. If Gentleman

人所许退军者,以女妻之。张生非慕小姐颜色,岂肯建区区退军之策?兵退身安,夫人悔却前言,岂得不为失信乎?既然不肯成其事,只合酬之以金帛,令张生舍此而去。却不当留请张生于书院,使怨女旷夫,各相早晚窥视,所以夫人有此一端。目下老夫人若不息其事,一来辱没相国家谱,二来张生日后名重天下,施恩于人,忍令反受其辱哉!使至官司,夫人亦得治家不严之罪。官司若推其详,亦知老夫人背义而忘恩,岂得为贤哉?红娘不敢自专,乞望夫人台鉴:莫若恕其小过,成就大事,捆之以去其污,岂不为长便乎?

【麻郎儿】秀才是文章魁首,姐姐是仕女班头,一个通彻三教九流,一个晓尽描鸾刺绣。

【幺篇】世有、便休、罢手,大恩人怎做敌头?起白马将军故友,斩飞虎叛贼草寇。

Zhang didn't admire lady, how would he propose the plan of withdrawing the rebels. When the rebels are defeated and everyone is safe, the old lady regrets for what you said before. Isn't losing faith to other people? Since you didn't agree with the marriage, you should just show your gratitude by giving him gold and silver, and ask him to leave. However, you allow gentleman to stay in the study room, so that you made your daughter grieving and Gentleman Zhang desolate everyday. Two people peep at each other day and night. So that's your faults, my old lady. At the moment, if you don't agree with this affair, it will bring shame to the family tree of the prime minister. Moreover, if Gentleman Zhang gain fame in the future, wouldn't it bring shame to him too? Even if we bring the case to the lawsuit, the old lady will be guilty for not strictly governing the family. If looking deeply into this lawsuit, everyone will know my old lady's faithless. Could you be called able and virtuous again? Red Maid dare not speak for myself, but wish that my old lady is able to judge wisely. If you could forgive our little mistakes, we can achieve happiness, which I mean if you granted their marriage, wouldn't it be a good thing for all of us?"

[Tune of the Pocked Face Song] "The scholar is Number One Scholar in writing articles, and sister is the head of the maid. One is an expert of the three religions and the nine schools of thoughts, and the other one has viewed all kinds of embroideries."

[Tune of Spinner Song] "Since Gentleman Zhang and Ying Ying have already made love with each other, the old lady has to stop interfering. How could she makes the benefactor of the family into

【络丝娘】不争和张解元参辰卯酉，便是与崔相国出乖弄丑。到底干连著自己骨肉，夫人索穷究。

（夫人云）这小贱人也道得是。我不合养了这个不肖之女。待经官呵，玷辱家门。罢，罢，俺家无犯法之男，再婚之女，与了这厮罢！红娘，唤那贱人来！（红见旦云）且喜姐姐，那棍子则是滴溜溜在我身上，吃我直说过了，我也怕不得许多。夫人如今唤你来，待成合亲事。（旦云羞人答答的，怎么见夫人？（红云）娘跟前有甚么羞！

【小桃红】当日个月明才上柳梢头，却早人约黄昏后。羞的我脑背后将牙儿衬著衫儿袖。猛凝

an enemy, who is friend of White Horse General."

[Tune of the Silk Maid] "If you do not agree with the marriage, it should bring shame to the prime minister family. Not to mention she is your flesh and blood, the old lady, you had better not get at the root of the thing."

[The Old Lady says] "What this little bitch said makes sense. Be it so! I have brought up an unfilial daughter. If there is a lawsuit, it must bring shame to our family. Ok. Ok. In the history of our family, we have no man who committed crime, nor woman who married again. Give Ying Ying to this man. Red Maid, please bring that wretched girl here."

[Red Maid meets Ying Ying and says] "Congratulation, my sister. Good things will happen. That stick should have beaten on my body, but the old lady is convinced by me. I am unable to fear about the consequences, so I tell the truth. The old lady asked me to call you and arrange a wedding for you."

[Ying Ying says] "I feel so ashamed for myself. How do I have face to meet my mother?"

[Red Maid says] "There is no need to be shy in front of your mother."

[Tune of Red Peach blossoms Song] "That night, when the moon just climbs up on the top of the willow branches, you can not wait for meeting with the other one after the sunsets. It makes me feel so shamed when you made love with him that I clutched my sleeves many times. In a sudden I look back, I see your small feet.

眸,看时节则见鞋底尖儿瘦。一个恣情的不休,一个哑声儿厮耨。呸!那其间可怎生不害半星儿羞?

(旦见夫人科)(夫人云)莺莺,我怎生抬举你来?今日做这等的勾当!则是我的孽障,待怨谁的是!我待经官来,辱没了你父亲,这等事,不是俺相国人家的勾当。罢罢罢,谁似俺养女的不长俊!红娘,书房里唤将那禽兽来!(红唤末科)(末云)小娘子,唤小生做甚么?(红云)你的事发了也。如今夫人唤你来,将小姐配与你哩。小姐先招了也,你过去。(末云)小生惶恐,如何见老夫人?当初谁在老夫人行说来?(红云)休佯小心,过去便了。

【小桃红】既然泄露怎干休,是我相投首。俺家里陪酒陪茶到搁就,你休愁,何须约定通媒媾?我弃了部署不收,你元来"苗而不秀"。呸!你是个银样镴枪头。

One is making love recklessly, and the other is groaning in the bedclothes. Puah! Why don't you feel shamed at that time?"

[Ying Ying meets Old Lady] [The Old Lady says] "Ying Ying, How I did you a favour by praising you! What have you done! You are my sin. If I call a lawsuit, I am afraid to ruin your father's reputation. What you have done is not in line with the family's tradition. Okay. Why doesn't my daughter give me face? Red Maid, please call that amorist to come too."

[Red Maid calls on Zhang Gong.][Zhang Gong says] "My sister, what does you call me for?"

[Red Maid says] "The old lady has known your affair. Today, she asked you to come, and marry the lady to you. The lady confessed first. Please come as soon as possible."

[Zhang Gong says] "I am so flustered. How dare I have the face to meet the old lady? Who exposed this affair to her?"

[Red Maid says] "Don't be worried. Please just come."

[Tune of Red Peach Blossoms Song] "If this affair is known by the old lady, how would the old lady forgive you? It is me who confessed first. Now, our family will serve you with tea and wine, and arrange the marriage as soon as possible. Don't be worried. There is no need for an engagement. Since then, I will not give advice to you. You are really a corn which does not bear grain. Puah, you are an impressive-looking but a useless person in reality!"

（末见夫人科）（夫人云）好秀才呵！岂不闻"非先王之德行不敢行"？我待送你去官司里去来，恐辱没了俺家谱。我如今将莺莺与你为妻，则是俺三辈儿不招白衣女婿，你明日便上朝取应去，我与你养著媳妇。得官呵，来见我，驳落呵，休来见我。（红云）张生早则喜也。

【东原乐】相思事，一笔勾，早则展放从前眉儿皱，美爱幽欢恰动头。既能勾，张生，你觑兀的般可喜娘庞儿也要人消受。

（夫人云）明日收拾行装，安排果酒，请长老一同送张生，到十里长亭去。（旦念隔语西河堤畔柳，安排青眼送行人。（同夫人下）
（红唱）

【收尾】来时节画堂箫鼓鸣春昼，列著一对儿鸾交凤友。那其间才受你说媒红，方吃你谢亲酒。

（并下）

[Zhang Gong meets Old Lady] [The Old Lady says] "What a good scholar! Have you ever heard that we dare not do anything that is against the virtue of previous kings? I have intended to give you a lawsuit, but afraid to bring shame to our family tree. Today, I will marry Ying Ying to you. However, in our three generations, we have not had any commoner without a rank as son-in-law. You may leave to go to the capital and take the imperial examination tomorrow, and I will raise your wife for you. If you get a position in the officialdom, you are able to come and meet me. If you fail, don't see me again."

[Red Maid says] "Gentleman Zhang, congratulation!"

[Tune of Joy of The East Plain Song] "Since then, the love sickness is written off at one stroke. The knitted eyebrows are being unfolded. The beautiful love and happy meeting just begin. If you are attached to my lady, you should bear the time for short separation for the marriage."

[The Old Lady says] "Tomorrow, pick up your luggage and go on your journey. I will prepare for some fruits and drinks. Let's send Gentleman Zhang off with the abbot to the Ten-li Road Side Pavilion ten-li away." [Exeunt]

[Ying Ying says] "I will send my missing words to you near the willows on the Xi River's bank, to see you off with my tearful eyes.[Exit]
[Red Maid sings]

[Tune of Epilogue]"When you first came, there was pipe singing in the monastery hall and a pair of love birds painting on the wall. You said to reward me with heavy gold for being the match maker. Now, I will receive your reward by eating your wine."[Exeunt]

第三折

(夫人长老上云)今日送张生赴京,十里长亭安排下筵席。我和长老先行,不见张生、小姐来到。(旦末红同上)(旦云)今日送张生上朝取应,早是离人伤感,况值那暮秋天气,好烦恼人也呵!悲欢聚散一杯酒,南北东西万里程。

【正宫】【端正好】碧云天,黄花地,西风紧,北雁南飞。晓来谁染霜林醉?总是离人泪。

【滚绣球】恨相见得迟,怨归去得疾。柳丝长玉骢难系。恨不倩疏林挂住斜晖。马儿迍迍的行,

Scene Three

[The Old Lady and the abbot enter] "Today, we are sending Gentleman Zhang off to the capital. We have prepared for the banquet in the Ten-li Road Side Pavilion. I have arrived first with the abbot, but not seeing Gentleman Zhang and my daughter."

[Ying Ying enters with Red Maid][Ying Ying says] "Today, I am seeing Gentleman Zhang off for the imperial examination. I feel so sentimental for parting, especially this is the late autumn. How troublesome it is. Joys and sorrows of gathering and parting can only be wiped off by a glass of wine. It is a journey of thousands of miles all around the country."

[Tune of Calm dignity Song] "The sky is cloudless blue and the land is covered with yellow leaves. The west wind blows hard, and wild geese fly from the north to the south. In the morning, who dyes the maple trees red? It must be tears from the people who are going to part with each other."

[Tune of Rolling Ball Song] "I am regretful for meeting you so late, and blaming you for leaving me so early. The willow branches are long, but they cannot stop the horses which are parting far away. How I wish that the setting sun hang on the dense forests. The horse of Gentleman Zhang is walking slowly, and my cart is following behind quickly. The bitterness of lovesickness is just cured, however, the sorrow of parting comes again. Upon hearing that 'He is gone', suddenly I grow very thin. Looking at the Ten-li

车儿快快的随。却告了相思回避,破题儿又早别离。听得一声"去也",松了金钏。遥望见十里长亭,减了玉肌。此恨谁知!

(红云)姐姐,今日怎么不打扮?(旦云)你那知我的心里呵!

【叨叨令】见安排著车儿、马儿,不由人熬熬煎煎的气,有甚么心情花儿、靥儿,打扮的娇娇滴滴的媚,准备著被儿、枕儿,则索昏昏沉沉的睡,从今后衫儿、袖儿,都揾做重重叠叠的泪。兀的不闷杀人也么哥,兀的不闷杀人也么哥!久已后书儿、信儿,索与我恓恓惶惶的寄。

(做到见夫人科)(夫人云)张生和长老坐,小姐这壁坐,红娘将酒来。张生,你向前来,是自家亲眷,不要回避。俺今日将莺莺与你,到京师休辱末了俺孩儿,挣揣一个状元回来者。(末云)小生托夫人馀荫,凭著胸中之才,视官如拾芥耳。(洁云)夫人主见不差,张生不是落后的人。(把酒了,坐)(旦长吁科)

Li Pavilion roadside, I am thinner than before. Who can understand such sorrow of parting?"

[Red Maid says] "Sister, why don't you make up today?"

[Ying Ying says] "You will never understand what I am thinking in my mind!"

[Ying Ying sings]

[Tune of Murmuring Song] "Seeing the horse and carts ready, I feel heartbroken and have no mood to put on flowers on my head and paint colour on my face so, so as to be made up as a delicately pretty woman. I want to bury myself under the quilt and pillow, just wishing to dope off day and night. Since then, my dress and my sleeves will wipe endless parting tears. Why are these worries not killing people? Why are these worries not killing people? Since then, if there are letters from Gentleman Zhang, please send them to me as soon as possible."

[Having arrived at Ten-li Road Side Pavilion, Gentleman Zhang bows to the old lady] [The Old Lady says] "Gentleman Zhang, you sit with the abbot, and my daughter sit with me. Red Maid, please bring wine. Gentleman Zhang, come to me, we are a family now, and there is no need to avert suspicion. Today, I marry Ying Ying to you. When you reach the capital city, don't bring shame to the family. You must try your best to win a Number One Scholar before you come back." [Zhang Gong says] "Thanks to the old lady's great blessing, and my good talent, getting the scholarly honor of an official rank will be as easy as picking up a grass. [Abbot says] "The old lady is far-sighted enough. Gentleman Zhang are sure not to lag behind."

【脱布衫】下西风黄叶纷飞，染寒烟衰草萋迷。酒席上斜签著坐的，蹙愁眉死临侵地。

【小梁州】我见他阁泪汪汪不敢垂，恐怕人知。猛然见了把头低，长吁气，推整素罗衣。

【幺篇】虽然久后成佳配，奈时间怎不悲啼。意似痴，心如醉，昨宵今日，清减了小腰围。

（夫人云）小姐把盏者。（红递酒，旦把盏长吁科云）请吃酒。

【上小楼】合欢未已，离愁相继。想著俺前暮私情，昨夜成亲，今日别离。我谂知这几日相思滋味，却元来此别离情更增十倍。

[After filling the wine in the cup, Ying Ying sighs deeply]

[Tune of Doffing off Clothes Song] "The west wind blows, and yellow leaves meander in the sky. With frost falling, everywhere is dry yellow grass. Gentleman Zhang sits on the banquet and knits his eyebrows, in extremely a low spirit."

[Tune of small Liang Zhou] "I see him trying his best not to allow his tears falling down on his cheek, afraid to be noticed. All of a sudden, he lowers down his head, sighs deeply, and wipes his tears, as if pretending to arrange his white silk coat."

[Tune of Petty Song] "Though we will be man and wife in the future, at this moment of parting, how could people not feel sad? My mind with him is infatuated, and my mood with him is intoxicated. Only one night passed, my waist is more slender than before."

[The Old Lady says] "Red Maid, please fill the cup with wine."

[Red Maid brings the flagon to Ying Ying. Ying Ying holds up the cup in her hands and sighs] "Please have a cup of drink."

[Tune of Ascending the Attic Song] "It doesn't take long for the union, but the sadness of parting follows successively. Thinking of the night before yesterday, we secretly made engagement with each other. Last night, we became a married couple, but today, we are going to separate. These days, I have experienced the bitterness of love sickness. Who knows the grief of parting is ten times bitter than love sickness."

【幺篇】年少呵轻远别,情薄呵易弃掷。全不想腿儿相挨,脸儿相偎,手儿相携。你与俺崔相国做女婿,妻荣夫贵,但得一个并头莲,煞强如状元及第。

(夫人云)红娘把盏者。(红把酒科)
(旦唱)

【满庭芳】供食太急,须臾对面,顷刻别离。若不是酒席间子母每当回避,有心待与他举案齐眉。虽然是厮守得一时半刻,也合著俺夫妻每共桌而食。眼底空留意,寻思起就里,险化做望夫石。

(红云)姐姐不曾吃早饭,饮一口儿汤水。(旦云)红娘,甚么汤水咽得下。

【快活三】将来的酒共食,尝著似土和泥。假若便是土和泥,也有些土气息,泥滋味。

【朝天子】暖溶溶玉醅,白泠泠似水。多半是相思泪。眼面前茶饭怕不待要吃,恨塞满愁肠胃。蜗角虚名,蝇头微利,拆鸳鸯在两下里。一个这壁,一个那壁,一递一声长吁气。

[Tune of Petty Song] "Ah, a young man tends to take light of parting and abandon his first wife if they are not together forgetting all about the sweetness of getting together with touching legs, cuddling faces as well as clutching hands. You have become the son-in-law of the prime minister's family. Wife will be honored if husband is noble. I only hope we can never part with each other like twin lotus flowers on one stalk. It is much better than winning the Number One Scholar."

[The Old Lady says] "Red Maid, please fill the cup." [Red Maid fills the cup] [Ying Ying sings] "It is too fast to fill the cup and serve the meal. Now we sit face to face, but later we are separating from East and West. How much do I wish to tell you my heart-felt feeling if my mother wasn't there? Though we can only be together for just a few moment, we have shared same meal as husband and wife. I can only pass the love message through my eyes. Thinking of the twists and turns of this marriage, I am nearly turned into a stone waiting for the return of my husband."

[Tune of Happiness Three Song] "The food and drinks on the table tastes like earth and dust. If they are really earth and dust, they should have that smell and taste, but they do not."

[Homage to the Emperor Song] "The warm and good wine tastes as light as water. It must have been full of the tears of love sickness. I do not want to eat the food and take the drink in front. Only turbulent sorrows are overwhelming my mind. For the empty fame, my mother tears the husband and wife apart. One is here and the other is there. Both keeps sighing for a long time."

（夫人云）辆起车儿，俺先回去，小姐随后和红娘来。（下）（末辞洁科）（洁云）此一行别无话儿，贫僧准备买登科录看，做亲的茶饭，少不得贫僧的。先生在意，鞍马上保重者。从今经忏无心礼，专听春雷第一声。（下）

（旦唱）

【四边静】霎时间杯盘狼藉，车儿投东，马儿向西。两意徘徊，落日山横翠。知他今宵宿在那里? 有梦也难寻觅。

张生，此一行得官不得官，疾便回来。（末云）小生这一去，白夺一个状元。正是：青霄有路终须到，金榜无名誓不归。（旦云）君行别无所赠，口占一绝，为君送行：弃掷今何在，当时且自亲。还将旧来意，怜取眼前人。（末云）小姐之意差矣，

[The Old Lady says] "Hitch up the cart. I am leaving first. Red Maid, you come back with the lady later." [Exit]

[Gentleman Zhang says goodbye to Fa Ben] [Fa Ben says] "I have no other words to say to you when you leave this time. I intend to buy the register of the members who pass the imperial examine. The food and drinks of the marriage between you and the lady cannot do without me. My gentleman, take care of yourself on the journey. Since then, I have no mood to recite the Buddhist scriptures, but to follow the good news of you everyday. "[Exit]

[Tune of Four Side Tranquility] "They remove the wine and dishes instantly. My cart will go east, and his horse west. Two lovers are too unwilling to part with each other. The rays of the setting sun fall on the greenery mountainside. Where is he going to stay tonight? Even if in the dream, it is hard to find him."

[Ying Ying says] "Gentleman Zhang, no matter you pass the official exam or not, please come back as soon as possible."

[Zhang Gong says] "I am sure to return with the Number One Scholar this time. There is an old saying, 'There is a way to come to the blue sky eventually, and I swear never to come back if I am not in the list of successful scholars in the imperial examination'."

[Ying Ying says] "I have nothing to present you as a gift for your leaving, but I compose verses to send you off. 'Where is the man who forsakes me first? He is so affectionate to me before. He is using the same kindness towards me, to face a new lover in front of him.'"

张珙更敢怜谁?谨赓一绝,以剖寸心:人生长远别,孰与最关亲?不遇知音者,谁怜长叹人?
(旦唱)

【耍孩儿】淋漓襟袖啼红泪,比司马青衫更湿。伯劳东去燕西飞,未登程先问归期。虽然眼底人千里,且尽生前酒一杯。未饮心先醉,眼中流血,心里成灰。

【五煞】到京师服水土,趁程途节饮食,顺时自保揣身体。荒村雨露宜眠早,野店风霜要起迟。鞍马秋风里,最难调护,最要扶持。

【四煞】这忧愁诉与谁?相思只自知,老天不管人憔悴。泪添九曲黄河溢,恨压三峰华岳低。到晚来闷把西楼倚,见了些夕阳古道,衰柳长堤。

[Zhang Gong says] "My lady, you are wrong. How dare I love a new one? I will make verses of four lines to express my determination, 'There is hardly any parting in the life. Whom I will show affection for? If not meeting my soul mate, who will have pity for a poor scholar?"

[Ying Ying sings]

[Tune of Playing with the Child Song] "My sleeves is wet with crimson tears, wetter than yours, those of blue grown. The butcher bird is flying eastward, and the swallow is flying westward. Before you start to leave, I ask the date of your return. Though the man before my eyes is going afar, I just toast you a cup of wine to show my heart. However, before drinking, I am already drunk. There is blood in my tears, and the flame of heart extinguishes like cold ashes."

[Tune of Last Stanza but Five] "When you reach the capital, I hope you can have acclimatization, to walk faster, eat healthier, and take care of yourself. If you stay in inns in wild villages, you should sleep earlier. If it is snowy outside, you should get up late. When you are riding in the autumn wind, it is more difficult to keep balance. All in all, please take care of yourself."

[Tune of Last Stanza but Four] "Whom should I tell these sorrows? The love sickness is only curved in the mind. The heaven god doesn't care if people are wane and weak. The tears of parting will flood the Yellow River. The resentments will suppress the three peaks of Hua Mountain. Under the sunset, I lean upon the west building, looking far away the ancient road under the setting sun.

【三煞】笑吟吟一处来，哭啼啼独自归。归家若到罗帏里，昨宵个绣衾香暖留春住，今夜个翠被生寒有梦知。留恋你别无意，见据鞍上马，阁不住泪眼愁眉。

（末云）有甚言语，嘱付小生咱？
（旦唱）

【二煞】你休忧文齐福不齐，我则怕你停妻再娶妻。休要一春鱼雁无消息，我这里青鸾有信频须寄，你却休金榜无名誓不归。此一节君须记：若见了那异乡花草，再休似此处栖迟。

（末云）再谁似小姐，小生又生此念？
（旦唱）

【一煞】青山隔送行，疏林不做美，淡烟暮霭相

as well as the declined willows along the long banks."

[Tune of Last Stanza but Three] "I come to send Gentleman Zhang off with a smile on the face, but tears keep rolling down when I go home alone. If I go back to my room and enter the bed curtain, I will remember sweetness with you in the embroidery quilt that lovely night. Tonight, the quilt will be as cold as ice, making people difficult to sleep. You have climbed the horse saddle. I keep knitting my eyebrows and shedding my tears."

[Zhang Gong says] "What else do you want to tell me?"

[Tune of Last Stanza but Two] "Don't worry about imperial examination, because you have talent. What you need is just luck. I am only afraid that you will forsake me, and marry someone else instead. Please don't go away without sending a letter. I will keep sending letters to you. Don't swear that you will never come back if you don't pass the imperial exam. One thing you should remember: if you met other lady in the other town, don't linger long as you did here."

[Zhang Gong says] "Who can be compared to my lady? How dare I have such thoughts?"

[Ying Ying sings]

[The Tune of Last Stanza but One] "The high mountains and forests stand between you and me, preventing my eyesight from seeing you off. The light smoke mingles with evening mist. The setting sun slants on the ancient road without a human voice, the

遮蔽。夕阳古道无人语，禾黍秋风听马嘶。我为甚么懒上车儿内？来时甚急，去后何迟！

（红云）夫人去好一会，姐姐，咱家去。

（旦唱）

【收尾】四围山色中，一鞭残照里。遍人间烦恼填胸臆，量这些大小车儿如何载得起？

（旦红下）（末云）仆童，赶早行一程儿，早寻个宿处。泪随流水急，愁逐野云飞。（下）

第四折

（末引仆骑马上开）离了蒲东早三十里也，兀的前面是草桥，店里宿一宵，明日赶早行。这马百般儿不肯走。行色一鞭催去马，羁愁万斛引新诗。

rustling of autumn wind blows with the horse neighing. Why should I be too reluctant to get on the cart? I was in such a hurry to come, but too slow to leave."

[Red Maid says] "The old lady has gone for a long time. Sister, Let's go home now."

[Ying Ting sings]

[Tune of Epilogue] "Emerging into the scenery of the mountains, the horse is far away in the setting sun. The troubles of the whole world all rushes into my mind. How could such a small cart be capable to carry them?"

[Ying Ying and Red Maid exit] [Zhang Gong says] "My servant Boy, let's hurry up to travel a distance and find a place to rest tonight in shortest time. Tears are shedding down on my face like running water. Full of sorrows, I am chasing the wild clouds far away." [Exeunt]

Scene Four

[Zhang Gong enters with his servant boy] "It has been thirty li since I left Pu Dong Town. I saw a cottage in front of me. Let's have a rest in the cottage, and start off for the capital earlier tomorrow. The horse is too tired to move. I will whip the horse, to urge it to move faster. At the bottom of my heart, the sorrows are as deep as ten thousand cups of wine."

【双调】【新水令】望蒲东萧寺暮云遮，惨离情半林黄叶。马迟人意懒，风急雁行斜。离恨重叠，破题儿第一夜。

想著昨日受用，谁知今日凄凉！

【步步娇】昨夜个翠被香浓薰兰麝，欹珊枕把身躯儿趄。脸儿厮揾者，仔细端详，可憎的别。铺云鬓玉梳斜，恰便似半吐初生月。

早至也。店小二哥那里？（小二哥上云）官人，俺这头房里下。（末云）琴童，接了马者。点上灯，我诸般不要吃，则要睡些儿。（仆云）小人也辛苦，

[Double Tune of New Water Song] "Looking back at Pu Jiu Monastery, I see it is shrouded by the clouds. The half woods have turned yellow, which makes the parting more unbearable. The horse is slow and I am lazy. The wind is harsh and wild geese fly slantingly. The pain of separation is miserable. Today is the first night that I separate from the lady.

Who knows how happy we were last night, and how sad it is tonight!"

[Tune of Charming Paces Song] "Last night, the green silk quilt was scented with the fragrant smell of my lady's body, and today, I crawl up on the pillow to avoid the coldness of night. I still remember her face and her pair of watery eyes lowering down for shyness, but tonight we are torn apart from each other. I remember how Ying Ying was combing her cloudy hair and put a jade hairpin on her bun, which looks like a crescent moon on her head.

Having arrived the inn earlier. Where is the cottage keeper?"

[The cottage keeper enters and says] "My guests, will you stay in my cottage tonight?"

[Zhang Gong says] "Yes, we will. The servant boy, feed the horse and light the lamp. I don't want to eat anything, just wishing to sleep earlier."

[The Servant Boy says] "I am tired too. I will do after taking a little rest."

[The Servant Boy spreads up his bedding in front of Zhang Gong's bed and falls asleep first][Zhang Gong says] "How am I able to sleep tonight?"

待歇息也。(在床前打铺做睡科)(末云)今夜甚睡得到我眼里来也!

【落梅风】旅馆欹单枕,秋蛩鸣四野,助人愁的是纸窗儿风裂。乍孤眠被儿薄又怯,冷清清几时温热!

(末睡科)(旦上云)长亭畔别了张生,好生放不下。老夫人和梅香都睡了,我私奔出城,赶上和他同去。

【乔木查】走荒郊旷野,把不住心娇怯,喘吁吁难将两气接。疾忙赶上者,打草惊蛇。

【搅筝琶】他把我心肠扯,因此不避路途赊。瞒过俺能拘管的夫人,稳住俺厮齐攒的侍妾。想著他临上马痛伤嗟,哭得我也似痴呆。不是我心邪,自别离已后,到西日初斜,愁得来陡峻,瘦得来咍嗻。则离得半个日头,却早又宽掩过翠裙三四褶。谁曾经这般磨灭。

【锦上花】有限姻缘,方才宁贴,无奈功名,使人离缺。害不了的愁怀,却才觉些掉不下的思量,

[Tune of Wind Blowing Down the Plum Flowers Song] "Sleeping on the single pillow in the cottage, I hear grasshoppers singing everywhere. Tonight, I sleep alone, and the quilt is thin and cold. When could it get warm?"

[Zhang Gong falls asleep][Ying Ying enters] "Since parting with Gentleman Zhang in the Road Side Pavilion, I cannot take my mind at ease. My mother and Red Maid are all sleeping. I secretly elope out of the town, wishing to catch up with him and go to the capital together."

[Tune of Brushwood Song] "Walking in the wild countryside alone, I feel scared and cold. I have walked so fast that I can hardly breathe. I beat the grass, for fear of snakes."

[Tune of Playing Pipa Song] "My heart is all on him, so that I am not scared of the long journey. I was successful in deceiving my strict mother, and avoiding the maid who stays with me together. Thinking of him crying and sighing on the horse, I shed tears like a fool. It's not that I am wretched. Since his departure in the morning till the sun setting down from the sky, I have been too sorrowful to take up my spirit, and too thin to wear my old dresses. Just parting for half a day, my clothes are too large to wear. Who brings such troubles to us?"

[Tune of Flower on the Brocade Song] "We just completed our short union of marriage, however, the pursuit of scholarly honour separates the couple apart. The sorrows are unboundless. All of a

如今又也。清霜净碧波，白露下黄叶。下下高高，道路曲折。四野风来，左右乱飐。我这里奔驰，他何处困歇？

【清江引】呆答孩店房儿里没话说，闷对如年夜。暮雨催寒蛩，晓风吹残月，今宵酒醒何处也？

（旦云）在这个店儿里，不免敲门。（末云）谁敲门哩？是一个女人的声音，我且开门看咱。这早晚是谁？

【庆宣和】是人呵疾忙快分说，是鬼呵合速灭。

（旦云）是我。老夫人睡了，想你去了呵，几时再得见，特来和你同去。

sudden, I feel the worries flashing in my mind again. The clear frost cleans the grass, making it as if blue waves, and white dew presses yellow leaves down. I walk up and down on the winding road. The wild wind is blowing from all directions, as if knives cutting people's faces. I am running, and wondering where he is going to rest tonight."

[Tune of Clear River Song] "Dull as I am in the sleeping room, with no one to talk to. The night is as long as a year. The evening rain hastens the cold cricket, and the morning breeze blows on the waning moon. Where shall I sober up tonight?"

[Ying Ying says] "He must stay in this cottage. I have to knock the door."

[Zhang Gong asks] "Who is knocking the door? I heard it was a woman's voice. I should go and see. Who is coming at this time of the day?"

[Tune of Celebration of the Harmony Song] "If you are a human, please speak up quickly. If you are a ghost, I kill you as soon as possible."

[Ying Ying says] "It's me. The old lady is sleeping. I have been thinking when shall we meet again after your leaving. So I come to see you, and wish to go with you together."

[Zhang Gong says] "As soon as I hear the voice, I open the door and

(末唱)

听说罢将香罗袖儿拽,却元来是姐姐、姐姐。难得小姐的心勤!

【乔牌儿】你是为人须为彻,将衣袂不藉。绣鞋儿被露水泥沾惹,脚心儿管踏破也。

(旦云)我为足下呵,顾不得迢递。(旦唧唧了)

【甜水令】想著你废寝忘餐,香消玉减,花开花谢,犹自觉争些。便枕冷衾寒,凤只鸾孤,月圆云遮,寻思来有甚伤嗟?

【折桂令】想人生最苦离别!可怜见千里关山,犹自跋涉。似这般割肚牵肠,到不如义断恩绝。虽然是一时间花残月缺,休猜做瓶坠簪折。不恋豪杰,不羡骄奢,生则同衾,死则同穴。

hug her in my arms. It is my lady. How nice to meet you tonight!"

[Tune of Pseudo-melody Song] "You love me so much that you don't even care about going in rags. Your beautiful embroidered shoes are soaked by water and soiled by mud. The arches of your feet are scratched through."

[Ying Ying says] "For your sake, I have no mind to care about the great distance."

[Ying Ying sings]

[Tune of Sweet Water Song] "I am missing of you all the time, so that I forget to sleep and eat the whole day. I am waning and wasting day by day. The flowers blossom and fade only to vie for something. Since your departure, I always feel like something is missing in my mind. The pillow is cold, and the quilt is broken. The saddest thing in the world is parting with beloved one in life. The bright round moon is covered by clouds. I wonder why I should sigh all the time!"

[Tune of Picking Laurel Song] "The hardest thing in the life is a pair of lovers to be torn apart. I have climbed up thousands of miles in the mountain, and trudged along a crooked path with difficulty. If I had known this love has caused you so much unease, and the parting is so painful, I would rather break you off decisively. I am not admiring great heroes, nor longing for a luxury life, but only wishing you to share the same quilt with me when we are alive; if I died, I wish we would be able to be buried will me cave together."

（外净一行扮卒子上叫云）恰才见一女子渡河，不知那里去了，打起火把者！分明见他走在这店中去也。将出来！将出来！（末云）却怎了？（旦云）你近后，我自开门对他说。

【水仙子】硬围著普救寺下锹撅，强当住咽喉仗剑钺。贼心肠馋眼脑天生得劣。

（卒子云）你是谁家女子，黉夜渡河？（旦唱）休言语，靠后些！杜将军你知道他是英杰，觑一觑著你为了醯酱，指一指教你化做酱血——骑著匹白马来也。

（卒子抢旦下）（末惊觉云）呀，元来却是梦里。且将门儿推开看，只见一天露气，满地霜华，晓星初上，残月犹明。无端喜鹊高枝上，一枕鸳鸯梦不成。

[One soldier enters and says] "Just then, I saw a woman crossing the river. Where is she going? Please light the torch! She must have gone inside this cottage. I will go and have a look. Please come out!"

[Zhang Gong asks] "What shall we do now?"

[Ying Ying says] "Please stay behind me. I will open the door and speak to him."

[Tune of Song of Narcissus Song] "Besieging the Pu Jiu Monastery, the soldiers looted and killed. With the courage, she faces the thieves as if with a sword in her hand. If the wicked solider has a vicious desire, he is sure to be punished by nature."

[The soldier asks] "Whose family are you from? Why do you cross the river at night?"

[Ying Ying sings] "Stop talking. Please stand away and disappear. Have you heard of General Du? If you dare to stare at me, you will become his meat pulp. If you dare to hurt my one finger, you will turn into a blood river. Here, he is coming with a white horse now."

[The soldier ties the Ying Ying and exits][Zhang Gong wakes up from sleep with a start] "Ah, I was dreaming. He opens up the door, and sees the night full of dew and frost. The morning star just climbs up the sky, and the waning crescent moon still hangs bright. The magpies are climbing up the tree branches and twittering. He realized that his love dream was broken."

【雁儿落】绿依依墙高柳半遮，静悄悄门掩清秋夜，疏剌剌林梢落叶风，昏惨惨云际穿窗月。

【得胜令】惊觉我的是颤巍巍竹影走龙蛇，虚飘飘庄周梦蝴蝶，絮叨叨促织儿无休歇，韵悠悠砧声儿不断绝。痛煞煞伤别，急煎煎好梦儿应难舍冷清清的咨嗟，娇滴滴玉人儿何处也？

（仆云）天明也，咱早行一程儿，前面打火去（末云）店小二哥，还你房钱，鞴了马者。

【鸳鸯煞】柳丝长咫尺情牵惹，水声幽仿佛人呜咽。斜月残灯，半明不灭。唱道是旧恨连绵，新愁郁结恨塞离愁，满肺腑难淘泻。除纸笔代喉舌，千种相思对谁说！（并下）

[Tune of Falling Swan Song] "The green willows half lean on the high walls, and the quiet door is shined by the light autumn night. The bleak autumn wind blows down the leaves from the trees, and in the darkness the half cloud-covered moon sheds light into my room through the window."

[Tune of Triumphant Song] "The shaking shadows of the bamboo trees look as if dragons and snakes walking on the wall. I have dreamed of butterflies just as the sage Chuang Tsze did long ago. The chirping of crickets is unceasing at night. The washing woman's pounding is echoing in the empty air. My heart is full of grief. How am I too reluctant to wake up from the sweat dream! When waking up, I have to sigh again. Where is my sweet and charming lady?"

[The Servant Boy says] "The day is bright. Let's go on earlier to see if there is an inn ahead to have a lunch."

[Zhang Gong says] "The cottage keeper, this is your house rent. Please loose my horse."

[Tune of Lover Birds' Epilogue] "My grief is as long as the willow branches. The flowing water sounds like a human weeping. The setting moon in the sky and the expiring lamp in my hands are half bright and half put out. Old love sickness continues for a long time. The old and new sorrows make parting even harder. There is no way to express my feelings, except using rice paper and writing brush as my voice, or could I make my lady know my thousands of love sickness!" [Exeunt]

【络丝娘煞尾】都则为一官半职,阻隔得千山万水。

  题目 小红娘成好事 老夫人问由情
  正名 短长亭斟别酒 草桥店梦莺莺

[Tune of Spinner Epilogue] "Just for the sake of fame certain official positions, the lovers are separated by numerous mountains and rivers."

The Red Maid makes a good match, and the old lady asks for the reason.

Saying goodbye in the long pavilion and drinking for the leave of the lover, In the cottage, Zhang Sheng dreams of Ying Ying.

张君瑞庆团圆杂剧　五剧第五本

Act Five

楔　子

　　(末引仆人上开云)自暮秋与小姐相别,倏经半载之际,托赖祖宗之荫,一举及第,得了头名状元。如今在客馆,听候圣旨御笔除授。惟恐小姐挂念,且修一封书,令琴童家去,达知夫人,便知小生得中,以安其心。琴童过来,你将文房四宝来,我写就家书一封,与我星夜到河中府去。见小姐时,说:"官人怕娘子忧,特地先著小人将书来。"即忙接了回书来者。过日月好疾也呵!

【仙吕】【赏花时】相见时红雨纷纷点绿苔,别离后黄叶萧萧凝暮霭。今日见梅开,别离半载。

　　琴童,我嘱付你的言语记著:则说道特地寄书来。(下)

　　(仆云)得了这书,星夜望河中府走一遭。(下)

Prologue

[Zhang Gong enters and says] "How time flies! Since separation with my lady in last autumn, it has already been half a year. Thanks for the blessing of my ancestors, I have won the Number One Scholar in the imperial examination. Now I am staying at the inn, and waiting for the imperial edict to arrange an official position for me. I decide to write a letter to my lady first, ask the Servant Boy to go home, and tell the lady the good news so that she would not worry about me. Boy, come here. Please take out the four treasures of the study, and I will write a letter home. Please set out with the letter to the He Zhong Prefecture without delay. When you meet the lady, please tell her, 'My master is afraid that my lady will be anxious, so he asked me to send the letter home as soon as possible.' When you get her letter in reply, please send it back to me quickly!"

[Tune of Appreciating Flowers in Company of Fairies] "When we first met, the falling red petals of flowered tints the greenery moss. When we parted with each other, the yellow leaves rustled in the wind condensing the evening haze. Today, I saw plum blossom open. It has been half a year since we parted with each other.

Boy, I exhort you again. Please remember my words. Just tell the lady that I write to her especially." [Exit]

[The Servant Boy says] "After getting the letter, I have to walk to the He Zhong Prefecture under starlight." [Exit]

第一折

（旦引红娘上开云）自张生去京师，不觉半年，杳无音信。这些时神思不快，妆镜懒抬，腰肢瘦损，茜裙宽褪，好烦恼人也呵！

【商调】【集贤宾】虽离了我眼前，却在心上有不甫能离了心上，又早眉头。忘了时依然还又，恶思量无了无休。大都来一寸眉峰，怎当他许多颦皱？新愁近来接著旧愁，厮混了难分新旧。旧愁似太行山隐隐，新愁似天堑水悠悠。

（红云）姐姐往常针尖不倒，其实不曾闲了一个绣床，如今百般的闷倦。往常也曾不快，将息便可，不似这一场，清减得十分利害。

Scene One

[Ying Ying enters with Red Maid. She says] "Since Gentleman Zhang has gone to the capital city, half a year has been passed unknowingly. However, there is no news of him at all. These days, I feel worried and anxious, too lazy to make up and my waist grows too slender to wear my former skirt. How much I am suffering from love sickness now!"

[Tune of Gathering the Sage Together Song] "Though he is out of my eyesight, he is still staying in my heart. I am unable to get rid of his image, so it makes my eyebrows knitted. When I am about to forget him for a moment, he appears in my mind again. If I think of him, the thoughts will be endless. My eyebrows are knitting like a mountain, which keeps frowning all the time. Recently, new worries overlap with the old ones, which mingle together, making me hard to tell which one is old and which one is new. The old sorrows are just like concealed Tai Hang Mountain, and the new ones flow like water in a natural moat."

[Red Maid says] "Sister, usually, you keep needling. You never stay idle on the embroidered bed. However, now you look so lazy and tired. You had been unhappy before, but after taking a nap, you will feel better. You are never like this. After serious illness, you become too slim."[Ying Ying sings]

（旦唱）

【逍遥乐】曾经消瘦，每遍犹闲，这番最陡。

（红云）姐姐心儿闷呵，那里散心耍咱。

（旦唱）

何处忘忧？看时节独上妆楼，手卷珠帘上玉钩，空目断山明水秀。见苍烟迷树，衰草连天，野渡横舟。

（旦云）红娘，我这衣裳，这些时都不似我穿的。（红云）姐姐，正是"腰细不胜衣"。

（旦唱）

【挂金索】裙染榴花，睡损胭脂皱纽结丁香，掩过芙蓉扣线脱珍珠，泪湿香罗袖杨柳眉颦，人比黄花瘦。

（仆人上云）奉相公言语，特将书来与小姐。恰才前厅上见了夫人，夫人好生欢喜，著人来见小姐，早至后堂。（咳嗽科）（红问云）谁在外面？（见科）（红见仆人，红笑云）你几时来？可知道昨夜灯花报，今朝喜鹊噪。姐姐正烦恼哩。你自来？和哥哥来？（仆云）哥哥得了官也，著我寄书来。（红

[Tune of Free Enjoyment Song] "My previous leanness can be recovered, but this time the illness is the most dangerous one."

[Red Maid says] "Sister, if you feel gloomy in your mind, let's go out and have a little fun."

[Ying Ying says] "How could I forget my sorrows? When the same day in the memory arrives, I will climb up the chamber room myself. I roll up the bead door curtain and put it on the jade hook. My empty eyesight watches the picturesque scenery in front of me. I only see the smoke obscuring the trees, the withered grass reaching the sky, and a small boat anchoring the ferry wharf in the wild village."

[Ying Ying says] "Red Maid, these clothes of mine are not like what I wore before."

[Red Maid says] "Sister, this is because your waist is too slim to wear these clothes."

[Tune of Golden Chain Song] "Her dress is dyed with the colour of pomegranate flower. After the broken sleep, the rouge is condensed into lilac flower, covering the tears as if broken pearls, and wetting the fragrant silk sleeves. She herself is thinner than yellow flowers outside."

[The Servant Boy enters] "I follow the order of my master, and send a letter to my lady especially. Just then, I met the old lady in the front hall, and she was so happy for the news. She asked me to call on the young lady in the back hall as soon as possible."

[The Servant Boy coughs out of the door]

云）你则在这里等著，我对俺姐姐说了呵，你进来。（红见旦笑科）（旦云）这小妮子怎么？（红云）姐姐大喜，大喜！咱姐夫得了官也！（旦云）这妮子见我闷呵，特故哄我。（红云）琴童在门首，见了夫人了，使他进来见姐姐，姐夫有书。（旦云）惭愧，我也有盼著他的日头！唤他入来。（仆入见旦科）（旦云）琴

[Red Maid asks] "Who is coughing outside?"

[She opens the door, and meets the Servant Boy] "When do you come? Last night, the candlewick snuffed, and this morning, the magpies chirped to bring good tidings. My sister is feeling worried at the moment. Do you come alone? Where is brother?"

[The Servant Boy says] "My master gets an official position. He asked me to send a letter to the lady."

[Red Maid says] "You can wait for me here. I will talk to my lady. You can come in with me."

[Red Maid smiles at Ying Ying][Ying Ying says] "What happened?"

[Red Maid says] "Sister, Great happiness. Brother-in-law gets a position in the officialdom."

[Ying Ying says] "The dear girl sees me so gloomy, that she deliberately cajoled me!"

[Red Maid says] "If you don't believe me, the Servant Boy is just standing at the door. He has met the old lady. I will ask him to come in, and brother-in-law has a letter for you."

[Ying Ying says] "How shameful I am. I never expect that he would have the made a rise in life. Please call the servant boy in."

[The Servant Boy meets Ying Ying][Ying Ying says] "Boy, when did you leave the capital city?"

[The Servant Boy says] "I have left for more than one month. When I was here, brother was parading on the street."

童,你几时离京师?(仆云)离京一月多也。我来时,哥哥去吃游街棍子去了。(旦云)这禽兽不省得,状元唤做夸官,游街三日。(仆云)夫人说的便是。有书在此。(旦做接书科)

【金菊香】早是我只因他去减了风流,不争你寄得书来又与我添些儿证候。说来的话儿不应口,无语低头,书在手,泪凝眸。(旦开书看科)

【醋葫芦】我这里开时和泪开,他那里修时和泪修,多管阁著笔尖儿未写早泪先流,寄来的书泪点儿兀自有。我将这新痕把旧痕溻透,正是一重愁翻做两重愁。

(旦念书科)"张珙百拜,奉启芳卿可人妆次:自暮秋拜违,倏尔半载。上赖祖宗之荫,下托贤妻之德,举中甲第。即目于招贤馆寄迹,以伺圣旨御笔除授。惟恐夫人与贤妻忧念,特令琴童奉书驰报,庶几免虑。小生身虽遥而心常迩矣,恨不得鹣鹣比翼,邛邛并躯。重功名而薄恩爱

[Ying Ying says] "This amorist always make me remembering with concern. As the Number One Scholar, he acted as a grandiloquent official and paraded on the street for three days for celebrating!"

[The Servant Boy says] "My lady, you are right. Here is a letter for you."

[Ying Ying receives the letter]

[Tune of Golden Chrysanthemum's Fragrance Song] "Before, for his sake, I was sick at heart as lovesickness, but the letter that you sent to me has added once again the symptom of my sickness. I can not express my mind with any words at this moment, so I have nothing to say with lower my head and taking the letter in my hand and being full of tears in my eyes."

[Ying Ying opens the letter]

[Tune of a Gourd of Vinegar Song] "When I open the letter, the tears are dried. When he finished writing the letter, his tears had just stopped shedding. For many times, before he picked up the writing brush, his tears had already overwhelmed his eyes. The letter that he sent to me has the spots of tears. My new tears falls on the old tears on his letter paper. That is to say one sorrow has turned into two."

[Ying Ying reads the letter] "Zhang Gong bows to my lady. I show my greatest respect to my beautiful lady. Since parting with you in the last autumn, it has already been half a year. Thanks to the blessing of my ancestors and the virtue of my great wife, I have won the Number One Scholar in the imperial examination. At the moment, I am staying in the Recruitment Hall and waiting for the

者,诚有浅见贪饕之罪。他日面会,自当请谢不备。后成一绝,以奉清照:玉京仙府探花郎,寄语蒲东窈窕娘。指日拜恩衣昼锦,定须休作倚门妆。"

【幺篇】当日向西厢月底潜,今日向琼林宴上挝。谁承望跳东墙脚步儿占了鳌头?怎想道惜花心养成折桂手?脂粉丛里包藏著锦绣?从今后晚妆楼改做了至公楼!

(旦云)你吃饭不曾?(仆云)上告夫人知道:早晨至今,空立厅前,那有饭吃?(旦云)红娘,你快取饭与他吃。(仆云)感蒙赏赐,我每就此吃饭。夫人写书,哥哥著小人索了夫人回书,至紧,至紧。(旦云)红娘,将笔砚来。(红将来科)(旦云)书却写了,无可表意。只有汗衫一领,裹肚一条,袜

emperor to appoint me an official title. I am afraid that old lady and my virtuous wife will worry about me, so I ask my servant boy to send you a letter and pass the message to ease your worries. Though I am staying far away, my heart is still with you. How I wish we could turn into two legendary birds flying wing to wing or to lie on a small mount side by side. Those who value fame and rank and belittle affectionate love will be guilty of of being shortsighted as well as gluttonous. Some other day when we meet each other, I will show my gratitude to you in person. Here I have composed verses of four lines for you, hoping you could give me some advice. 'The Number One Scholar in the capital city, send a letter to my beautiful lady in Pu Dong Town. Soon I will return with fine array, and you must not lean on the door doing your make-up'."

[Tune of Petty Song] "At that day, I was staying in the western chamber, and hiding under the moonlight. Today, I am attending the scholars' banquet held by the emperor. I didn't expect to be the first man entering her boudoir by jumping over the east wall,nor did I ever think of becoming a lucky one for my cherishing beauty. Is it because the beautiful brocade was hided in cluster of rouge and powder? Since then, the evening dressing room had been turned into our dating room."

[Ying Ying asks] "Have you eaten dinner?"

[The Servant Boy says] "I am telling the lady that from morning till now I am just standing in the hall, with nowhere to have a meal."

[Ying Ying says] "Red Maid, go and get him something to eat as soon as possible."

儿一双，瑶琴一张，玉簪一枚，斑管一枝。琴童，你收拾得好者。红娘，取银十两来，就与他盘缠。(红娘云)姐夫得了官，岂无这几件东西，寄与他有甚缘故？(旦云)你不知道，这汗衫儿呵，

【梧叶儿】他若是和衣卧，便是和我一处宿但，粘著他皮肉，不信不想我温柔。

(红云)这裹肚要怎么？
(旦唱)

常则不要离了前后，守著他左右，紧紧的系在心头。

[The Servant Boy says] "Thanks for lady's care. I will eat here. Lady, please write a letter, and brother asks me to take it back to him as soon as possible."

[Ying Ying says] "Red Maid, please bring me my writing brush and ink-slab."

[Red Maid comes with the writing brush and the ink-slab][Ying Ying says] "When I am about to write, I find no words to express my feelings. I have only one undershirt, one bellyband, a pair of stockings, one ancient zither, one jade hairpin and one writing brush to send to him. Servant Boy, please take these things carefully. Red Maid, please give him ten taels of silver as travelling expenses."

[Red Maid says] "Since brother in law gets a postition in the officialdom, doesn't he have these things in his residence? Why should you send him these things for?"

[Ying Ying says] "You don't know. This undershirt—"

[Tune of Plane Leaves Song] "If he sleeps with this undershirt, he is sleeping just like with me together now. It clings to his skin and flesh. I just wonder if he will forget my gentleness."

[Red Maid asks] "How about the bellyband?"

[Ying Ying sings]

"He will always wear it on his body, as if I am following him by his side. He has deeply twined by me in his mind."

(红云)这袜儿如何?

(旦唱)拘管他胡行乱走。

(红云)这琴他那里自有,又将去怎么?(旦唱)

【后庭花】当日五言诗紧趁逐,后来因七弦琴成配偶。他怎肯冷落了诗中意,我则怕生疏了弦上手。(红云)玉簪呵,有甚主意?

(旦唱)我须有个缘由,他如今功名成就,则怕他撇人在脑背后。

(红云)斑管,要怎的?

(旦唱)湘江两岸秋,当日娥皇因虞舜愁,今日莺莺为君瑞忧。这九嶷山下竹,共香罗衫袖口——

[Red Maid says] "How about these stockings?"

[Ying Ying says] "To restrain him from going astray."

[Red Maid says] "He has a ancient zither in his baggage. Why do you send him one again?"

[Ying Ying sings]

[Tune of Backyard Flowers Song] "At that night, I followed his rhythm and made a verse with five characters in each line, however, I had to leave quickly. Later, after hearing his ancient zither music, I finally understand his feelings, and became deeply attached to him. How could he neglect the meaning of the verses and become unfamiliar with ancient zither music?"

[Red Maid asks] "How about the jade hairpin?"

[Ying Ying says] "I have a reason. Now, since he has achieved success and won fame, I am afraid that he will forsake me behind."

[Red Maid asks] "What about the writing brush?"

[Ying Ying sings] "One day in autumn, at both banks of Xiang Jiang bank, Empress E Huang shed tears for the death of her husband Shun. Today, I feel the same sorrow for my husband Zhang. The writing brush's holder is made of bamboo from Jiu Yi Mountain. It left the ink's sweetness on both our sleeves."

【青哥儿】都一般啼痕浥透。似这等泪斑宛然依旧,万古情缘一样愁。涕泪交流,怨慕难收。对学士叮咛说缘由,是必休忘旧。

(旦云)琴童,这东西收拾好者。(仆云)理会得。(旦唱)

【醋葫芦】你逐宵野店上宿,休将包袱做枕头,怕油脂腻展污了恐难酬。倘或水浸雨湿休便扭,我则怕干时节熨不开褶皱。一桩桩一件件细收留。

【金菊花】书封雁足此时修,情系人心早晚休?长安望来天际头,倚遍西楼,人不见,水空流。

(仆云)小人拜辞,即便去也。(旦云)琴童,你见官人对他说。(仆云)说甚么?

[Tune of Blue Song] " Same as Empress Er Huang, Ying Ying would wet her tears sleeves with her tears. The tear stains today are still the same as those long ago trees. All romance relationships through the ages share sorrows alike. Tears and mucus flow down together and missing and love mingle in the mind too. I must urge my scholar again and again, telling him the reason why he should not forget his former lover."

[Ying Ying says] "Servant Boy, please take care of these things."

[The Servant Boy says] "Take it easy. I can handle it."

[Ying Ying sings]

[Tune of a Gourd of Vinegar Song] "If you take rest in cottages in wild places, don't take the package as your pillow, in case you will make it dirty and greasy. If it is soaked in water, don't rinse, in case the crease cannot be removed when it is dried. You should pack these things one by one."

[Tune of Golden Chrysanthemum's Fragrance Song] "I hope the letter will be sent by a crane flying in the sky, so that the love expressed will reach Scholar Zhang's hands quickly. Chang An is as far as the end of the horizon. Standing on the western chamber, I can see no one, and only leave the water flowing in vain."

[The Servant Boy says] "My lady, I will leave now."

[Ying Ying says] "When you meet my husband, please tell him."

[The Servant Boy asks] "What should I tell him?"

(旦唱)

【浪里来煞】他那里为我愁,我这里因他瘦。临行时啜赚人的巧舌头:指归期约定九月九,不觉的过了小春时候。到如今悔教夫婿觅封侯。

(仆云)得了回书,星夜回俺哥哥话去。(下)

第二折

(末上云)画虎未成君莫笑,安排牙爪始惊人。本是举过便除,奉圣旨,著翰林院编修国史。他每那知我的心,甚么文章做得成!使琴童递佳音,不见回来。这几日睡卧不宁,饮食少进,给假在驿亭中将息。早间太医院著人来看视,下药去了。我这病,卢扁也医不得。自离了小姐,无一日心闲也呵!

[Tune of Rolling Waves Song] "He feels sorrows for me over there, and I am getting thinner for him here. On the day when we parted with each other, he lied to me: He would come back on Ninth of September in lunar calender. Unknowingly, it has already passed October. Now, I deeply regret for allowing my husband to seek fame and honor."

[The Servant Boy says] "Got it. I am leaving to answer my brother at the starry night. [Exeunt]

Scene Two

[Zhong Gong enters] "Don't laugh at a person who intends to paint a tiger but doesn't finish. When he starts to draw the tiger's pawns and teeth, people begin to show surprise. I had thought after that becoming Number One Scholar in the imperial exam, I would be appointed to a position in the officialism. However, getting the imperial edict, I was asked to compile the history of dynasty as a member of the Imperial Academy. How His Majesty knows what I am thinking in my heart? How am I able to do the job well? I asked the Servant Boy to send the good message for me, but I haven't seen him back. These days, I cannot sleep well or eat well, so I ask for a sick leave and take a rest in the cottage. In the morning, the imperial physician came and prescribed some medicine for me. This sickness of mine can not be cured even by Bian Que, a famous physician in ancient times. Since leaving my lady, there is not a day of leisure."

【中吕】【粉蝶儿】从到京师,思量心旦夕如是,向心头横躺著俺那莺儿。请医师,看诊罢,一星星说是。本意待推辞,则被他察虚实不须看视。

【醉春风】他道是医杂证有方术,治相思无药饵。莺莺,你若是知我害相思,我甘心儿死、死。四海无家,一身客寄,半年将至。

(仆上云)我则道哥哥除了,元来在驿亭中抱病。须索回书去咱。(见了科)(末云)你回来了也。

【迎仙客】疑怪这噪花枝灵鹊儿,垂帘幕喜蛛儿,正应著短檠上夜来灯爆时。若不是断肠词,决定是断肠诗。

[Tune of Pink Butterflies Song] "Since arriving at the capital city, I have been constantly missing my lady from morning to evening. There is always beautiful Ying Ying in my mind. When the imperial physician came, he talked about my symptom, and everything he said was right. I intended to reject his coming, but he had already seen through my plight and said that I needed no further treatment."

[Tune of Intoxicating to the Spring Wind Song] "He said there is always a way to cure miscellaneous diseases, but no remedy for love sickness. Ying Ying, if you could know how I suffer from love sickness, I would rather die for you, die for you. There is no home for me anywhere in the four seas, and I am a lonely lodging guest here. This situation has remained for almost half a year."

[The Servant Boy says] "I have known my brother has accepted the official position. Now he is resting in the cottage after getting a sick leave. I should have to respond to him as soon as possible."

[The Servant Boy meets Zhang Gong][Zhang Gong says] "You have come back."

[Tune of Waiting for the Immortals Song] "I have seen the magpie climbing up the branches of flowers, and an auspicious spider appearing on the falling curtains. There is a burst of light when the lamp first lighted at night. These must bring good tidings. If what the lady wrote is not a heartbroken poem, it must be a heartbroken song."

（仆云）小夫人有书至此。（末接科）

写时管情泪如丝。既不呵，怎生泪点儿封皮上渍？

（末读书科）"薄命妾崔氏拜覆，敬奉才郎君瑞文几：自音容去后，不觉许时，仰敬之心，未尝少怠。纵云日近长安远，何故鳞鸿之杳矣？莫因花柳之心，弃妾恩情之意。正念间，琴童至，得见翰墨，始知中科，使妾喜之如狂。郎之才望，亦不辱相国之家谱也。今因琴童回，无以奉贡，聊有瑶琴一张，玉簪一枚，斑管一枝，裹肚一条，汗衫一领，袜儿一双，权表妾之真诚。匆匆草字欠恭，伏乞情恕不备。谨依来韵，遂继一绝云：阑干倚遍盼才郎，莫恋宸京黄四娘。病里得书知中甲，窗前览镜试新妆。"那风风流流的姐姐！似这等女子，张珙死也死得著了。

[The Servant Boy says] "Lady has a letter for you." [Zhang Gong receives the letter]

"When I wrote the letter, my love sickness makes my tears fall down like silk. If not, why does it stain the cover paper?"

[Zhang Gong continues reading the paper] "'Unlucky woman Cui Ying Ying bows to the talented man Zhang Jun Rui: Since parting with you, time has passed very slowly. My respect towards you doesn't wane through the time. I am looking in the direction of Chang An, which is so far away. Why there is no letter from you? Please do not wander among the streets of ill reputes in the capital city, and forget my love towards you. When I was just thinking of you, the servant boy came in. When I saw your letter, I finally got the news that you have become Number One Scholar in the imperial examination. I am too happy to be crazy. My husband's talent doesn't bring shame to the family tree of the Prime Minister. I asked the servant boy to go back. There is nothing to offer you, but one ancient zither, one jade hairpin, one writing brush, one bellyband, one undershirt and pair of stockings to express my sincerity of love. If the letter is short, please forgive me for my inconsideration. Just following your rhythm in the poem you sent to me, I have composed a verse of same style for you too: I am leaning on the banisters and waiting for the talented young man, please never cling to Lady Huang Si in the capital city. I got the news that you have become the Number One scholar when I was sick, so I start to remake up in front of the mirror.' My amorous and beyond comparison lady, Zhang Gong is willing to die for you!"

【上小楼】这的堪为字史,当为款识,有柳骨颜筋,张旭张芝,羲之献之。此一时,彼一时,佳人才思,俺莺莺世间无二。

【幺篇】俺做经咒般持,符箓般使。高似金章,重似金帛,贵似金赏。这上面若佥个押字,使个令史,差个勾使,则是一张忙不及印赴期的咨示。

(末拿汗衫儿科)休说文章,则看他这针黹,人间少有。

【满庭芳】怎不教张生爱尔,堪针工出色,女教为师。几千般用意针针是,可索寻思。长共短又没个样子,窄和宽想象著腰肢,好共歹无人试。想当初做时,用煞那小心儿。

小姐寄来这几件东西,都有缘故,一件件我都猜著。

【白鹤子】这琴,他教我闭门学禁指,留意谱声诗。调养圣贤心,洗荡巢由耳。

[Tune of Ascending Attic Song] "Her handwriting is like a calligraphist which can be inscribed on the implement. It resembles the writing techniques of top calligraphists such as Liu Gongquan, Yan Zhenqing. It also shows the charms seen in the calligraphic works of Zhang Xu and Zhang Zhi as well as those of Wang Xizhi and his son Wang Xianzhi. Circumstances change with the time, but the sharp wit of Ying Ying is peerless in the world."

[Tune of Petty Song] "I will treat her letter as a scripture or incantation, and use it as as magic a figure drawn by a Taoist monk. They are as high-valued as a gold seal of the officialdom, as heavy as golden silks, and as expensive as gold treasures. If having an official signature on it, and sending a courier with it to a receiving officer, it will turn to be an official document needing immediate dealing with."

[Zhang Gong takes out the undershirt and says] "Setting aside the hand writings, just look at her needleworks, it is rare in this world."

[Tune of Courtyard Full of Fragrance Song] "How could you make me not love you? You are so good at needleworks that you can teach other women as a master. Every stitch and thread is entrusted with your feelings, and full of your kisses, which are unforgettable for a long time. You did not have my size or model to decide whether it is too long or too short, all you had to do was just to estimate my waistline. Fit or not, you could not have me to try it in place. I could imagine that she had put all her heart on doing it."

[Tune of White Crane Song] "About this ancient zither, she asks me to play ancient zither music within the door. She reminds me to pay attention to the music and poetry, to build up a sage's heart, and keep my ears refined."

【二】这玉簪，纤长如竹笋，细白似葱枝，温润有清香，莹洁无瑕毗。

【三】这斑管，霜枝曾栖凤凰，泪点渍胭脂：当时舜帝恸娥皇，今日淑女思君子。

【四】这裹肚，手中一叶绵，灯下几回丝，表出腹中愁，果称心间事。

【五】这鞋袜儿，针脚儿细似虮子，绢帛儿腻似鹅脂，既知礼不胡行，愿足下当如此。

琴童，你临行，小夫人对你说什么？（仆云）著哥哥休别继良姻。（末云）小姐，你尚然不知我的心哩！

【快活三】冷清清客店儿，风淅淅雨丝丝，雨儿零风儿细梦回时，多少伤心事！

[Tune of Second Stanza] "The jade hairpin is as long as bamboo shoots and as white as shallots. It is mild and fragrant, clean and without flaws."

[Tune of Third Stanza] "The holder of this writing brush was a frosted bamboo branch on which a phoenix had once perched, and her tears had steeped the rouge. When Emperor Shun died, Empress E Huang was grief stricken. Today, my lovely lady misses me in the same way."

[Tune of Four Stanza] "This bellyband was made out of a piece of cotton cloth in her hands,thread by thread,she did it hard at night under the lamp,only to express her love sickness in the heart."

[Tune of Five Stanza] "About this pair of stockings, its line of stitches is as thin as a louse, and the cloth is as soft as the fat of a goose. She hopes me to know the manner, and restrains me from going astray."

Servant Boy, when you was leaving, what did lady say to you?"

[The Servant Boy says] "She asked me to tell brother not to marry another one."

[Zhang Gong says] "Lady, you still don't know my heart."

[Tune of Happiness Three Song] "I can never forget the cold and lonely cottage in the village, when it blows hard with rain falling down heavy . Many times in my dream, I dream of you, which reminded me of how many heartbroken things happened before!"

【朝天子】四肢不能动止,急切里盼不到普救寺。小夫人须是你见时,别有甚闲传示?我是个浪子官人,风流学士,怎肯带残花折旧枝。自从、到此,甚的是闲街市。

【贺圣朝】少甚宰相人家,招婿的娇姿?其间或有个人儿似尔,那里取那温柔,这般才思?想莺莺意儿,怎不教人梦想眠思。

琴童来,将这衣裳东西收拾好者。

【耍孩儿】则在书房中倾倒个藤箱子,向箱子里面铺几张纸。放时节须索用心思,休教藤刺儿抓住绵丝。高抬在衣架上怕吹了颜色,乱穰在包袱中恐刬了褶儿。当如此,切须爱护,勿得因而。

【二煞】恰新婚才燕尔,为功名来到此。长安忆念蒲东寺。昨宵爱春风桃李花开夜,今日愁秋雨

[Tune of Homage to the Emperor Song] "I can't control my hands and feet. I am so worried that I want to go back to Pu Jiu Monastery as soon as possible. My lady, when you see me, what are you going to say to me? You should have thought that I am an official and a libertine, as well as a romantic talented scholar, how can I have many love affairs? It's not like this. There is no need to walk astray on the street."

[Tune of Congratulation to the Imperial Court Song] "Are there charming daughters at the home of the current Prime Minister? The answer is yes! However, among them, who can have such tenderness and talent as you? Pondering Ying Ying's meaning, I cannot help dreaming of her at night."

Servant Boy, please pack the clothes and other things properly."

[Tune of Playing with the Child Song] "Please be hurry to empty the rattan box and put several papers inside first. When you put these clothes into the box, please take good care of it, not to let the rattan to collide or tangle the cotton silk thread. If put the clothes on the high hanger, I am afraid that the wind would blow away the colors. If put them leisurely in the package, I am afraid they will be creased. You must take good care of these clothes, and do as I tell."

[Tune of Two stanza] "I Just enjoyed a newly married life, but for the sake of fame, I arrive here. When I am in Chang An City, my dream is still in the Pu Jiu Monastery. Last night, I appreciated peach and plum blossoming in the blow of the spring wind, and tonight I am feeling sorrow for leaves of phoenix trees falling down

梧桐叶落时。愁如是，身遥心迩，坐想行思。

【三煞】这天高地厚情，直到海枯石烂时。此时作念何时止，直到烛灰眼下才无泪，蚕老心中罢却丝。我不比游荡轻薄子，轻夫妇的琴瑟，拆鸾凤的雄雌。

【四煞】不闻黄犬音，难传红叶诗，驿长不遇梅花使。孤身去国三千里，一日归心十二时。凭栏视，听江声浩荡，看山色参差。

【尾】忧则忧我在病中，喜则喜你来到此。投至得引人魂卓氏音书至，险将这害鬼病的相如盼望死。（下）

in the shower of autumn rain. I am so sorrowful that my body is here and my mind is far away. When I sit or stand, I think of you all the time."

[Tune of Three Stanza] "This love is higher than the sky, and deeper than the sea. It will last till the ocean is dried and the stone is broken. I don't know when I can stop thinking of you. The candle is shedding tears until it is burnt out. The silkworm cannot make silk until it is dead. I am not a flimsy and fickle young man. I value the harmony relations between husband and wife, and hate the separation of a pair of phoenix birds."

[Tune of Four Stanza] "Not hearing the barking of yellow dog, I find no one coming. It is difficult to pass the lover's verses in the autumn. I want to walk three thousand miles alone, wishing to arrive home in twelve hours of a day. Leaning on the banister, I hear the mighty sound of waves in the lake, and gaze at the different heights of mountains far away.

[Tune of Epilogue Song] "What worries me is that I am still in the sickness. However, I feel happy to receive your letter. Thanks to this servant boy who sends me letter here, otherwise, I will die for love sickness."[Exit]

第三折

（净扮郑恒上开云）自家姓郑，名恒，字伯常。先人拜礼部尚书，不幸早丧。后数年，又丧母。先人在时，曾定下俺姑娘的女孩儿莺莺为妻，不想姑夫亡化，莺莺孝服未满，不曾成亲。俺姑娘将著这灵榇，引著莺莺，回博陵下葬。为因路阻，不能得去。数月前写书来，唤我同扶柩去。因家中无人，来得迟了。我离京师，来到河中府，打听得孙飞虎欲掳莺莺为妻，得一个张君瑞退了贼兵。俺姑娘许了他。我如今到这里，没这个消息便好去见他。既有这个消息，我便撞将去呵，没意思。这一件事，都在红娘身上。我著人

Scene Three

[Zheng Heng enters and says] "My family name is Zheng, given name is Heng, and nickname is Bo Chang. My father was in the position of General Secretary of the Department of Rites, however he died earlier. After a few years, my mother died too. When my father was alive, he made an engagement between me and my aunt's daughter Ying Ying, however, my uncle died suddenly, so Ying Ying was still wearing mourning dresses. Our marriage has been delayed. My aunt has carried the coffin with Ying Ying, planning to bury it in Bo Ling. As the road is full of twists, she cannot go there, but stop on the way. Several months ago, they wrote to me and asked me to come to them and help to carry the coffin. As there was nobody at home, I arrived here late. When I departed from the capital city, and arrived at He Zhong Prefecture, I heard of the story that a rebel Sun Feihu had intended to kidnap Ying Ying as his wife, but he was withdrawn by a man called Zhang Junrui. My aunt engaged Ying Ying to him. Since I am here already, I will find out whether there is such a news. If it is not true, I am going to meet Ying Ying; if it is true, even though I rashly go to meet her, it is not interesting. This marriage is all up to Red Maid. I have sent someone for Red Maid. I will ask 'I come from the capital and dare not to visit my aunt without permissions. So I ask sister to come to my place, and consult you for some issues.' It has been for a long time, but she hasn't come back yet. Ying Ying must have something to urge her."

[Red Maid enters and says] "Brother Zheng Heng has arrived. He

去唤他，则说："哥哥从京师来，不敢来见姑娘，著红娘来下处来，有话去对姑娘行说去。"去的人好一会了，不见来。见姑娘和他有话说。（红上云）郑恒哥哥在下处，不来见夫人，却唤我说话。夫人著我来，看他说甚么。（见净科）哥哥万福。夫人道："哥哥来到呵，怎么不来家里来？"（净云）我有甚颜色见姑娘？我唤你来的缘故是怎生？当日姑夫在时，曾许下这门亲事。我今番到这里，姑夫孝已满了，特地央及你去夫人行说知，拣一个吉日，了这件事，好和小姐一答里下葬去。不争不成合，一答里路上难厮见。若说得肯呵，我重重的相谢你。（红云）这一节话再也休题。莺莺已与了别人了也。（净云）道不得"一马不跨双鞍"！可怎生父在时曾许了我，父丧之后母倒悔亲？这个道理那里有！（红云）却非如此说。当日孙飞虎将半万贼兵来时，哥哥你在那里？若不是那生呵，那里得俺一家儿来？今日太平无事，却来争亲。倘

doesn't come to visit the old lady, but call me here. My old lady asked me to come, to see what he is going to say."

[Red Maid meets Zheng Heng] "Long live happiness, brother Zheng. My old lady let me ask you 'since you have come, why don't you go to see her?'"

[Zheng Heng says] "I have no face to meet Ying Ying. Why do I call you? When uncle was alive, he had made an engagement between me and Ying Ying. Today I have arrived here, and the duration of Ying Ying's mourning time is terminated, so I ask you to request my aunt, to choose a lucky day and marry Ying Ying to me, so that I am able to bury my uncle's coffin with Ying Ying. If our union is postponed, it will be inconvenient for me to meet Ying Ying. The trip is so long that it is difficult for me to send the message. If you can pass the message to my aunt, I should have thanked you heavily."

[Red Maid says] "Never mention these words any more. Ying Ying has engaged with other gentleman."

[Zheng Heng says] "There is an old saying that two saddlers can not be put on the back of one horse! My uncle agree to such a marriage when he was alive, but after he died, why did my aunt regretted this marriage! What kind of reason it is!"

[Red Maid says] "It is not like this. Please listen to my explanation. When Sun Feihu led five thousand rebels to besiege the monastery, where is brother? If not that Gentleman Zhang to withdraw the rebels, how are our family able to survive? These days, we live in peace, but brother you come to fight for the marriage. If my lady was captured by the rebels, how are you going to fight with him?"

被贼人掳去呵,哥哥如何去争?(净云)与了一个富家,也不枉了,却与了这个穷酸饿醋,偏我不如他?我仁者能仁、身里出身的根脚,又是亲上做亲,况兼他父命。(红云)他到不如你?噤声!

【越调】【斗鹌鹑】卖弄你仁者能仁,倚仗你身里出身。至如你官上加官,也不合亲上做亲。又不曾执羔雁邀媒,献币帛问肯。恰洗了尘,便待要过门。枉腌了他金屋银屏,枉污了他锦衾绣裀。

【紫花儿序】枉蠢了他梳云掠月,枉羞了他惜玉怜香,枉村了他殢雨尤云。当日三才判,两仪初分乾坤,清者为乾,浊者为坤,人在中间相混。君瑞是君子清贤,郑恒是小人浊民。

(净云)贼来,怎地他一个人退得?都是胡说!

[Zheng Heng says] "If Ying Ying is married to a rich family, it is fair. However, she is married to a poor scholar. Why am I not as good as him? I am kind and born well. Moreover, it will cement our relative ties by marriage by her father's order."

[Red Maid says] "Why is he not as good as you? Please listen to me!"

[Tune of Fighting the Quail Song] "You are showing off that you are kind and well born. However, even if you are promoted many a time, you are still not fit for the marriage. When did you come to invite a match maker with heavy gifts and propose for the marriage? When did you send us betrothal gifts to ask whether Ying Ying is willing to marry you or not. You just arrived, and said that you want to marry Ying Ying. If so, it will wrong his gold house and silver screen; stain his silk quilt and embroidered bundle."

[Tune of Violet Flower Song] "You will wrong his ability of combing clouds and flying over the moon as stupid. You will wrongly humiliate his cherishing beauty. You will mistake his worries about rain and clouds as a fuss. Three Basic Factors appeared when the world was divided into heaven and earth, heaven was clear and earth was muddy, and human beings are in the middle. Among them, Jun Rui is an upright gentleman as if in heaven, and Zheng Heng is just a base person on earth."

[Zheng Heng says] "How is he able to withdraw the rebels himself? That is totally nonsense."

（红云）我对你说。

【天净沙】把河桥飞虎将军，叛蒲东掳掠人民，半万贼屯合寺门，手横著霜刃，高叫道要莺莺做压寨夫人。

（净云）半万贼，他一个人济甚么事？（红云）贼围之甚迫，夫人慌了，和长老商议，拍手高叫："两廊不问僧俗，如退得贼兵的，便将莺莺与他为妻。"忽有游客张生，应声而前曰："我有退兵之策，何不问我？"夫人大喜，就问其计何在。生云："我有一故人白马将军，见统十万之众，镇守蒲关。我修书一封，著人寄去，必来救我。"不想书至兵来，其困即解。

[Red Maid says] "You are wrong."

[Tune of Clear Sand over the Sky Tune] "General Sun Feihu guarding the Pu River Bridge rebelled against Pu Dong Town and plundered the people. His five thousand rebelling soldiers besieged the monastery with five thousand rebelling soldiers, holding swords and sabres in their hands, shouting loudly to demand Ying Ying to be the wife of the him soldiers."

[Zheng Heng says] "What can he do with five thousand rebelling soldiers alone?"

[Red Maid says] "When the rebelling soldiers was besieging the monastery, the old lady was deeply troubled. So she discussed with the abbot in the monastery and called out loudly, 'People standing in the long corridor, whether you are monks or oridnary people, I will marry Ying Ying to the one who is able to withdraw the rebelling soldiers.' At this moment, there was a traveler called Zhang Gong coming in front. He said, 'I have a plan to withdraw the rebels, why doesn't the old lady ask me?' The old lady was very happy and asked what the plan was. Gentleman Zhang said, 'I have an old friend, who is called White Horse General. He is leading one hundred thousand soldiers, and guarding the Pu Pass. I will write a letter to him, and ask him to come here. When the letter arrives, he is sure to come and save me.' No one expected when the letter arrived, the soldiers indeed came too, so they rescued us from the besiege."

[Tune of Red Peach Blossom Song] "The talented scholar of West

【小桃红】洛阳才子善属文,火急修书信。白马将军到时分,灭了烟尘。夫人小姐都心顺,则为他威而不猛,言而有信,因此上不敢慢于人。

(净云)我自来未尝闻其名,知他会也不会!你这个小妮子,卖弄他偌多!(红云)便又骂我!

【金蕉叶】他凭著讲性理《齐论》《鲁论》,作词赋韩文柳文,他识道理为人敬人,俺家里有信行知恩报恩。

【调笑令】你值一分,他值百十分,萤火焉能比月轮?高低远近都休论,我拆白道字辩与你个清浑。

(净云)这小妮子省得甚么拆白道字?你拆与我听。(红唱)君瑞是个"肖"字这壁著个"立人",你是个"木寸"、"马户"、"尸巾"。

Luo City is good at composing articles. He hurried to write a letter to the general. The general on the White Horse arrived in time, and withdrew the rebels. Both the old lady and the young lady were greatly relieved, for Gentleman Zhang is mighty but not fierce, and as good as his words, so we dare not show indifference to him."

[Zheng Heng says] "I never heard of him. I don't believe what you said. Your little bitch, you are just boasting him off!"

[Red Maid says] "Here you are!"

[Tune of Golden Banana Leaves Song] "He talked about human relationships and classic knowledge with a sense, or making verses like famous poets Han Yu and Liu Zongyuan in the ancient time. He is sensible, who treats others with respects. Our family keeps promises to return his favor for good."

[Tune of Song of Flirtation] "You are worthy of one penny, and he is worthy of hundreds of pennies. How can a firefly be compared with the moonlight? I will not argue with you who is noble and who is base, I will just predict your fortunes by analysing the component parts of Chinese characters of your names."

[Zheng Heng says] "Your little bitch, how are you going to analyse the components parts of Chinese characters of our names? I am listening."

[Red Maid says] "His given Jun Rui are composed of two characters: one is 'similar' and the other is a 'standing human being', if put together, the meaning is 'smart'. Yours are composed of a piece of wood, the household that keeps official horses as servitude, and

343

（净云）木寸、马户、尸巾,你道我是个"村驴
屌"?我祖代是相国之门,倒不如你个白衣饿夫
穷士?做官的则是做官!

（红唱）

【秃厮儿】他凭师友君子务本,你倚父兄仗势欺
人。齑盐日月不嫌贫,治百姓新民、传闻。

【圣药王】这厮乔议论,有向顺。你道是官人则
合做官人,信口喷,不本分。你道穷民到老是穷
民,却不道"将相出寒门"!

（净云）这桩事,都是那长老秃驴弟子孩儿,
我明日慢慢的和他说话。

（红唱）

【麻郎儿】他出家儿慈悲为本,方便为门。横死
眼不识好人,招祸口不知分寸。

the body scarf."

[Zheng Heng says] "A piece of wood, the household that keeps official horses as servitude, and the body scarf. Are you calling me a donkey in the village? I was born in the family of the former prime minister in the dynasty. How am I not as good as that commoner without a rank who is a hungry man and poor scholar? The man in the official position should be respected for his position!"

[Red Maid sings]

[Tune of Bold Head Song] "He is a gentleman doing his duty who depends on his teachers and friends, while you are bullying others because of titles of your brothers and father. Gentleman Zhang does not complain of being poor, while he governs people, he is famous for his celebrity."

[Tune of Sovereign Medicine Song] "This man keeps arguing and has prejudices. You are saying that only official family can keep on the position of officialdom. You are wagging your tongue too freely, not content with your lot. What you meant is that the poor man will live poor forever. But your never know that a lot of prime ministers and generals come out of poor family."

[Zheng Heng says] "It must be the bold ass—that abbot who allows the affair happen. Tomorrow, I will lesson to him slowly."

[Red Maid sings]

[Tune of Pocked Face Song] "The abbot has shown mercy and convenience for others. I hate those who doesn't judge good people

（净云）这是姑夫的遗留，我拣日，牵羊担酒，上门去，看姑娘怎么发落我！

（红唱）

【幺篇】讪筋，发村，使狠，甚的是软款温存。硬打捱强为眷姻，不睹事强谐秦晋。

（净云）姑娘若不肯，著二三十个伴僧，抬上轿子，到下处脱了衣裳，赶将来，还你一个婆娘！

（红唱）

【络丝娘】你须是郑相国嫡亲的舍人，须不是孙飞虎家生的莽军。乔嘴脸、腌躯老、死身份，少不得有家难奔。

（净云）兀的那小妮子，眼见得受了招安了也。我也不对你说，明日我要娶，我要娶！（红云）不嫁你，不嫁你！

from bad. If you meet trouble for your unkind words, don't blame that I have reminded you before."

[Zheng Heng says] "The engagement is the dying words of my uncle. I will choose a lucky day, take the sheep and carry wine, and propose for the marriage. I will see how Ying Ying is going to deal with me?"

[Red Maid sings]

[Tune of Petty Song] "Vexed and angry, if you act ruthlessly, you cannot win her tenderness. Even if Ying Ying is forced to the marriage, you are not going to live in a harmony."

[Zheng Heng says] "If Ying Ying is not willing to marry me, I will get twenty or thirty monks to carry her into the sedan chair. The moment she gets off the sedan chair, I will take off her clothes. And then, I will return you a married woman."

[Red Maid sings]

[Tune of Spinner Song] "You are the son of honorable former prime minister Zheng, not one of the rebels like Sun Feihu. You have an ugly face, an old body and a dead official position. You are sure to roam without a home in the future."

[Zheng Heng says] "This little bitch, she must have been bewitched by that commoner. I will not talk to you any more. Tomorrow, I will marry Ying Ying, marry Ying Ying."

[Red Maid says] "She is not going to marry you. Not going to marry you!'

【收尾】佳人有意郎君俊，我待不喝采其实怎忍。

（净云）你喝一声我听。（红笑云）你这般颓嘴脸，则好偷韩寿下风头香，傅何郎左壁厢粉。（下）（净脱衣科云）这妮子拟定都和那酸丁演撒！我明日自上门去见俺姑娘，则做不知。我则道："张生赘在卫尚书家，做了女婿。"俺姑娘最听是非，他自小又爱我，必有话说。休说别个，则这一套衣服也冲动他。自小京师同住，惯会寻章摘句。姑夫许我成亲，谁敢将言相拒？我若放起刁来，且看莺莺那去！且将压善欺良意，权作尤云殢雨心。（下）（夫人上云）夜来郑恒至，不来见我，唤红娘去

[Tune of Epilogue Song] "The beautiful lady has amorous love towards that handsome gentleman. I cannot wait for applauding to them."

[Zheng Heng says] "Dare you applaud for once?"

[Red Maid laughs] "With this ugly face of yours, you can never marry a beautiful girl but pick up those who were thrown away by both handsome gentlemen Han Shou and He Yan."[Exit]

[Zheng Heng takes off clothes and says] "This bitch must have flirted with that poor scholar. Tomorrow, I will visit my girl, pretending not to know anything. I just said, 'Gentleman Zhang has become son-in-law of Minister Wei's family.' My girl is always suspicious of these things, and she liked me since she was a child. She must have something to say when she heard that. Not to mention other things, just for the splendid attire, I am sure to marry her. We lived together in the capital city since we were children, and used to write in cliches. Uncle has made an engagement between us. If I insist, who dare to be against? Everything I do is for Ying Ying' sake.[Exit]

[The Old Lady enters and says] "Last night, Zheng Heng arrived. He doesn't meet me, but inquire Red Maid for the marriage. I agree with Ying Ying's marriage with Zheng Heng whole-heartedly, not to mention the engagement was promised by my husband. I am acting against my husband's will. As the manager of the household, I am not a proper one. Ying Ying and Zhang Gong has

问亲事。据我的心,则是与孩儿是况兼相国在时已许下了。我便是违了先夫的言语。做我一个主家的不著,这厮每做下来。拟定则与郑恒,他有言语,怪他不得也。料持下酒者,今日他敢来见我也。(净上云)来到也,不索报覆,自入去见夫人。(拜夫人哭科)(夫人云)孩儿,既来到这里,怎么不来见我?(净云)小孩儿有甚嘴脸来见姑娘!(夫人云)莺莺为孙飞虎一节,等你不来,无可解危,许张生也。(净云)那个张生?敢便是状元?我在京师看榜来,年纪有二十四五岁,洛阳张珙,夸官游街三日。第二日,头答正来到卫尚书家门首,尚

made a secret wedding. Ying Ying broke off the engagement with Zheng Heng first, so if he has some complaints, I can not blame him. Please prepare the feast for Zheng Heng. I believe that he will visit me today." [Zheng Heng enters] "I am coming. There is no need to report to my aunt beforehand. I am going to visit her myself."

[Zheng Heng kneels down to the old lady, and bursts out crying] [The Old Lady says] "My nephew, since you have arrived, why didn't you come to see me?" [Zheng Heng says] "How did I have face to meet my girl!"

[The Old Lady says] "Because of the incident aroused by Sun Feihu, we were waiting for you in vain, when I had no way to put off the pressing danger, I asked help from Gentleman Zhang and married Ying Ying to Gentleman Zhang." [Zheng Heng says] "Who is this Gentleman Zhang? Is he the Number One Scholar? When I was in the capital city, I had read the imperial notice of announcement. There is a gentleman Zhang called Zhang Gong, from Luo Yang City. He was parading on the street with music for three days. On the second day, he arrived at Minister Wei's family gate. The daughter of Minister Wei's family is about eighteen years old. She was standing on the decorated balcony and throwing an embroidered ball onto the street. That ball just hit him. I was riding the horse there at that moment, that ball nearly hit me too. Minister Wei asked more than ten maids to drag Gentleman Zhang into the gate of his house. Gentleman Zhang was shouting, 'I already have a wife. I am the son-in-law of former prime minister Cui's family.' That Minister Wei was so powerful that he didn't listen to Gentleman Zhang, who was forced to the marriage. To be honest, Gentleman Zhang had no other choice. Minister Wei said, 'My

书的小姐十八岁也,结著彩楼,在那御街上,则一球正打著他。我也骑著马看,险些打著我。他家粗使梅香十馀人,把那张生横拖倒拽入去。他口叫道:"我自有妻,我是崔相国家女婿!"那尚书有权势气象,那里听?则管拖将入去了。这个却才便是他本分,出于无奈。尚书说道:"我女奉圣旨,结彩楼,你著崔小姐做次妻。他是先奸后娶的,不应取他。"闹动京师,因此认得他。(夫人怒云)我道这秀才不中抬举,今日果然负了俺家。俺相国之家,世无与人做次妻之理。既然张生奉圣旨娶了妻,孩儿,你拣个吉日良辰,依著姑夫的言语,依旧入来做女婿者(净云)倘或张生有言语,怎生?(夫人云)放著我哩。明日拣个吉日良辰,你便过门来。(下)(净云)中了我的计策了。准备筵席茶礼花红,克日过门者。(下)(洁上云)

daughter is to marry you and you will make Ying Ying as a second wife according to the imperial decree. He had tarnished Ying Ying's innocence first, so he shouldn't marry Ying Ying as a first wife.' This affair shocked the whole capital. That's how I got to know Gentleman Zhang."

[The Old Lady says angrily] "This scholar doesn't know to appreciate our kindness, and he lets Ying Ying down. As a member of former prime minister's family, how could she be the second wife of him? Since Gentleman Zhang has married a wife by the imperial decree, my nephew, you may choose a lucky day, and marry Ying Ying as it was planed before."

[Zheng Heng says] "If Gentleman Zhang looks for trouble, what shall we do?"

[The Old Lady says] "Please take it easy. I can handle it. Tomorrow is a good time, and you can marry Ying Ying immediately."[Exit]

[Zheng Heng says] "The old lady has fallen into the trap. I will prepare for the good food and drinks, and the next day, I will marry Ying Ying home."[Exit]

[Fa Ben says] "I bought the imperial notice of announcement yesterday. I saw Gentleman Zhang has become the Number One Scholar. He has been appointed as the magistrate of He Zhong Prefecture. However, who knows the old lady has changed her mind, and will marry the young lady to Zheng Heng. The old lady is reluctant to greet Gentleman Zhang for his returning home and getting on the new position, but I will prepare for good food and drinks, taking them to the Ten-li Road Side Pavilion, and greeting the government

老僧昨日买登科记看来，张生头名状元，授著河中府尹。谁想夫人没主张，又许了郑恒亲事。老夫人不肯去接，我将著肴馔，直至十里长亭，接官走一遭。(下)(杜将军上云)奉圣旨，著小官主兵蒲关，提调河中府事，上马管军，下马管民。谁想君瑞兄弟一举及第，正授河中府尹，不曾接得。眼见得在老夫人宅里下，拟定乘此机会成亲。小官牵羊担酒，直至老夫人宅上，一来庆贺状元，二来做主亲，与兄弟成此大事。左右那里？将马来，到河中府走一遭。(下)

第四折

(夫人上云)谁想张生负了俺家，去卫尚书家做女婿去。今日不负老相公遗言，还招郑恒为婿。今日好个日子，过门者。准备下筵席，郑恒敢待来也。(末上云)小官奉圣旨，正授河中府尹。今日衣锦还乡，小姐的金冠霞帔都将著，若见呵，双

official." [Exit]

[General Du enters and says] "By imperial decree, I was appointed commander to the Pu Pass before. Now, I am promoted to supervise He Zhong Prefecture. I am about to charge military and civilian affairs at the same time. I heard my brother Jun Rui has won the Number One Scholar in the imperial exam. He is just appointed as He Zhong Prefecture magistrate. I haven't congratulated him yet. At the moment, the old lady of Cui prime minister's family is staying in a house in He Zhong Prefecture. She must take this opportunity to marry the young lady to Jun Rui. I will take sheep and carry wine to the old lady's house, for one thing to congratulate the Number One Scholar, for another to arrange the marriage for my brother. Where are my servants? Please bring my horse here. I will take a ride to He Zhong Prefecture. [Exit]

Scene Four

[The Old Lady enters and says] "I never expected that Gentleman Zhang has betrayed our family, and become the son-in-law in Minister Wei's family. I will not act against my husband's last will, and marry Ying Ying to Zheng Heng. Today is a lucky day. Zheng Heng will become the son-in-law in our family. Please prepare for the banquet, and wait for Zheng Heng to come."

[Zhang Gong enters] "By imperial decree, I have been appointed as He

手索送过去。谁想有今日也呵！文章旧冠乾坤内，姓字新闻日月边。

【双调】【新水令】玉鞭骄马出皇都，畅风流玉堂人物。今朝三品职，昨日一寒儒。御笔亲除，将名姓翰林注。

【驻马听】张珙如愚，酬志了三尺龙泉万卷书莺莺有福，稳请了五花官诰七香车。身荣难忘借僧居，愁来犹记题诗处。从应举，梦魂儿不离了蒲东路。

（末云）接了马者。（见夫人科）新状元河中府尹婿

Zhong Prefecture magistrate. Today, I am able to return home in glory. I am carrying my lady's phoenix coronet and robes of rank with me. If I meet my lady, I will present them to her with my own hands. Who knows a previous poor scholar will have such glory today? Still wearing the old hat, I am a well learned scholar, full of noble aspiration in my mind, and my name has become well known everywhere under the sun and moon."

[Tune of New Water Song] "Taking the jade whip and riding on the good steed, I come out of the capital city. People all talk about me as an outstanding personage in imperial palace. Today, I take the official position of third rank, but yesterday, I was just a poor scholar without a penny in my hands. Using a imperial writing brush, the Emperor himself added my name in the list the members of the Imperial Academy."

[Tune of Halting Horse Song] "I am a foolish man. I only read countless classics and poetry. How lucky Ying Ying is! I have secured her an official title of Five-flower and a Seven-fragrance chariots to ride. I will never forget my staying in the Pu Jiu Monastery. When love sickness came into my mind, I could still remember the days when I made verses with Ying Ying together. Since I got the Number One Scholar, my dream has never left the road leading to Pu Dong Road."

[Zhang Gong says] "Please take the horse."

[When he meets the old lady, he bows to her] "The new Number One Scholar and He Zhong Prefecture magistrate, your son in law bows to my old lady."

张珙参见。

（夫人云）休拜，休拜！你是奉圣旨的女婿，我怎消受得你拜！

（末唱）

【乔牌儿】我谨躬身问起居，夫人这慈色为谁怒？我则见、丫鬟使数都厮觑，莫不我身边有甚事故？

（末云）小生去时，夫人亲自饯行，喜不自胜。今日中选得官，夫人反行不悦，何也？（夫人云）你如今那里想著俺家？道不得个"靡不有初，鲜克有终"。我一个女孩儿，虽然妆残貌陋，他父为前朝相国，若非贼来，足下甚气力到得俺家？今日一旦置之度外，却于卫尚书家作婿，岂有是理！（末云）夫人听谁说？若有此事，天不盖，地不载，害老大小疔疮！

【雁儿落】若说著丝鞭士女图，端的是塞满章台路。小生呵此间怀旧恩，怎肯别处寻亲去。

【得胜令】岂不闻"君子断其初"，我怎肯忘得有

[The Old Lady says] "Don't bow to me. Don't bow to me. You are the son-in-law by imperial decree. How can I be worthy of your bow?"

[Zhang Gong sings]

[Tune of Pseudo-Melody Song] "I bow to you with my full love and respect. My kind old lady, whom are you so angry with? I see the servants and maids exchanging their glances. What happened?"

[Zhang Gong says] "When I was leaving Pu Dong Town, the old lady saw me off personally. You looked more than happy. Today, I get a position in the officialdom. Why are you not happy instead?"

[The Old Lady says] "Do you still have of us in your mind now? There is a saying which goes 'everyone has his initial goal, but not everyone gets to the end'. I have a girl, though she is ugly and wears broken make-up but his father was the former prime minister in the dynasty. If the rebelling soldiers didn't come, how were you able to get our daughter? Today, you forget all of this, and become the son in law of Minister Wei's family. How outrageous it is!"

[Zhang Gong says] "My old lady, from whom do you hear this? If there was such a thing happen, I will neither be blessed by the heaven nor held by the earth. I will grow malignant over my body."

[Tune of Falling Swan Song] "I am sending the lady with silken whip, but you are suspecting that I came from a whorehouse. I am full of gratitude of the kindness of you and Ying Ying given to me before, how dare I accept other girl as my wife?"

[Tune of Triumphant Song] "Haven't you heard about the saying that the noble gentleman will not cut off his first love. How can I

恩处？那一个贼畜生行嫉妒，走将来老夫人行厮间阻？不能勾娇姝，早共晚施心数说来的无徒，迟和疾上木驴。

（夫人云）是郑恒说来，绣球儿打著马了，做女婿也。你不信呵，唤红娘来问。（红上云）我巴不得见他。元来得官回来，惭愧，这是非对著也。（末背问云）红娘，小姐好么？（红云）为你别做了女婿，俺小姐依旧嫁了郑恒也。（末云）有这般跷蹊的事！

【庆东原】那里有粪堆上长出连枝树，淤泥中生出比目鱼，不明白展污了姻缘簿？莺莺呵，你嫁个油炸猢狲的丈夫。红娘呵，你伏侍个烟薰猫儿的姐夫。张生呵，你撞著个水浸老鼠的姨夫。这厮坏了风俗，伤了时务。

forget your kindness? Which is the beast who is jealous of me, and come to my old lady to disturb my marriage. He couldn't arouse the attraction of the young lady, so he worked out the base plan and acted as a scoundrel. Sooner or latter, he is sure to ride on the wooden donkey."

[The Old Lady says] "It is Zheng Heng who told me this. He said the embroidered ball hit your horse, so you became the son-in-law of Minister Wei's family. If you do not believe what I said, you can ask Red Maid."

[Red Maid enters and says] "I am anxious to meet him. So you come back as an official. What a shame. This is not right."

[Zhang Gong asks Red Maid secretly] "Red Maid, how is the lady?"

[Red Maid says] "As you have become son-in-law in someone else's family. The lady will marry Zheng Heng according to the previous engagement."

[Zhang Gong says] "How strange this matter is!"

[Tune of Celebrating the East Plain Song] "How can the trees whose branches interlock with each other grow on a dunghill? How can flatfish live in the mud? Wouldn't it tarnish the marriage book? Ah, Ying Ying you will marry a monkey husband in the fried pot. Red Maid, you will serve a sooty cat brother-in-law. Gentleman Zhang, you have met a drowned rat in the water. This guy breaks the custom of time, and destroys the good affair."

[Red Maid sings]

（红唱）

【乔木查】妾前来拜覆,省可里心头怒。间别来安乐否?你那新夫人何处居?比俺姐姐是何如?

（末云）和你也葫芦题了也。小生为小姐受过的苦,诸人不知,瞒不得你。不甫能成亲,焉有是理?

【搅筝琶】小生若求了媳妇,则目下便身殂。怎肯忘得待月回廊,难撇下吹箫伴侣。受了些活地狱,下了些死工夫。不甫能得做妻夫,见将著夫人诰敕,县君名称,怎生待欢天喜地,两只手儿分付与,你划地到把人赃诬。

（红对夫人云）我道张生不是这般人,则唤小姐出来自问他。（叫旦科）姐姐,快来问张生。我不信他直恁般薄情。叫见他呵,怒气冲天,实有缘故。（旦见末科）（末云）小姐间别无恙?（旦云）先生万福。

[Tune of Brushwood Song] "I am bowing to you to ease your anger. Just calm down. How are you since we parted with each other? Where does your new wife live? How is she compared to my sister Ying Ying?"

[Zhang Gong says] "You are muddle-headed too. How I suffered for your lady! If other people don't know, you should have known it. Finally, I don't have a chance to marry my lady right now, but... This is really outrageous!"

[Tune of Playing Pipa Song] "If I had married other lady as a wife, I will die immediately. How am I able to forget our romance in the corridor under the moonlight? How can I forget the days of playing the ancient zither music for my mistress? After suffered the hell like hardship in the real life, and exerted myself without mirth, I am able to marry Ying Ying finally. If I didn't want to marry Ying Ying, why did I report my lady's name to the Emperor, who gave her the title as the first lady of the county. How happy we will be. We will hold each other hand in hand, but how do I know I would get slandered when I am back?"

[Red Maid tells the old lady] "I don't think Gentleman Zhang is such a faithless person. Please call lady to question him herself."

[Calling Ying Ying] "Sister, come here to ask Gentleman Zhang yourself quickly. I don't think he is as fickle as he was said. Please come to see him. He is in a towering rage now. There must be a reason."

[Ying Ying meets Zhang Gong.] [Zhang Gong asks] "How are you, my lady?"

（红云）姐姐有的言语，和他说破。（旦长吁云）待说甚么的是！

【沉醉东风】不见时准备著千言万语，得相逢都变做短叹长吁。他急攘攘却才来，我羞答答怎生觑。将腹中愁恰待伸诉，及至相逢一句也无。则道个"先生万福"。

（旦云）张生，俺家何负足下？足下见弃妾身，去卫尚书家为婿，此理安在？（末云）谁说来？（旦云）郑恒在夫人行说来。（末云）小姐如何听这厮？张珙之心，惟天可表！

【落梅风】从离了蒲东路，来到京兆府，见个佳人世不曾回顾。硬揣个卫尚书家女孩儿为眷属，曾见他影儿的也教灭门绝户！

[Ying Ying says] "Wish you all happiness, sir."

[Red Maid says] "Sister, if you have something to say to him, please ask him directly."

[Ying Ying sighs and says] "What am I going to say?"

[Tune of Intoxicating the East Wind Song] "When I haven't seen him, I have prepared so much to say. When I meet him in person, I have forgotten everything, and kept sighing all the time. He comes here in a hurry, and how bashful I am to peep at him secretly. There is no way to express the thousands of sorrows in my mind, so that I am silent again. I just uttered a greeting, 'Wish you all happiness, sir'."

[Ying Ying says] "Gentleman Zhang, how did my family fail you? Why do you forsake me and become the son-in-law of Minister Wei's family. Is there any reason for that?"

[Zhang Gong asks] "Who said that?"

[Ying Ying says] "Zheng Heng said so to my mother."

[Zhang Gong says] "My lady, why do you believe such a guy? My heart to you can be witnessed by heaven and earth."

[Tune of Wind Blowing Down the Plum Blossom Song] "Since leaving Pu Dong Town, and arriving at the capital city, I never looked a beautiful woman over my shoulder. I was rumored to having married the daughter of Minister Wei's family, if ever I had seen her shadow, my entire family will be exterminated and no descendants can survive."

（末云）这一桩事都在红娘身上，我则将言语傍著他，看他说甚么。红娘，我问人来，说道你与小姐将简帖儿去唤郑恒来。(红云)痴人！我不合与你作成，你便看得我一般了。

【甜水令】君瑞先生，不索踌躇，何须忧虑。那厮本意糊突俺家世清白，祖宗贤良，相国名誉。我怎肯他根前寄简传书？

【折桂令】那吃敲才怕不口里嚼蛆，那厮待数黑论黄，恶紫夺朱。俺姐姐更做道软弱囊揣，怎嫁那不值钱人样齄驹。你个东君索与莺莺做主，怎肯将嫩枝柯折与樵夫。那厮本意嚣虚，将足下亏图，有口难言，气夯破胸脯。

（红云）张生，你若端的不曾做女婿呵，我去夫人根前一力保你。等那厮来，你和他两个对证。(红见夫人云)张生并不曾人家做女婿，都是郑恒谎，等他两个对证。(夫人云)既然他不曾呵，等郑恒那厮来对证了呵，再做说话。(洁上云)谁想

[Zhang Gong says] "It must be Red Maid who did this. I will try to argue with her iwasn words to see what she is going to say. Red Maid, I have asked someone, who told me that you acted as a match maker and sent the lady's letter to Zheng Heng."

[Red Maid says] "What an idiot you are. If I ought not help you to fulfill your wishes, you will treat me as a cheap maid."

[Tune of Sweet Water Song] "Gentleman Jun Rui, don't be hesitated, nor be worried. That guy just wanted to bring shame to our family and virtue of our ancestors. How was I willing to send my lady's letter to him?"

[Tune of Picking Laurel Song] "That damned guy isn't afraid of chewing maggots in the mouth, who counts black as yellow, and hates the color purple plundering the red one. Though my sister is tender and weak, how is she willing to marry that beast? You have asked the Emperor to give a title for Ying Ying, how can we marry our delicate lady to that guy as if plucking a burgeon to give a woodman? That guy has intended to take advantage of the opportunity, and foul your name, making you unable to speak in self-defense. Finding this, I nearly burst with anger."

[Red Maid says] "Gentleman Zhang, if you really didn't become Minister Wei's son-in-law, I will do my best to help you in front of the old lady. When that guy arrives, you may have a confrontation with each other."

[Red Maid meets the Old Lady and says] "Gentleman Zhang hasn't become Minister Wei's son-in-law. It is Zheng Heng who is lying. Let's wait for them to confront each other with questions."

张生一举成名,得了河中府尹。老僧一径到夫人那里庆贺。这门亲事,几时成就?当初也有老僧来,老夫人没主张,便待要与郑恒。若与了他,今日张生来,却怎生?(洁见末叙寒温科)(对夫人云)夫人今日却知老僧的是,张生决不是那一等没行止的秀才。他如何敢忘了夫人?况兼杜将军是证见,如何悔得他这亲事?(旦云)张生此一事,必得杜将军来方可。

【雁儿落】他曾笑孙庞真下愚,若是论贾马非英物,正授著征西元帅府,兼领著陕右河中路。

【得胜令】是咱前者护身符,今日有权术。来时节定把先生助,决将贼子诛。他不识亲疏,啜

[The Old Lady says] "If he really didn't, we'd better avoid making a decision until Zheng Heng arrives and makes his argument."

[Fa Ben enters and says] "No one has expected Gentleman Zhang can become famous just after one imperial examination? He gets the official position as He Zhong Prefecture magistrate. I will walk to the old lady and congratulate her. When will this marriage be held? I have played a role in it before. However, the old lady had no idea, and intended to marry Ying Ying to Zheng Heng. If she is to marry to Zheng Heng, why does Gentleman Zhang come here today?"

[Fa Ben meets Gentleman Zhang and greets him good day] [He says to the Old Lady] "Old lady, you finally know I am right today. Gentleman Zhang is definitely not a misbehaved scholar. How dare he forget the old lady? Moreover, it was General Du has witnessed this engagement, how can he regret for this marriage?"

[Ying Ying says] "This matter can only be resolved by General Du let's wait for him ."

[Tune of Falling Swan Song] "General Du has once laughed at the stupidity of Sun Feihu, and regarded Jia Yi and Si Ma Xiangru as no heroes. He has been appointed as Westward Expedition Army's Chief Commander, and the civilian head of He Zhong Prefecture."

[Tune of Triumphant Song] "General Du was my amulet before, and today he is able to use his wisdom and power to help me again. When he comes, he is sure to solve the puzzle, and punish the bad man, who doesn't know his values, but deceives a good man's wife. He cannot distinguish between the good and bad,and believes in the old saying that 'Ruthlessness is the mark of a truly great man'."

赚良人妇。你不辨贤愚,无毒不丈夫。

(夫人云)著小姐去卧房里去者。(旦下)(杜将军上云)下官离了蒲关,到普救寺,第一来庆贺兄弟咱,第二来就与兄弟成就了这亲事。(末对将军云)小弟托兄长虎威,得中一举。今者回来,本待做亲。有夫人的侄儿郑恒,来夫人行说道,你兄弟在卫尚书家作赘了。夫人怒欲悔亲,依旧要将莺莺与郑恒,焉有此理?道不得个"烈女不更二夫"。(将军云)此事夫人差矣。君瑞也是礼部尚书之子,况兼又得一举。夫人世不招白衣秀士,今日反欲罢亲,莫非理上不顺?(夫人云)当初夫主在时,曾许下这厮,不想遇此一难。亏张生请将军来,杀退贼众。老身不负前言,欲招他为婿。不想郑恒说道,他在卫尚书家做了女婿也,因此上我怒他,依旧许了郑恒。(将军云)他是贼心,可知道诽谤他。老夫人如何便信得他?(净上云)

[The Old Lady says] "Please bring the lady to her chamber."[Exit]

[General Du enters and says] "Since I left Pu Pass, I have arrived at Pu Jiu Monastery immediately. For one thing, I come to celebrate my brother for his success; for another, I will arrange the marriage for him."

[Zhang Gong says to General Du] "By brother's blessing, I have become the Number One Scholar in the imperial examination. Today, I come back to be married. However, the nephew of my old lady told her that I have become the son-in-law of Minister Wei's family. The old lady is so angry that she wants to marry Ying Ying to Zheng Heng as previously arranged. How outrageous it is! There is an old saying that " A chaste maid can never marry a second husband."

[The General Du says] "My old lady, you make a mistake this time. Jun Rui is the son of General Secretary of the Department of Rites and today, he has become the Number One Scholar. Old lady, you didn't accept an intelligent young man without an official title as son- in-law before, but now how can you regret for such a marriage when my brother has become the Number One Scholar? There is no reason for that."

[The Old Lady says] "When my husband was alive, we had made an engagement between my daughter and my nephew. However, I never expected that we had experienced such a misfortune in the

打扮得整整齐齐的,则等做女婿。今日好日头,牵羊担酒,过门走一遭。(末云)郑恒,你来怎么?(净云)苦也!闻知状元回,特来贺喜。(将军云)你这厮,怎么要诳骗良人的妻子,行不仁之事,我跟前有甚么话说?我闻奏朝廷,诛此贼子。

(末唱)

【落梅风】你硬撞人桃源路,不言个谁是主,被东君把你个蜜蜂儿拦住。不信呵去那绿杨影里听杜宇,一声声道"不如归去"。

(将军云)那厮若不去呵,祗候拿下。(净云)不

Pu Jiu Monastery. Owing to Gentleman Zhang who requested you to withdraw the rebels, we avoided the danger. I would keep my promise, intending to accept Gentleman Zhang as son-in-law. However, Zheng Heng said that he has become the son-in-law of Minister Wei's family, so I am in extremely anger for his ingratitude, and still marrying Ying Ying to Zheng Heng as planned before."

[The general Du ays] "Zheng Heng is a ruffian. He is slandering my brother. Old lady, how can you believe him?"

[Zheng Heng enters and says] "I have carefully made up today, eager to marry Ying Ying. It is a lucky day. I have taken sheep and brought wine, coming here to visit to the old lady."

[Zhang Gong says] "Zheng Heng, why do you come?"

[Zheng Heng says] "What a misfortune! I have heard that Number One Scholar has arrived, so I am coming to offer you my congratulations."

[General Du says] "You little boy, why dare you deceive a good man's wife? I will report to the imperial court, and kill you the thief!"

[Tune of the Wind Blowing off the Plum Flower Blossoms Song] "You have rashly intruded to the Peach Garden, not knowing who the garden's master is. You little bee who intended to suck honey are stopped by the master. If you don't believe it, just hear the cuckoo's cracking in the green willow trees. It keeps singing 'It is better to go home'."

[General Du says] "If this ruffian doesn't go, I will make an arrest of him." [Zheng Heng says] "Don't do it. I will break off the marriage

必拿，小人自退亲事与张生罢。(夫人云)相公息怒，赶出去便罢。(净云)罢，罢！要这性命怎么，不如触树身死。妻子空争不到头，风流自古恋风流。三寸气在千般用，一日无常万事休。(净倒科)(夫人云)俺不曾逼死他，我是他亲姑娘，他又无父母，我做主葬了者。著唤莺莺出来，今日做个庆喜的茶饭，著他两口儿成合者。(旦红上，末旦拜科)(末唱)

【沽美酒】门迎著驷马车，户列著八椒图，四德三从宰相女，平生愿足，托赖著众亲故。

【太平令】若不是大恩人拔刀相助，怎能勾好夫妻似水如鱼。得意也当时题柱，正酬了今生夫妇。自古相女配夫，新状元花生满路。(使臣上科)

engagement by myself, and return Ying Ying to Gentleman Zhang."

[The Old Lady says] "General Du, don't be angry. Just drive him out of here."

[Zheng Heng says] "OK. OK. What does I ask this life for? It's better to end my life by dashing my head to the tree, rather than living the shame. It is in vain to strive for a wife. The beauty loves heroes. I racked my brain, trying to devise a cheme and win a wife. But one incident has made everything come to an end." [Zheng Heng falls down on the floor, dead]

[The Old Lady says] "I have never wanted him to die. I am his aunt. He has no mother or father, so I will hold his funeral. Please call Ying Ying out. Let's hold a congratulatory banquet, and the couple."

[Ying Ying and Red Maid enters. Zhang Gong and Ying Ying bow to the old lady, and to each other] [Zhang Gong says]

[Tune of Buying the Good Wine Song] "Carriages driven by a team of four horses crowded on the street, and noble ladies' chambers are spread all over the courtyard. I have married a virtuous wife who is the daughter of prime minister, and my dream has been fulfilled, thanks to the help of my relatives and old friends."

[Tune of Peaceful Song] "Had not General Du drawn his sword to give assistance to me, how are we be able to marry happily together? When we are pleased, we shall not forget to write inscription on the column, to celebrate the happiness of being husband and wife.

（末唱）

【锦上花】四海无虞，皆称臣庶诸国来朝，万岁山呼行迈羲轩，德过舜禹圣策神机，仁文义武。朝中宰相贤，天下庶民富万里河清，五谷成熟户户安居，处处乐土凤凰来仪，麒麟屡出。

【清江引】谢当今盛明唐圣主，敕赐为夫妇。永老无别离，万古常完聚，愿普天下有情的都成了眷属。

Since the ancient time, being married to the daughter of a prime minister, the new Number One scholar will be perfectly satisfied and have a promising future."

[The imperial envoy enters, and all bow to him.] [Zhang Gong sings]

[Tune of the Flower on the Brocade Song] "Whole country is in totally peace. Other countries around the world all declare them a vassal and come to pay tribute to the Emperor. The emperor is as sage as ancient emperors Fu Xi and Xuan Yuan, and his virtue is higher than that of ancient emperors Shun and Yu. Both political and military achievements of our dynasty are in line with the Confucian principles of benevolence and righteousness.The prime ministers are all men of virtue and righteous ness. Common people live an abundant life, and the ten thousand miles rivers are clear. The five cereals are ripe, and every family lives in happiness. Lands of happiness are everywhere across the country so that the phoenix arrives in the sky, and Chinese unicorn often appears too."

[Tune of a Clear River Song] "Thanks to the sage emperor in the dynasty for granting an imperial order allowing me to marry Ying Ying, we are able to become a couple. Since then, we will hold hands together till we grow white hairs. We will be united forever. Wish that all lovers in the world could eventually get married."

【随尾】则因月底联诗句,成就了怨女旷夫。显得有志的状元能,无情的郑恒苦。(下)

  题目 小琴童传捷报 崔莺莺寄汗衫
  正名 郑伯常干舍命 张君瑞庆团圆
  总目

张君瑞要做东床婿

法本师住持南瞻地

老夫人开宴北堂春

崔莺莺待月西厢记

[Tune of Epilogue Song] "Composing poems under the moonlight makes a happy marriage of a grumbling maid and a desolate man. The aspiring Number One Scholar is talented and happy, while the heartless Zheng Heng's life is miserable."

[Exeunt]

The lute bearer sends the good news, Ying Ying gives Zhang Gong a vest as present.

Zheng Heng lost his life in deep depress Zhang Gong celebrates for his happiness.

Zhang Gong finds a good chance to be the son in love of a rich family, Abbot Fa Ben fulfills his duty. The old lady holds a feast in te northern flawer, And Ying Ying waits under the moonlight in the western chamber.